FORBIDDEN NIGHT WITH THE WARRIOR

Michelle Willingham

MILLS
BOON®

First published in Great Britain 2017
By Mills & Boon, an imprint of HarperCollins*Publishers*
1 London Bridge Street, London, SE1 9GF

Large Print edition 2017

© 2017 Michelle Willingham

ISBN: 978-0-263-06796-5

MIX
Paper from
responsible sources
FSC **FSC™ C007454**
www.fsc.org

This book is produced from independently certified FSC paper to ensure responsible forest management. For more information visit www.harpercollins.co.uk/green.

Printed and bound in Great Britain
by CPI Group (UK) Ltd, Croydon, CR0 4YY

Warriors of the Night

Surrender to seduction…

Let Michelle Willingham sweep you away
with her brand-new, thrillingly passionate
Warriors of the Night miniseries. Be
entranced by these darkly sexy warrior
heroes, and follow them as they face their
biggest challenge yet—falling in love!

Forbidden Night with the Warrior

Available now

Forbidden Night with the Highlander

Coming soon

Author Note

Forbidden Night with the Warrior is the first in a new series inspired by *Indecent Proposal*. When Rosamund de Courcy falls in love with Warrick de Laurent as a maiden her father forbids a union between them. The star-crossed lovers try to wed in secret, but Rosamund is forced to marry another man.

In this book I wanted to explore the idea of what might happen if a dying lord desperately needed an heir and offered a night with his wife to the man she'd always loved. It's a story about second chances and wanting to right the wrongs of the past. And then, too, there is the question of which marriage was real…

Look for the second book in this series, *Forbidden Night with the Highlander*, which tells the story of Rhys de Laurent and Lianna MacKinnon. If you'd like me to email you when I have a new book out, please visit my website at michellewillingham.com to sign up for my newsletter. As a bonus, you'll receive a free story just for subscribing!

RITA® Award finalist **Michelle Willingham** has written over twenty historical romances, novellas and short stories. Currently she lives in south-eastern Virginia with her husband and children. When she's not writing, Michelle enjoys reading, baking and avoiding exercise at all costs. Visit her website at: michellewillingham.com.

Books by Michelle Willingham

Mills & Boon Historical Romance
and **Mills & Boon Historical** *Undone!* **eBooks**

Warriors of the Night

Forbidden Night with the Warrior

Warriors of Ireland
(Linked to *The MacEgan Brothers*)

Warrior of Ice
Warrior of Fire

The MacKinloch Clan

Claimed by the Highland Warrior
Seduced by Her Highland Warrior
Craving the Highlander's Touch (Undone!)
Tempted by the Highland Warrior

The MacEgan Brothers

Her Irish Warrior
The Warrior's Touch
Her Warrior King
Her Warrior Slave (prequel)
Taming Her Irish Warrior
Surrender to an Irish Warrior
Warriors in Winter

Visit the Author Profile page
at millsandboon.co.uk for more titles.

To Barb Massabrook, a bright spirit with a ready smile, a love for Scotland, and gorgeous men in kilts. You are one of the nicest women I've ever met, and I am so glad to call you my friend. As you fight this battle, know that we are with you always.

Chapter One

England—1174

'You cannot ask this of me.' Rosamund de Courcy stared at her husband in disbelieving shock. 'It is a sin.'

Alan de Courcy, the Baron of Pevensham, leaned back against the pillow of their bed. His brown hair hung limply against his face, and his grey eyes were shielded with unending pain. He had grown weaker over the past three months, and though Rosamund prayed each night for his recovery, the shadow of death lingered over him. It terrified her to imagine him gone, for he had been a true friend through her darkest nightmares.

Now he wanted her to lie with another man to conceive the child they so desperately needed. The very idea was unthinkable.

'We need an heir, *ma petite.* And I am incapable of giving you one.' Her husband spoke of the proposition as if it were a business arrangement. 'I will not let my brother inherit everything I have built. Owen would ruin Pevensham within a year.'

Rosamund paced before the hearth, her heart racing at the very thought of Alan's command. How could he even imagine she would betray him in that way? She was a woman of honour, not an unfaithful wife.

Whispers of guilt pulled at her conscience, reminding her of the mistakes she had made as a young woman. But Alan knew nothing of them, and she had always been true to him during their marriage. She had paid the price for her sins, but the heartbreak haunted her still.

'I have been nothing but loyal to you,' she insisted to Alan. 'For three years, I have obeyed you. Why would you ask this of me?'

'Because you do not want Owen to inherit, either. You know what he would do to you when I am gone.' His voice held a trace of ice, and she understood his unspoken words. If Owen took possession of Pevensham, he would force his unwanted attentions upon her. She suppressed a shiver of revulsion.

'But…to lie with another man when I am married to you? You ask too much of me. I could never do such a thing.' She closed her eyes, gripping the edges of her skirt. The union between a man and a woman was not painful, but she had never enjoyed it with Alan. He had been so careful, treating her with such gentleness. But there was no thrill of passion between them, hardly more than a gesture of marital comfort.

Alan had tried to please her, though he'd sensed her distance when he had claimed her body. Because of it, he had not asked that she share his bed often. And in the half-year since he'd fallen ill, she had not lain with him once.

'I have asked Warrick de Laurent to come to Pevensham. He will be here within a sennight.'

An icy chill suffused her skin, and she felt lightheaded for a moment. Warrick was the man she had loved since she was a maiden. Tall and strong, with dark hair and piercing blue eyes, she had wanted him desperately. Never had she forgotten the fierce warrior who had haunted her dreams. Or the way his kiss had awakened her body, arousing her blood.

'I cannot lie with him,' Rosamund insisted. For if she did, it would threaten the very foundation of her marriage. Her throat constricted with a flood of memories she couldn't face. She had closed off her heart to what would never be, accepting Alan and becoming a proper wife.

For him to ask this of her evoked such a fury, she could hardly speak.

Alan *knew* what this would mean. He knew it, and yet he was forcing her to confront the past.

If she let Warrick touch her, she would no longer be able to trust herself. It would be impossible to guard her feelings and behave as if the union meant nothing. Even the memory of his touch made her pulse quicken and her body tremble.

For a time, Alan was silent. She heard only the sound of his laboured breathing and the rustle of sheets. 'I know you did not want to marry me, *ma petite*. I was never the man you wanted.'

No, he wasn't. Everyone had known it, though she had obeyed her father's command and married the man of his choosing. There had been no other way.

The pain in Alan's voice weighed upon her, cooling the anger. She remained beside the hearth, closing her eyes as she chose her words carefully. 'You have always been kind to me. I could not have asked for a better husband.'

But the arranged marriage had forced her to put aside the broken dreams and start anew. Warrick had joined the king's forces, fighting in Normandy, and she had not seen him again. Instead, Rosamund had accepted this new life with a man who cared for her, and it should have been enough.

He expelled a sigh. 'The words do not make it true, Rosamund. I know you wanted to wed Warrick de Laurent.'

It was far more than that, she thought, but didn't say so.

'That was a long time ago,' she said quietly. She couldn't understand why Alan was bringing up the ghosts of the past. 'When you took me as your wife, I tried to be everything you wanted.'

'And you have been, Rosamund. But I was never what *you* wanted.' His voice was quiet, rimmed with sadness.

She hated to hear it, for this man had become her friend as well as her husband. Alan had never raised a hand against her, and he had given her dominion over the castle and household. 'You have always been good to me.'

'But we have no children,' he said softly. 'And now, we will find another way. There must be a child to keep Owen from inheriting Pevensham.'

She didn't stop the tears now, for it had been nearly three years since she had delivered a babe that was stillborn. It was a resounding ache in her heart, and time had never diminished the emptiness. Perhaps the loss might have faded if she had carried a child to term, but after the death of her daughter, she had never conceived again. It was as if God were punishing her for her disobedience as a young maiden.

A part of her was grateful that she had not become pregnant again. The idea of bearing another child terrified her, for she had given birth too soon. All the pain and blood had resulted in nothing but death.

'Look at me, Rosamund,' Alan demanded. When she turned, his expression held apology. 'It was my fault, never yours. I was not a virtuous man before we wed. I had my share of women, maids, and willing serving girls. Not once did any of the women bear a bastard child. And there were many opportunities.'

He was trying to blame himself, and she didn't want that. 'Both of us share the failure.'

'You have already conceived a child once before, and you will do so again. But I know that the only man you would take into your bed is Warrick de Laurent.'

The blood roared in her ears, and she turned away again. Battered emotions poured across her soul at the thought of letting him touch her. 'I cannot. And he will not agree to this, either.' She couldn't imagine that a man as proud as Warrick would let himself be used in that way.

'I will ask him,' Alan said quietly. 'He may agree to it with adequate compensation. I want him to marry you when I am gone. He will defend Pevensham from our enemies, and he can protect you from Owen.'

Rosamund gripped her shaking hands together. He had everything planned out, didn't he? One wicked night of sin, a man to take his place, and a child who would inherit everything under the pretence of being a true-born heir.

Tears of anger and frustration burned in her eyes at the thought of this deception. 'Alan, no.'

'I am going to die, Rosamund. Both of us know it.'

She didn't want to face it, though she feared the worst. It was easier to imagine that it wouldn't happen. She could bind herself with this life and shut out harsh reality.

'I have prayed for you—'

'Prayers will not change it. But before I go, I can ensure that Owen never inherits my property. I will provide someone to protect you, someone who would give his life for yours.'

She moved to sit beside him on his bed. Fear gripped her hard, even as she took his hand in hers. 'Do not ask me to betray you, Alan. I will not. You deserve better than this.'

'So did you.' In his tone, she heard compassion and love. 'I wanted to marry you, Rosamund, and God help me I did everything to make you love me.'

'I do,' she whispered.

'Not in the way you loved him.'

Rosamund bit her lip so hard she tasted blood. He was right, though she wanted to deny it. She had loved Alan like a brother, and their marriage rested upon pillars of friendship and affection, but not love. For the past three years, she had tried to make the best of her marriage and forget about Warrick.

Alan squeezed her palm, and before she could protest, he touched a finger to his lips. 'I know you care for me, Rosamund, and I will take that with me to my grave. But before I die, you must obey me in this.' His face hardened. 'You will do everything possible to ensure that we have a child to inherit. Swear to me that you will lie with him.'

She said nothing, not wanting any part of this devil's arrangement. It was unthinkable, and if the adultery were discovered, she could lose everything.

'Swear it,' he demanded. 'If you have any loyalty or obedience towards me, I demand this of you.'

She bit her lip, wanting to lash back at him. But despite his rigid tone, she sensed the regret behind his words. This was about more than conceiving a son to inherit. He was trying to right the wrong, to give her back the man she had wanted to wed. And the arrangement would irrevocably bind her to Warrick.

With all her heart, she wanted to refuse him. But when she looked into his pain-filled grey eyes, she realised that her words held the power to give a dying man peace. He loved her enough to make this sacrifice, even knowing the Pandora's box it would open.

If she refused his proposition, it would intensify his worries and weigh down upon his spirit. But if she lied and voiced her agreement, it would soften his fears. What harm was there in speaking a lie? He need never know whether she had kept her vows.

She pushed back her apprehension, knowing that she held the power to refuse his request. If words would grant him comfort, then she could give him that much.

'All right,' she said softly. 'I will allow him to claim me.'

* * *

'Why would I kill a man for your sake?'

Warrick de Laurent gripped the hilt of his sword while staring at Owen de Courcy. The man had summoned him to his settlement at Northleigh, a rotting fortress that reeked of old rushes and neglect. Owen was a younger man with cold grey eyes and dark brown hair cut short to his ears. His beard had not fully grown in, and his lips were pursed like a pouting child.

'Because I will give you land in return,' Owen said. 'And because you may take Rosamund de Courcy as your battle prize.'

Warrick was careful not to reveal any reaction to the mention of Rosamund. For three years, he'd tried to forget her, but the memory of her beautiful face still haunted him at night.

She made her choice, and it wasn't you, his mind taunted.

'I have no need of a woman.' He spoke the words without emotion, as if she meant nothing to him.

Owen appeared dismissive. 'As you will. I am certain I can find another of my men who will… take care of her.'

The barb struck true, and his instincts rose up in warning. No, he didn't want to see Rosamund again, but that didn't mean he would let another man harm her. Before he could snarl at Owen, the man continued. 'Kill my brother, and you shall have everything you've ever wanted. You have killed many men in battle already. Why would one more matter?'

It didn't surprise Warrick to learn that Owen wanted his brother dead, for he would inherit Pevensham and vast holdings across south-west England. Although Owen already possessed the small estate at Northleigh, it was clear that it was falling into disrepair. All around, he saw the signs of a man who lacked wealth of his own.

'Your brother is already dying,' he told Owen. 'Everyone knows it. You need only wait, and you will have what you want.'

'I have debts that must be paid.' His expression narrowed with distaste. 'And I grow weary of living like a swine in this place. If Alan's wife bears a child, I inherit nothing.'

A sudden flare of possessiveness washed over him at the mention of Rosamund. Warrick didn't want to imagine her giving birth to another man's son. His fists clenched and blood roared through him when he thought of Alan de Courcy touching her. Three years had done nothing to diminish his fury.

'What if she has already conceived?' he asked.

Even as he spoke the words, Warrick suspected Owen would ensure that she lost the child. This was a man who was determined to get what he wanted, no matter the cost.

At his question, a slow smile spread over Owen's face. 'She will not give birth to an heir. I will see to it.' His servant returned and handed him a message. Owen poured a cup of ale and handed it to Warrick. 'My servants intercepted this missive a few days ago. My brother has invited you to Pevensham as his guest. While you are there, you will have every opportunity to take his life.'

Warrick accepted the parchment, and saw that the broken wax held Alan de Courcy's seal. Within the message, de Courcy mentioned that he had a special task for Warrick, one that would bring him a vast sum.

He had no interest in whatever 'task' Alan de Courcy desired him to complete. Ever since Rosamund had married de Courcy, Warrick had not spoken to either of them.

'You will see to it that Alan does not survive this fortnight. Rosamund will be isolated from him until I can be certain she is not with child. He must not have an heir,' Owen said.

'Why now?' He could not understand why the man was determined to see his brother dead so soon—especially within a short time. It made him wonder if Owen was facing a threat of his own.

'King Henry will be returning from Normandy soon. We must be ready to prove our alliance.'

The pieces started to fall into place. If Owen commanded two estates, he would be a valuable ally to the king. Or perhaps he intended to side with the rebellious sons of Henry, in the hopes of securing a higher place for himself.

'And you want to cast no blame upon yourself. If I am caught, *I* would be executed for murder, not you.'

The man seemed unconcerned. 'I would suggest that you do not get caught. Let them believe Alan's death occurred from a natural means.' Owen studied him a moment. 'You could kill him in his sleep, and no one would know the truth.'

Warrick still wanted nothing to do with this man. 'I do not kill innocent men.'

Owen eyed him with a sly expression. 'You've done it many times in the service of your king. How many have you slaughtered in battle? They call you the Blood Lord, do they not?'

Tension knotted within him, but he betrayed no emotions. 'I am no lord.'

'Indeed you are not. And that is why you will help me—because you possess nothing at all. I will give you land in Ireland where your poverty will not matter. You can begin again as the lord you always wanted to be.'

It was true that he *did* want land. The desire for his own demesne burned through his blood. As the youngest son, he possessed hardly anything, and he had no wish to live with his father or his older brother Rhys.

But Warrick wasn't about to reveal this to de Courcy. His hand returned to his sword. 'If land was all I wanted, I could take it for myself.'

'You haven't enough men to lay siege to a fortress,' Owen pointed out. 'And it isn't only land that you want. You want vengeance against Rosamund and the man who stole her from you. I am giving you the chance to take her back. Punish her if it makes you feel better.'

He did still harbour anger towards Rosamund, after the night she had turned her back on him. But he could not help but wonder why Alan de Courcy had summoned him. What did the man want? Undoubtedly, it was connected to Rosamund.

Warrick knew that the moment he set eyes upon her again, it would only rub salt in his wounded pride. He had tried to spend time with other women, attempting to forge a life without Rosamund. And yet, he could never forget the way she had smiled at him with love, pressing her hands against his heart. He had wound his hand around her long black hair, kissing her until she made soft sounds of yearning. Those green eyes had looked upon him as if no other man in the world existed.

A part of him was still furious that she had chosen someone else. Her father had forbidden them to be together, since Warrick had nothing to offer her. But he'd believed that Rosamund would defy her family and stay with him. He had suffered a brutal whipping on her behalf after her father had caught them fleeing together. But instead of holding fast to the promises they had made on holy ground, she had denied everything and had chosen Alan de Courcy.

Warrick needed to look into those treacherous green eyes and understand why she had done it. Rosamund was married to a man of wealth, yet she had no children and now her husband was dying. Did she regret her choice after all these years?

'Find out what my brother wants,' Owen said. He tossed a heavy bag towards Warrick. 'Take this as proof of my offer.'

He opened it and found it full of silver—rather appropriate for blood money. Warrick placed the bag back on a nearby table and shook his head. 'I will not kill on your behalf.'

'Not even for her?' Owen ventured. 'Not even if it meant she would belong to you after her husband is dead?'

Warrick had already made up his mind to find out what Alan de Courcy wanted. But he had no interest in becoming Owen de Courcy's assassin.

'I will go to Pevensham,' he said. 'But only to satisfy my own curiosity. If you want your brother dead, it will not be by my hand.'

Owen's expression turned thoughtful. 'We shall see, de Laurent. We shall see.'

Rosamund had never been more uneasy in all her life, save her wedding night. She had prayed that Alan would change his mind about this reckless plan, but her husband was steadfast in his wishes. A part of her wished she had the courage to stand up to him and refuse his wishes. The lie weighed upon her conscience, but silence was easier than confrontation. Adultery was a graver sin than breaking a promise, and since her husband had put her in an impossible position, it was one or the other.

She had stared out of her window for hours, days, waiting for Warrick to arrive. It was evening when she saw him riding through the gates. From the tower, she could hardly see his face, but his posture made it evident that this was indeed the proud man she had once loved. His gaze lingered upon the inner bailey for a moment before he turned to stare at the tower. She froze, fully aware of the moment he locked eyes upon her. There was no doubt that he had seen her.

From the tower window, her blue kirtle was as visible as a banner flying above a troop of soldiers. She had chosen her best gown with long tapered sleeves and a silver girdle studded with sapphires. Around her throat she wore a silver chain with another sapphire hanging upon it. Her maidservant had braided her dark hair and coiled it on to her head like a crown.

Did Warrick know why he had been summoned? Her skin tightened with fear, for she had not forgotten the look of hatred in his eyes on the day she had married Alan. He had wanted her to walk away from the wedding, to leave behind her family and all she had known, for his sake.

Sometimes she wished she had. But it was too late to change it now.

Rosamund's fingers dug into the wooden window frame. Did he despise her still after all these years?

Her heart was beating rapidly in her chest, but she tried to calm her nerves. He would refuse Alan's proposition, she was certain. All she had to do was remain quiet and obedient, and Warrick would go away.

If only she could silence the doubts and fears roiling within her. But Warrick was a proud warrior, a man who would not forget the wrongs done to him. It didn't matter that she had agreed to wed Alan as a means of saving his life. Or that she'd had no choice in the matter. He remembered only that she had given promises to him and then broken them. Warrick was not the sort of man who would forgive her for it.

A knock sounded at the door and when her maid answered it, the steward bowed. 'My lady, Lord Pevensham wishes you to greet his guest in the Great Hall, since he is unable to leave his bed.'

'Of course,' Rosamund murmured. Inwardly, she wanted to curse Alan. He had done this on purpose, forcing her to face the man who frightened her most.

But with every step she took towards the stairs, she thought of her husband's unholy command. It reawakened her anger and frustration. She didn't want to obey Alan's wishes, despite his need for an heir. It was far better for her to remain a loyal wife, shielding herself from the heartache it would conjure.

I cannot betray him, she thought. *Even if Alan demands it of me.*

For she could not trust herself in this. The slightest touch would evoke all the years of buried desire. Warrick's very presence shook her to the core.

Rosamund entered the Hall, and from the moment she stepped inside, she could feel the warrior's gaze upon her. The air was charged with tension, but she walked to the dais as if nothing were wrong. Her heart was beating so fast, her knees were shaking beneath her skirts.

Calm down. He is only a man.

She focused her attention upon the clean rushes, steadying herself until she dared to look up. With her shoulders squared and a serene expression upon her face, Warrick would not see the fear beneath the surface.

'My lady,' he greeted her, bowing low. But even with the courtesy, she could feel his veiled anger. It was there in his blue eyes, in the fierce bearing of his stance. His dark hair was cut short, and he carried his helm beneath one arm as if ready for battle.

He remembers everything, she realised. The

taut lines of his muscles were filled with a rigid cast, as if he still blamed her for refusing his offer of marriage. Did he honestly believe she'd had a choice?

'It has been a long time, my lord.' She tried to muster a smile but couldn't quite manage it. *I never meant for it to end with you hating me,* she wanted to say.

It never should have ended, he seemed to answer. His blue eyes held an unnamed emotion, and he studied her as if trying to discern her feelings. She saw the edge of anger in his eyes, but there was something more.

'I received your husband's missive, asking me to come. But he never said why.' Warrick regarded her with open displeasure, waiting for her explanation.

'I will take you to my lord husband, and he will tell you.' She beckoned for him to follow, and two of his men-at-arms started to accompany them.

'Your men should remain here,' she advised. 'What my husband wishes to tell you is not for others to hear.'

He raised an eyebrow at that, but gave the order for his soldiers to stay back. Rosamund turned and led the way towards the stairs. From behind her, she heard his footsteps. She grasped her skirts and began walking up the spiral stairs. Just when she had reached the halfway point, he caught her hand and forced her to stop.

'Why am I here, Rosamund?' His voice resonated with shielded anger, and his grip tightened upon her palm.

'As I said before, my husband—'

'I care naught about de Courcy. I came for you.'

A ripple of fear crossed her spine at that. His words reminded her of the sensuality that had once been between them. Years ago, he had touched her like a starving man, as if she were his reason for being alive. Right now, she was fully aware of his closeness. His grasp softened upon her palm, and his thumb traced the veins on her wrist. The sudden tenderness undid her senses, and she felt as if he were caressing other parts of her bare skin. In the shadowed darkness of the stairs, she was caught up in memories of his kiss. Rosamund leaned back against the wall, and the cool stones were a stark contrast to his touch.

She had a terrible feeling that this proposition would not end well for either of them. Time had done nothing to diminish the feelings she had once held.

'Why did you turn from me?' He rested both

hands on either side of her, trapping her against the wall. 'All these years I've wanted to know.'

She stiffened her spine and faced him. 'My father forced me to deny everything as the price for your life.' There was no doubt in her mind that Harold de Beaufort had wanted to kill Warrick for claiming her innocence.

Her heart bled at the memory of the day she had left him. There were even more secrets she had kept from him, and God willing, he would never learn them.

But he pressed further. 'He would not have killed me, and you know it. But then, Alan had all this to offer you, whereas I had nothing.' He lifted his hands from the wall and gestured towards the castle. 'A castle of your own and lands that rival King Henry's holdings.' His blue eyes grew frosted. 'Was it worth it?'

He made it sound as if she had married Alan out of greed. There was so much he didn't know, and she could never, ever tell him what had happened.

Instead, she murmured, 'What's done is done.'

'Is it?' He drew his hand to her cheek, cupping her face. She could almost imagine the touch of his mouth against her throat, his hands upon her skin. And the guilt flooded through her for even envisioning it.

'Please let me go.' She straightened her shoulders and pulled herself back. Yet there was no mistaking the invisible bindings that drew her to him. Even now, she found it difficult to walk away.

But Warrick released her and followed her up the stairs. Rosamund led him to her husband's bedchamber, though it felt as though she were walking towards her own demise. Before she opened the door, she paused and faced him.

'My husband is dying,' she said in a low voice. 'But he is a good man. What he asks of you, please know that it was none of my doing. Refuse him, for my sake.'

He eyed her with undisguised curiosity. 'Really?'

She nodded. 'I am sorry that you have wasted a journey here. But I will compensate you and your men for your trouble.' Without giving him a chance to answer, she opened the door and motioned for him to stay behind.

Her husband was seated in bed with several cushions propping him up. Alan's expression was tired. Beside him, she saw food he'd barely touched and a cup of wine he hadn't even tasted. It pained her to see him suffering, hardly able to eat.

But she moved forward and greeted him with a

kiss upon his cheek. 'My lord husband, Warrick de Laurent is here at your summons.' She turned back and motioned for their guest to enter the room. There was a dark cast to Warrick's face, as if he resented being here. Rosamund decided it was best to leave, since she did not want to witness his reaction to this unholy proposition. She had nearly reached the door, when Alan stopped her.

'You will remain here, Rosamund.' He motioned for his servant to go, and soon enough, the three of them were alone.

Her skin tightened with raw nerves. This was the last place she wanted to be, and she wished with all her being that Alan had allowed her to leave.

'Pour our guest some wine,' Alan instructed. 'Warrick, would you come and sit beside me? I fear I lack the strength to greet you properly.' He motioned for the man to be seated in the chair next to the bed.

Rosamund poured wine into two goblets and offered one to Warrick and another to her husband. Then she retreated to the furthest corner of the room, hoping for an opportunity to disappear. She picked up her embroidery, but her hands were shaking so badly, she could hardly thread the needle.

Her husband began with pleasantries, asking about his journey. Then he continued with, 'I suppose you wish to know why I asked you to come to Pevensham.' To his credit, Warrick only met his gaze and waited. 'It was because of my wife.' He beckoned for her to come forward. 'Sit beside me, Rosamund.'

She felt ill inside, her skin frigid with fear. Her husband took her hand in his, as if to soothe her. But his touch did nothing to allay her anxiety. She wished she could run from the room and leave them to plot with one another.

'I know that I am dying, de Laurent. I know not how much time I have remaining, but I want someone to take care of my wife when I am gone.'

Warrick's silence stretched across the space, and she didn't dare look at him. Alan seemed unconcerned by his lack of a response. 'As it stands, my brother will inherit Pevensham when I am dead. Owen is eager for my death, and I have no doubt that he will slaughter any child Rosamund bears if it means protecting his own interests.'

That brought a response. 'She is with child, then?' His voice was flat, as if he cared nothing for her.

Alan avoided a direct answer, saying, 'It is my hope that she will one day bear a son. However, I do not think Rosamund will be safe here, even with those who have sworn to guard her. I need someone I can trust to escort her from Pevensham and ensure that she and her unborn child are under protection. I want you to take her away before Owen arrives at Pevensham.'

Alan reached out and took Warrick's hand, placing it on top of Rosamund's. 'And I want you to marry her after I am gone.'

Her hands trembled at his words, and the weight of Warrick's fingers lay heavy upon hers. Emotions welled up within her, not only sorrow at the thought of Alan's death, but also the understanding of what he was trying to do.

A sudden thought occurred to her, and she met his gaze. Was it possible that Alan knew she had not been a virgin on their wedding night? Her cheeks burned, but all she saw was a weary look upon his face.

For a moment, Warrick seemed to consider the proposition. She was aware of the subtle caress of his thumb against her palm, and the barest touch sent a yearning through her body. Her skin prickled beneath her kirtle, though she tried to force back the feelings.

His blue eyes stared into hers, and for a moment, she caught a glimpse of the young man she had once known. Her heart stumbled a moment as she tried to gather her composure. But the reassuring weight of his hand upon hers brought back a flood of sensual memories. A grim expression shielded his face, and he pulled his hand free. 'There is nothing between Rosamund and me. She made her choice years ago.'

Alan tried to sit up, and she helped arrange the pillows to support him. 'I suspected you might say this. But you also know that I was never the man she wanted.'

Rosamund closed her eyes, guilt sliding over her that she could not love him in the same way. She'd wanted to push aside her feelings for Warrick, but it had never come to pass.

'We will find another way,' she told her husband. 'Warrick has a life of his own now, and I expected this.'

But Alan ignored her. 'You wanted her enough to run away with her, de Laurent. She will not be safe with my brother, and you know this.'

'She is not my responsibility.' His words were cool, but she detected the bitterness within them.

'No. But if you protect her, I will grant you the land you always wanted.'

A faint smile came over his face, and he asked, 'In Ireland, I suppose?'

She didn't quite understand his amusement, and Alan's expression narrowed. 'How do you know about my lands in Ireland?'

Warrick crossed his arms and regarded her husband. 'Because Owen de Courcy offered the same bargain to me, along with your wife. As payment for killing you.'

Chapter Two

Warrick wasn't surprised when Rosamund stood up from the bed and glared at him. 'Get out.' Fury burned upon her reddened cheeks. 'I will not let you harm my husband.'

She looked like an avenging soldier, ready to gut him if he dared to lay a hand on Alan. Her determination only provoked his interest, for her green eyes seethed with anger and her lips tightened. Her hand rested upon her eating knife, and he didn't doubt she would use it if necessary.

'Calm yourself, my dear,' Alan intervened. 'If de Laurent intended to kill me, he wouldn't have told me this first. He could have done so already, and neither of us is strong enough to stop him.'

'Indeed.' But Warrick's attention was fixed upon Rosamund. 'Do you intend to stab me with that blade?'

'I might.'

He didn't miss the fury on her face. Rosamund might appear to be a soft, demure lady, but she had a spine of steel.

'I presume you have no intention of murdering me in my bed, de Laurent?' Alan mused softly.

'No. But I thought I should come and warn you of your brother's intent. He is no friend to you.'

'I am aware of this.' Alan's expression turned grim. 'Although he has his own property at Northleigh, Owen has fallen deeply into debt. I suspect the vultures are circling him for repayment, even now. He has coveted my lands and castle since our father died four years ago. I will do all that I can to prevent him from inheriting Pevensham.'

His voice took on a different tone and strangely, Rosamund took a step away from her husband's bedside. She looked pained at what he was about to say, as if she wanted to shrink back and retreat within the walls.

'You had another reason for summoning me here, didn't you?' Warrick predicted. He kept his gaze fixed upon Rosamund, knowing that she held the answers.

Alan gave a nod. 'It is a most…unusual request. But one that is necessary to protect my wife and my lands.' He gestured towards the chamber walls as if they were not there. 'If you agree, then all of this would belong to you.'

Lord Pevensham's offer made little sense. Warrick was no blood relative, nor was there any means of him inheriting a place like Pevensham.

'It's not possible,' he said. But his gaze passed over Alan and then Rosamund as he wondered what the pair of them had plotted.

'You understand why I do not wish for my brother to inherit,' Alan continued. 'He is a cruel man who would threaten my serfs, bring my estates to the brink of destruction, and harm my wife. I have worked all my life, alongside my father, to make Pevensham prosperous.' The sincerity upon the man's face made it clear that de Courcy was indeed the sort of lord who wanted to protect his people. 'When I am gone, I can arrange to give Pevensham into your hands, with Rosamund at your side.'

The offer struck him speechless. Why would Alan de Courcy consider such a thing? They were virtually strangers. It made no sense at all.

'If I were to marry Rosamund, Pevensham still would not be mine,' he argued. 'She might have a dower portion, but—'

'You would govern Pevensham until her son comes of age,' Alan said quietly. 'And you would live here as his guardian.'

'But she could bear a daughter,' he pointed out. 'What would happen then?'

Alan's expression turned cool. 'I leave that in God's hands. For now, Rosamund is not yet with child. That is our first priority.'

The revelation confused him. 'But you said it was your hope that she would bear a son. Is she not already—?'

'Not yet,' Alan said. From the narrowed gaze upon the baron's face, Warrick could not understand what this conversation was about. Was he intending to have Warrick command the forces of Pevensham until Rosamund became pregnant?

Alan hesitated, and Warrick noticed that Rosamund had gone pale, her eyes downcast. 'I want *you* to give her a child.'

The words stunned him. How could any man ever contemplate an arrangement like this?

The baron's voice was quiet, filled with reluctance. 'If you agree to this, Rosamund will share your bed until she conceives. And your son will inherit Pevensham under the pretence of my name.'

* * *

Rosamund expected Warrick to refuse the proposal and leave Alan's bedchamber. Instead, his silence terrified her. Dear God, did this mean he was considering it? He—he couldn't. Not after all that had happened between them.

She stared down at her hands, praying for him to deny the request. But she felt the intensity of his stare upon her and the unspoken question.

When at last she looked at him, his blue eyes held a flare of desire. He was watching her, and his gaze moved down her body. 'You knew of this proposition, Rosamund?'

What was there to say? That she understood her husband's desire for a child and his willingness to sacrifice everything to save Pevensham? She couldn't bring herself to speak, but nodded. Every part of her wanted to protest, for this was a bargain she had never desired.

She had voiced her agreement to her husband, though it had never been her choice. Alan had been relieved at her assent, and she had seen a visible change in him, like a man who was confident that all would be well. And perhaps that was what he needed—reassurance that after he was gone, someone would take care of her.

Warrick regarded her with an unreadable expression. 'I would like to speak alone with Rosamund.'

No. She didn't want that at all. She'd rather walk barefoot across shards of broken glass than answer the questions he would pose.

But Alan had no such qualms. 'Of course.' He appeared eager to allow it, almost glad that Warrick had not made an outright refusal.

She sent her husband a pleading look, which he ignored, nodding for her to follow Warrick outside the bedchamber.

She gritted her teeth and obeyed. It occurred to her that she could be truthful with Warrick, making him understand why she had gone along with Alan's plan. Then, at least, he would know not to hold any expectations.

He continued walking down the hallway until she led him into the solar. His powerful stride revealed his impatience, and she sensed that he had a great deal to say to her.

Rosamund dismissed her maid, Berta, who was inside, and afterwards, Warrick closed the door behind him. He studied her for a moment, and then said, 'Was this your idea, Rosamund? Do you want a child that badly?'

Her frustration roared back. How could he possibly believe such a thing? 'No, not at all.' She took a deep breath, trying to force away her anger and calm herself. 'I understand what Alan wants. Pevensham means everything to him. Even more than me.' She couldn't quite hide the bitterness in her voice. 'He thinks a child will save his estate from Owen. But it will not happen.'

Warrick studied her a moment, and then his gaze passed over her body. 'Have you ever conceived a child before?'

His question caught her unawares, and she clenched her hands to keep them from trembling. This was not a question she wanted to face, especially from him. The shadow of grief had never left her heart, and she had wanted to keep that part of her buried, along with her baby.

She didn't want to tell him anything at all. If she spoke a single word, her fragile control would shatter. But she feared he would continue to demand answers, and she couldn't bear that. Instead, she gathered her composure and tried to hide the gleam of tears. 'I had a stillborn babe once.'

She was grateful when he didn't press her for more. He rested his hand upon her shoulder and offered, 'I am sorry for your loss.'

The kindness undid her, and she let the tears fall in silence. Warrick moved his hand from her shoulder, and she wished she could lean against him, taking solace in an embrace. But she didn't want to reveal weakness in front of him. Not now. Instead, she wiped her tears away, trying to push away the empty devastation.

Lifting her chin, she admitted, 'I don't want to have another child. There's a part of my heart that is gone forever.' She bit her lip and blurted out, 'I know Alan wants an heir, but… I don't know if I can do this again.'

He stared at her, betraying none of his thoughts. His blue eyes were like river stones, and she could not understand what he wanted from her.

Then he took a step nearer. 'If you were my wife, I would never give you to another man. I would slaughter him where he stood.'

She felt his penetrating gaze like an invisible touch. And from the heat of his stare, she knew that he still wanted her, even after all these years. Whether he spoke with jealousy or anger at the choice she had made, the result was the same. 'Alan is only trying to protect Pevensham,' she murmured. 'And me. He knows he is incapable of giving me a child.' She rubbed at her arms, feeling the chill of the room. 'I understand why he asked this of me, but what he wants is wrong.'

His expression grew shielded, and she could

not tell what he was thinking now. His blue eyes never strayed from her face. 'What do *you* want, Rosamund?'

'I told Alan I would agree to his wishes...but I lied.' Her face burned with humiliation, but she forced herself to finish. 'I cannot betray my marriage vows. Not even with you.'

He didn't seem at all surprised. 'And what if Alan dies? Where will you go?'

She couldn't let herself think that far ahead. 'I intend to stay by his side, until the very last moment. I hope to remain here, but with Owen, I don't know...' Her words trailed off and she took a steadying breath. 'I don't want Alan to die, Warrick. I owe him my loyalty. He has always been good to me.'

He moved closer then, so close that she sensed the heat of his body. 'I know you want me to go away and leave you alone.'

His voice was sensual, flooding her mind with visions of the past. Her heartbeat quickened with fear of what he would do. She swallowed and tried to take a step backwards. But Warrick's hands moved to her waist, holding her in place.

'I am not the man I once was, Rosamund.' The heat of his hands burned through her kirtle, making her remember what it was to have his touch upon her skin. 'I watched you marry another man, and it changed me.'

He drew his hands up her spine in a soft caress. 'Do you remember what it was like between us? You used to press yourself close to me, kissing me until we could hardly breathe.'

'You spoke words of love, and I believed them.' His hands stroked down again, moving towards her hips. 'Or have you forgotten the promises you made? That *I* would be your husband and no other man.'

The words came to her lips, the truths she was too afraid to speak. When her father had learned that she had given her innocence to Warrick, his rage had been so strong, she had no doubt at all that Harold would have killed him. She had never seen him so furious, and she saw that same anger mirrored in Warrick's eyes now.

'I was there on the day you married Alan. I stood and watched while de Courcy claimed you as his wife. I joined the guests at the wedding feast, and every bite was like dust in my mouth. And when they took you away to share his bed—' Warrick's voice broke off, and it was filled with such frustration and rage, it frightened her.

But then his expression turned sensual. 'I know full well that you do not want me.' His hands encircled her waist and he held her closer, making her aware of his desire. 'But I do not believe it has anything to do with honour. You are afraid of remembering what it was like between us.'

She was shocked at the response of her own body to the pressure of his hips. His sinful words brought back memories of the forbidden, of skin upon skin. She ached at the sensation of his hard body pressed to hers, and it made her heart beat faster. Her breasts grew tight against her gown, yearning for his touch.

Alan had never made her feel anything at all in their marriage bed. She had endured her husband's attentions but never had he made her feel alive—only guilty. And during her pregnancy, she had given excuses for him not to share her bed.

Warrick traced his finger over her cheek and down her throat. In a low voice he said, 'I find myself wanting to say yes to your husband's proposition. For you are bound to obey, are you not? Especially when it means saving this castle.'

'I don't want you,' she gritted out. 'Not like this.'

But the words were a lie. Her blood was coursing through her body, making her remember the fierce response that only he could conjure. In the past, his kiss had echoed within her skin, arousing her until she had cried out with desire. He knew just how to draw out her response, though she tried to force back the feelings.

Warrick threaded his hands in her hair, leaning in so close, she felt the planes of his hard body against hers. 'I would have Alan's full permission to claim you, in the hopes of conceiving a child. But he would never know what truly happens between us.'

His hands moved down her spine, and with the heat of his skin, she felt herself awakening beneath his touch.

'I want you to know what you've been missing during these three years. You chose the wrong man, Rosamund. And when I touch you, you'll wish to God you had stayed with me instead.'

'Don't do this.' She would not stand for his threats, not now. In one motion, she unsheathed her knife and held it to his heart. 'I may be Alan's property, but I am not yours.'

'Not yet,' he murmured.

And when he released her, leaving her behind, the blade clattered from her fingertips.

She was shaking so badly, she could hardly stand. God help her now.

Warrick returned to de Courcy's bedchamber, his mood grim. An honourable man would refuse this bargain and walk away—he knew that. But in three years, he hadn't forgotten the fury at watching the woman he loved marry someone else. He had endured countless lashes for her sake, believing she would remain true to him. And after it was done, his father had watched him bleed.

'She was never going to wed a man like you. Rosamund de Beaufort is too high-born.'

The agony of his wounds was so harsh, he could say nothing. But his father's words cut deeper than any lash.

'I should have ordered them to kill you instead. Your life is worth nothing.'

He had grown accustomed to his father's hatred, after all these years. Edward de Laurent believed the lies of his wife, not the truth. Warrick had long ago given up the idea that his father would ever see him as a man of worth.

But he had been mistaken in thinking that Rosamund would be different.

She claimed she had married Alan to save Warrick's life…and that might have held some truth, but why had she not fought to stay with him? This beautiful maiden, who had met with him in stolen moments, promising to love him for the rest of her life, had suddenly grown cold. She had turned from him, leaving him to spend years with only a sword for company.

And now Alan wanted him to sire a child upon her? It was the strangest turn of fate he'd ever imagined.

He had wanted to ignore this summons to Pevensham, truthfully. He had no place upon an estate such as this. Although he was of noble birth, he would never be anything more than a warrior. There were no estates he could inherit, no lands for him to rule. He was expected to marry and live with his brother Rhys.

Or die in battle, if his father had his way.

Over the years, his stepmother Analise had convinced Edward de Laurent that Warrick was simple-minded and incapable of leadership. Absently, he rubbed at the scar upon his wrist. His gut tightened at the memory of the woman, and he pushed back the darkness. She was dead now, and his father had taken a third wife.

But the fact remained—Edward de Laurent had believed Analise's claims, hardly giving any attention to Warrick. The need to prove his father wrong had drawn him into the king's service and into countless battles.

Now, he had been given an opportunity to control lands that spanned even greater a distance than his family's. No longer would Edward de Laurent look upon him as the spare son who would live at home, possessing no estates of his own. Warrick could command of his own castle, and be equal in status to his brother Rhys.

All he had to do was murder an innocent man… or sleep with the man's wife, he thought wryly. Neither was an honourable choice.

And yet, Alan was right. His brother Owen fully intended to take possession of Pevensham, and it was possible that he could harm Rosamund. Certainly, the man wouldn't hesitate to kill an unborn child if it threatened his inheritance.

Warrick reached for his sword, and he clenched the familiar hilt. If he agreed to sire a son with Rosamund, there were endless risks. She might not conceive, and all would be for naught. Or if she did, others might question the child's legitimacy. Even if it came to pass as Alan desired, it meant that the child would grow up believing that another man was his father.

There were no clear answers, yet he stood at Alan's bedside. It was best to speak the truth. 'I have spoken to Rosamund, and she does not wish to dishonour her marriage vows.'

'She will do it if I command it of her.'

Warrick had no intention of forcing any woman.

Even the woman he had once desired beyond all else. 'I will not take Rosamund against her wishes.'

'She understands what is necessary to protect Pevensham. This is her home, and she has no desire for Owen to inherit.' Despite his physical weakness, Alan possessed a will of iron. 'Rosamund is a woman who is loyal and virtuous. She does not understand the greater need. I want her to be protected and cherished when I am gone. You could do this, and you would receive wealth and lands in return. Any man would welcome this opportunity.'

'Why me?' he shot back. 'You could choose any unmarried man in England, and all would be willing to do this.'

'Because I want a man who will take care of her after I am gone. Someone who will put her needs first. If all I wanted was someone to get a child on her that would be naught of concern.' Alan's face grew tight with his own frustration. 'I care about Rosamund, and I will not let my brother hurt her.'

'Do you not trust your guards to keep her safe?'

'My men cannot protect her when she is alone in her chamber at night. Owen will find a way, and I will be unable to stop him after I am dead.'

Warrick said nothing. The man's behaviour

seemed impossibly selfless. He didn't understand how anyone could make such an offer—especially wedded to a woman like Rosamund. If he were in Alan's place, he would die before giving her to someone else. He would hire a hundred men to defend her, if needed.

'There are a dozen ways you could protect her,' he said. 'If you truly loved her, you would never force her to lie with someone else to conceive a child.'

At that accusation, Alan's face hardened. 'I love her enough to give her what she truly wants, above all else.' He sat up straighter in his bed. 'She might have spoken her vows, but her heart was never mine. She obeyed her father and married me.' Alan's tone turned dark. 'I wanted her—I won't lie. But it broke her heart to wed me. She is a dutiful, faithful wife, but she does not love me the way I love her. I thought time would change it, but now my life grows short.

'And because of the sacrifices she made, I want to give her back what she desires most of all. The life she wanted to have with you.'

There was no doubting the sincerity of Alan's words, but Warrick didn't believe that Rosamund would agree to marry him now. She had made her intentions clear enough when she had obeyed her father's command. And though Warrick had come to the wedding, she had never looked at him once.

'She made her choice years ago.' He understood that Pevensham wanted him to protect Rosamund after he was gone, but Warrick didn't delude himself into thinking Rosamund still held feelings towards him.

'I may be dying, but I am not blind,' Alan countered. 'I saw her misery on our wedding day, and I saw her reaction when you answered my summons. Once she recognises the necessity, I believe she will do what is necessary to protect our lands.'

But Warrick disagreed. 'Rosamund has no intention of dishonouring her marriage vows, no matter what she told you.'

'There must be a child,' Alan insisted. His frustrated anger was evident in the planes of his face, and his hands clenched. 'It is the only way to ensure that Pevensham does not fall into Owen's hands. And once she conceives, I want you to take her to my estate in Ireland. My steward will grant you both sanctuary until she gives birth.'

But Warrick was uncertain it was the best course of action. If he removed Rosamund from her home, it would only invite Owen de Courcy to pursue her.

Alan met Warrick's gaze evenly. 'Will you do this for us? For her?'

He had not yet decided whether to accept Alan's proposition. Not only was Rosamund adamant that she would not break her vows, there was no telling whether the plan would work, even if she did change her mind. At the moment, she believed that a simple lie would pacify her husband, and she had no intention of attempting to conceive.

'I will think about it,' he said at last. It was the best answer he could give. If Rosamund wanted his help, he would not deny her. But until then, he would bide his time.

The door to Alan's bedchamber swung open, and Rosamund entered the room. She had gathered her composure and took a seat upon a low stool beside the hearth. Then she picked up her sewing and began to embroider the linen. Nothing in her demeanour suggested the rebellion within her heart.

When Warrick studied her more closely, Rosamund's green eyes revealed a stubborn nature. She had unyielding loyalty and was not about to obey this command meekly.

Alan was asking him to lay siege to this woman's body and heart, with a child and a castle as the prizes to be won. But it was far more compli-cated than that.

'Rosamund, Warrick tells me that you have changed your mind about our agreement.' His ex-pression held annoyance. 'I thought you under-stood the necessity of this arrangement.'

At that, she set aside her sewing and stood from her stool. 'My lord husband, I told him that I am a woman of honour, and I—'

'You promised,' Alan repeated. He extended his hand to his wife, and she went to his bedside. 'This is not about your desires or mine, or even his. This is about protecting everything we have built. If I could give you a child, I would have done so by now, Rosamund.' His complexion had gone grey, and he leaned back against the pillows. 'If you wait until I am gone, it will be too late. The child's parentage will be questioned, and I cannot risk this.'

Warrick remained in place, feeling like an out-sider while Alan stroked his wife's hand. She leaned in, murmuring to him, and the man closed his eyes for a moment.

'Rosamund, does Warrick de Laurent frighten you?'

'Yes,' she admitted. But the look on her face was enigmatic, as if something else troubled her.

'Do you believe he would harm you?' Alan continued. 'Would you rather I chose another man?'

'No.' She shook her head. 'I could not imagine lying with anyone else.' The moment she spoke the words, her face reddened when she realised what she'd said.

Warrick remained silent, but he could see that she was not entirely immune to him. 'Lord Pevensham, I propose that we give Rosamund more time to think about this. And in the meantime, I will remain here with my men until she has made her decision.'

Alan didn't look pleased with his suggestion, but he had little alternative. Warrick wanted to speak with her again and learn whether it was honour that kept Rosamund from fulfilling her husband's desires—or fear of the feelings she had buried over the last three years.

Chapter Three

Three years earlier

Rosamund stared up at the Montbrooke donjon with wonder. The keep had a large rectangular tower and stood atop a hillside. The outer wall was three feet thick and stretched from the base of the mound nearly twenty feet high. Another tower stretched above the main gate with sentries posted.

The earl had invited her family here to witness the betrothal of his oldest son Rhys to Lianna MacKinnon, a Scottish heiress. Rosamund didn't know either of them, but her father was friends with Edward de Laurent. The betrothed couple would marry soon, which would help secure their lands at Eiloch.

She rode alongside her parents and sister across the drawbridge which spanned a deep moat filled with water. The portcullis was made of iron, and she saw dozens of sentries standing guard.

When they reached the inner bailey, several stable boys took their horses and helped them dismount. Rosamund stood with her sister while her father and mother went forward to greet Lord Montbrooke. Edward de Laurent had three children—a daughter Joan who was slightly older than Rosamund, his eldest son Rhys, and another son, Warrick.

It was Warrick who caught her attention from the first. He had dark hair and blue eyes that watched her with interest. He wore leather armour and had a sword at his belt, as if he had just come from the training field. She guessed he was twenty, and the longer he stared at her, the more her cheeks flushed. Never before had a handsome young man shown interest in her, and she wondered if he would speak with her later.

'Do not even consider it,' her younger sister Cecilia warned in a hard whisper. 'Father would never allow it.'

'Allow what?'

'Don't be coy. I saw the way you were looking at Warrick de Laurent.' Her sister reached out and gripped her hand. 'Father plans to betroth you to

Alan de Courcy. I heard he was already negotiating the marriage contract.'

The thought soured her stomach. Though she knew her marriage would be arranged, she had hoped to have a choice in it.

'So soon?' She couldn't hide the dismay in her voice.

'Within a year, so I've heard.' Cecilia spoke as if it had already happened. 'So do not imagine that he would settle for the youngest son of an earl— not when you could have a baron to wed.'

Rosamund ignored her younger sister and straightened her shoulders. Instead, when her parents brought them forward to be introduced, she kept a smile on her face when Warrick took her hand. He gave her fingers a slight squeeze, and her nerves twisted with a rush of giddiness.

Later, his eyes seemed to promise.

I will wait, she answered.

The opportunity came that afternoon when her family was invited to go riding across Lord Montbrooke's estate. Rosamund mounted her horse with the help of a groom and joined her sister, Cecilia. They waited with their parents and then began riding across the drawbridge. Her family was in the middle of the riders while Warrick de

Laurent rode with his father and sister. After a few minutes, she noticed that he had begun to drop back, slowing his pace to join her. When he risked a glance behind him, he nodded towards the rear of the travelling party, as if he wanted her to join him. But how could she do so without her sister's interference? Cecilia would never allow him to speak to her.

Fate intervened when her father brought Cecilia forward to introduce her to another member of the group. Rosamund seized the opportunity and slowed her horse even more. In time, Warrick drew his horse alongside hers, and they kept slowing down until they reached the last members of the group.

For a moment, they rode in silence, as if Warrick couldn't quite think of what to say. He had the demeanour of a soldier, Rosamund decided. Rather fierce and forbidding. She waited a little longer, and when finally she could bear it no longer, she asked, 'Is everything all right?'

He glanced at her and said, 'It is.'

'You look angry with me.' And he truly did. His blue eyes were glaring as he stared straight ahead at the travelling party.

'I'm not angry,' he gritted out.

She bit her lip, wondering if she had misread

his intentions. But when she studied him more closely, she saw that his cheeks were reddened. Was he...nervous?

He was one of the most handsome men she had ever seen. With his dark brown hair cropped short and his deep blue eyes, she felt her pulse race just by looking at him.

'Was there something you wanted?' she blurted out. 'Or shall I leave you in peace and rejoin my family?'

'Don't.' His words were clipped, and when she studied him more closely, she realised that he was struggling for words. In a way, he seemed frustrated with his inability to converse. It seemed to be an invisible shield of awkwardness between them.

'If you are not angry with me, was I wrong to join you? I mistakenly thought you wanted to speak with me.' She waited a moment, trying not to stare. His arms were corded with muscles, as if he spent hours training with the other men. Even his chainmail armour moulded against his body like another skin.

'I did want to speak with you,' he admitted, but he kept his attention fixed upon the horses ahead.

She waited a little longer, and when the silence

stretched again, she couldn't help her smile. 'Do you not know how to talk to women?'

Warrick turned back as if to snap at her, but when he saw that she was teasing, he shrugged. 'I've little experience with women.'

'Well, then, we should start with names. I am Rosamund de Beaufort.'

'I know who you are.'

'Of course you do, but it's a way of talking to a woman for the first time. Now tell me your name once more.'

His expression remained a block of granite. 'I am Warrick de Laurent.'

'There. That wasn't so hard, was it?' She brightened and was rewarded when he glanced back at her. His face still appeared uneasy, and she tried to start a conversation. 'Your lands are quite beautiful. I do love the forest here. Such tall trees. And look at the way the sunlight glimmers through the leaves. It's like the fairies cast a spell over them.' She continued to talk about whatever came into her mind, understanding that conversation was not easy for him. But then, when he still didn't say anything, she wondered if she was simply irritating him.

'Shall I stop talking?'

His blue eyes softened, and he shook his head. 'I like listening to you.'

The confession warmed her in ways she hadn't expected. There was more to this quiet man than she had realised.

Warrick reached out and took the reins of her horse. 'There's a forest path that cuts through the land over here, if you want to see it better. It ends along the same path as the others.'

She hesitated, wondering if she dared to part ways from her family with a man she barely knew. Though she wanted to explore the woods, she was uncertain whether it was wise.

'Or if you would rather stay with the others, it's all the same to me.' His tone was matter of fact, but she wondered what effort it had taken for him to voice the suggestion. Warrick truly was a man who didn't say a great deal.

'Only for a short while,' she said at last. 'My family will be angry with me if they discover I'm missing. And I cannot go far.'

At that, his mouth curved in a slight smile, and the sudden warmth stole her breath. 'For a moment, then.'

He walked his horse towards the right, and she saw a trail that led through the forest. Again, she glanced back at her father and sister, hoping they would not notice. Then she guided her horse behind Warrick's, following him into the woods. The moment she entered the trees, she slowed her pace and caught her breath. Moss covered the ground like an enchanted carpet, and lush ferns grew in the shadow of the trees. The sunlight painted the leaves gold, and she drank in the sight of the beauty. In her mind, she imagined creating a tapestry with the same bold colours, and she wondered if it could be done.

'I do love it here. It's beautiful,' she told him.

'Do you…want to see more?' he offered. 'Just for a moment or two?' He glanced back towards the open meadow where the rest of the riders were.

She nodded. 'But I cannot stay long. Both of us will be missed, and I don't want to cause you any trouble.'

'This forest runs parallel to their trail, so we will join up with them quickly.' He led her a little deeper into the woods, but she could still catch glimpses of the riders. Ahead of them was a small stream dotted with rocks. It ran along the edge of the path, and she stopped to watch the water slosh against the stones.

'This looks like the sort of place where one might encounter magic,' she said in a whisper.

'Or an enchantment. Thank you for bringing me here, Warrick.'

He remained stoic, but in his blue eyes, she saw an intensity that caught her interest. Of all the men she had ever encountered, he was the quietest. And yet, she sensed that there was far more beneath his serious exterior.

'I suppose we cannot stay any longer.' Her voice revealed her regret, and she turned her horse back to the pathway. 'Shall we race back to the others?' She didn't wait for him to agree, but spurred her horse quickly, not waiting for him to catch up.

'Rosamund, wait!' he called out. 'It's not safe to ride fast along the pathway.'

My goodness, she'd never heard him speak so many words in one sentence. She slowed down and turned to look at him. He was riding hard towards her, and then abruptly, he ducked in the saddle to avoid a low branch.

His horse reared up at the sudden motion and threw him off. Warrick went crashing to the ground, where he rolled down the embankment and into the cold stream.

Rosamund abandoned her horse and hurried towards him. He was lying in the water, and she guessed he had struck his head on one of the rocks.

'Warrick, are you all right?' She waded into the stream, heedless of her skirts, and rolled him over. Saints, but he could drown in this pool if he was unconscious.

His head was swollen and bleeding, but she breathed a sigh of relief when she heard him groan.

'Can you stand up?'

'I need a moment,' he answered. 'I'm feeling dizzy.'

'Then hold on to me,' she bade him. She sat on one of the rocks while the water coursed around both of them. He did hold her waist, steadying himself. Rosamund felt terrible for what had happened. He had only meant to show her the forest and now he'd been injured as a result. She could see the pain in the lines of his face, the taut tension in his hands.

But then, he seemed to gather control. Something shifted between them, and this time, he looked into her eyes. There was wonder in his expression, and a yearning she'd never expected. His hand moved to her cheek, and the coolness of his caress awakened a contrasting heat in her skin.

'So beautiful…' he breathed.

His dark hair was wet from the water, and droplets covered his bristled face. Those blue eyes burned into hers, as if he wanted to kiss her. Saints above, but he was handsome in a forbidding, almost dangerous way. She saw a tiny scar at his temple, as if he'd narrowly blocked a sword from slicing his face. Time was slipping away from them, and she was no longer aware of the freezing water or anything else but this man.

'Are you badly hurt?' she whispered.

'I don't even feel it.' His thumb edged her cheek, and his gaze slid over her face, down the lines of her body. She went motionless, not daring to move or even breathe. The heat of his eyes burned through her, and she felt an answering call within her body.

She grew sensitive to the slight touch upon her face and the gentle pressure of his thumb. For a moment, she closed her eyes, uncertain of whether she should pull away. But his palm lingered upon her face, learning the lines of her jaw and chin. A thousand warnings crashed through her, of what could happen while she was alone in the forest with a strange man.

And yet, not once had he threatened her. His touch was inviting, drawing her closer. She felt an invisible connection with this man, making her crave more.

Then he leaned forward and captured her mouth

with his. It started out gentle, a slight brush of his lips against hers. She was shocked to feel herself responding to the kiss, tasting his mouth in return. The unexpected kiss heightened her awareness of this man. The cold and the heat mingled together, and he cupped her face with his wet hands, stealing the very breath from her. His lips were firm, claiming her kiss as his own. Never had she imagined a moment like this, but Warrick de Laurent was clearly a man of actions, not words.

He *did* like her. And with the way he was stroking her wet hair, plundering her mouth, she hardly cared that he wasn't speaking. All she knew was that she wanted this kiss, wanted to know more about this man. His mouth had tempted her, drawing her closer to him. Heat and need poured over her like water wearing down the resolve of her virtue.

'I think we should—'

'No. Don't think.' He stood from the water and lifted her off the rock, bringing her to the banks of the stream. And when he lowered her to stand, she found that he was right. She couldn't think at all. Her thoughts slipped away like grains of sand.

'Why did you kiss me?' she murmured. 'We've only just met.'

'Because I wanted to.' He leaned down and stole

another hard kiss, and it was all she could do not to embrace him, pulling him as close as she dared. She didn't understand the desires he evoked in her, but this man reminded her of an ancient conqueror, seizing what he wanted.

'Why did you kiss me back?' he asked against her lips, nipping them lightly.

She didn't know what to say, truly. In the end, she was honest with him. 'Because I wanted to know what it was like to kiss a man.'

'I was your first.' His words weren't a question.

'Yes,' she admitted. Her cheeks bloomed with the flush of embarrassment. 'They will be looking for us now,' she said, feeling the rise of anxiety. 'We're both soaking wet, and you're hurt, and—'

'Rosamund,' he said, touching his finger to her lips. 'Do not be afraid. I'm not a threat to you.'

She grew silent, and Warrick led her back to her horse. His hands lingered upon her waist a moment before he helped her mount. He swiped at the blood on his head and winced before he returned to his own horse. So he *had* been hurt but was hiding his pain from her.

When they reached the path beyond the edges of the forest, she saw that the travelling party had stopped and everyone was staring. Shame suffused her, and she felt as if her actions were branded upon her face. 'What should we tell them?'

Warrick led the way and shrugged. 'The truth.' His eyes grew hooded as if in memory of the shared kiss. But there was a hint of amusement in his eyes.

'We cannot tell them that.' She was aghast at the idea. 'I will say that I wanted to see the forest, and you accompanied me. I fell into the stream, and you rescued me.'

'But you rescued me,' he contradicted, bringing his horse alongside hers.

'They will never believe that,' she argued. 'My father certainly won't. For my sake, please don't deny my story.'

'I will say nothing.' But as they drew closer to the group, he lowered his voice. 'Will you meet with me again?'

His words slid over her in an invisible caress. And although she knew she shouldn't do this, she felt a rush of forbidden desire for this man. She hardly knew him, and it wasn't at all wise. But her lips still tingled from the kiss.

'I don't know,' she whispered. 'My father would be angry.'

His expression sobered as if he had expected her to refuse. In his blue eyes, she saw the guarded look of a soldier who possessed no emotions at all. Looking at him now, she would never have imagined he had such hidden passion.

Someone had hurt this man in the past, she decided. And he had closed himself off from everyone because of it.

'All right,' she answered. 'Where?'

He appeared taken aback by her sudden change of heart. The coldness receded, and in its place was a look of disbelief. Then he answered, 'Meet me by the stream. Tomorrow at dawn.'

Over the next few weeks, they continued to meet in secret. Warrick was well aware that Rosamund's father, Harold de Beaufort, did not want him anywhere near his daughter. He had made it clear that Warrick was not to speak with her again.

But the man's insinuation, that he wasn't good enough for Rosamund, burned through him, igniting the desire for rebellion. Rosamund was the most beautiful woman he'd ever laid eyes on. From the first moment he'd seen her, one word had been branded upon his soul: *Mine*.

Her black hair held a slight wave to it and curled to her hips. Her green eyes held joy, and by the bones of St. Christopher, the woman never ceased talking. She talked enough for both of them, which was fine by him. He preferred to listen and to judge people by their actions.

But after Rosamund had rescued him from the stream, he'd given in to primal instincts. He'd craved the taste of her lips, and he'd taken them without any regret. What startled him was the fact that she'd kissed him back. Why this exquisite woman would grant him her favour was impossible to understand.

He knew better than to imagine she would care for a man like him, landless and hardly more than a soldier. But he savoured every moment of their meetings, knowing they would not last.

Today, Rosamund was seated upon the stone stairs that led towards the battlements. She had brought her sewing, and the light summer breeze lifted strands of hair back from her face. The very sight of her was a distraction that quickened his pulse. He knew she had come to watch him train with his brother and the other men. When he stole a look at her, there was a faint smile upon her face.

He wore chainmail armour this morn, and his brother Rhys came up behind him. 'Are you wanting her to watch, Brother?'

He turned and saw the knowing smile on Rhys's face. 'It matters not if she is there.'

'I've seen the way you stare at her.' Rhys handed him a quarterstaff. 'Spar with me a moment. I'll make you look good.'

'Her father would be furious if he saw her here. It's dangerous with so many men about.'

'That is her risk to take. And she does want to watch you.' Rhys grinned. 'I think we should show her more.'

He had no idea what his brother was talking about. Then Rhys stripped away his chainmail hauberk and tunic, until he stood bare-chested. 'If she's going to look, shouldn't you give her something to look at?'

He wasn't at all certain of this, but Rhys was already reaching to help him with his hauberk.

'I'll wager her gaze is upon you this very moment,' his brother said in a low voice.

'This is foolish.'

'Not for quarterstaffs,' Rhys argued. 'You don't need heavy armour.'

He was right. Although Warrick felt awkward about it, he stripped to his waist. Just as Rhys had predicted, he caught Rosamund eyeing him. She gave a secret smile and continued sewing.

At that moment, Rhys lunged at him, and Warrick deflected the blow out of instinct. His brother was merciless, striking with speed and strength.

Warrick dodged a blow and followed up with a hard strike to his brother's ribs.

Rhys grunted and retaliated by slicing the quarterstaff at Warrick's knees. He jumped out of the way, only for his brother to strike his back and knock him to the ground. He rolled away and caught his brother across the ankles, tripping him. 'I thought you were going to make me look good.'

His brother cursed and got to his feet just as Warrick did. 'I lied. But even so, she's watching you.'

Warrick turned his head and moved out of the way at the same time. His brother's blow missed him entirely, and Rosamund smiled.

He struck Rhys's quarterstaff over and over again, moving with speed and intensity, until his brother was forced to retreat. He lunged hard, about to knock his brother to the ground, but Rhys dodged the blow, laughing.

'Go and talk with her.' His brother clapped a hand on his back, half-pushing him towards the beautiful maiden.

Warrick gripped his quarterstaff, pausing a moment. Rosamund remained on the stairs but set her sewing down. Her face softened at the sight of him with the hint of another smile. God above, she was the most beautiful woman he'd ever seen.

He couldn't think of what to say to her, for his tongue tangled up.

The sparring match had ignited his desire for this woman. When he crossed the inner bailey, she stood to meet him. A faint blush stained her cheeks, but she never took her gaze from his. He stood two steps below her, and glimpsed the fallen sewing. It was like nothing he had seen before, with all the colours of the sky and clouds blended into a scene. It reminded him of a stained-glass window, with all the colourful pieces creating the whole.

'You fought well,' she said quietly.

Her face was so close to his, he could imagine sliding his hands through her thick dark hair and bringing her mouth to his. She was the sort of woman men would fight for, hoping to win her as a conquest.

Warrick wanted to tell her this or to compliment her sewing. But the words were caught in his throat, stifled by his own awkwardness.

Rosamund reached over her shoulder to pull a ribbon free from her braid. Her green eyes studied him with interest as she ordered, 'Hold out your arm.'

He obeyed, and she tied the ribbon to it. The light touch of her fingers against his bare skin evoked a searing ache. He wanted to press her back against the stairs and kiss her until she could no longer stand. But he was aware of the others watching over them.

When she had tied the ribbon, she let her hands linger a moment before she lowered them to her sides. The small scrap of silk was a visible binding to this woman. In a low voice she murmured, 'Now you have my favour.'

Warrick reached for her hand and held it a moment. His thumb brushed over the centre of her palm, and he answered, 'Just as you have mine, my lady.'

A blinding smile crossed her face, and she gripped his hand in answer. Several seconds passed before she released his palm. 'I should go now. My father will be looking for me, as will my mother. Or my sister Cecilia.'

Before he could speak a word, she grasped her skirts and walked down the stairs past him. 'Farewell, Warrick.'

Only after she had gone did he realise that she'd left her sewing behind. He picked it up, not knowing whether to follow Rosamund and return it.

He studied it, and his brother approached. 'Are you thinking of picking up a needle yourself, Warrick?' Rhys's tone held a teasing air.

'She dropped it,' was all he could say.

'Did she? Or did she leave it on purpose, to give you a reason to see her again?'

The thought hadn't occurred to him, but it was possible. He was about to pursue Rosamund when Rhys caught him by the arm. 'Not yet, Brother. Wait another day.'

Warrick reached for his tunic and pulled it over his head. 'I'll give it to one of the servants to return to her.'

'Why would you? She deliberately left it to you.' His brother shrugged. 'Claim a kiss from her as thanks.'

He wanted nothing more. But he was also a man of reason. 'Her father would never allow a match between her and a man like me.'

'You desire her. Just as she desires you,' his brother answered. 'At least one of us might have a good marriage.' Tension slid over his face, the tension of a man who welcomed execution over his own betrothal.

'Lianna MacKinnon is a beautiful woman.'

'With a heart of ice,' Rhys finished. 'She despises the air I breathe, and with good reason.' He shrugged. 'Were it possible, I would take her to Scotland and leave her there. That would make her happy.' But then he masked his frustration. 'One day, you will understand what it is to be powerless to command your own life. God help you then.'

Later that afternoon, Rosamund stood still while her maid braided her hair and tied it up with a new ribbon. Her mother shook her head in exasperation. 'Really, Rosamund, how could you lose a hair ribbon?' She chided her about being more careful, but Rosamund paid her no heed.

She hadn't forgotten the sight of Warrick sparring without his tunic. His skin held a darker cast, and every muscle appeared carved from stone. A sheen of perspiration had beaded upon his chest, and she had been spellbound by him. Though he spoke little, his eyes had burned into her as if he'd wanted to kiss her again. She had never experienced a kiss like his, and perhaps it was a sin to long for it again.

'Did you hear me, Rosamund?' her mother demanded.

'Of course,' she lied.

'Now remember, if you are among the women chosen for the game, you may grant a cake as your favour, but nothing more. And Cecilia may not be chosen. Even if she begs it of you, tell her no.' Agnes de Beaufort sent her a strong look of warning.

Rosamund mumbled her assent, though she had no idea what game her mother was speaking of. She was accustomed to games of skill like archery or swimming, but nothing involving a favour. It might be a game that was meant to kindle the courtship between Rhys de Laurent and his bride, Lianna MacKinnon. She knew that something had caused hatred between the pair of them, but could not imagine what it was.

'You look beautiful,' her mother pronounced, and took her by the hand to lead her from the chamber. 'And by this time next summer, you will be celebrating your own wedding to Alan de Courcy. He will make a fine husband for you.'

Rosamund slowed her steps, startled by her mother's words. Although her sister had mentioned it earlier, she hadn't paid Cecilia much heed. 'I have never met the man.' *And he isn't the one I want.* Her attention was caught by the stoic, handsome warrior who made her heartbeat quicken.

'He is wealthy and is a strong ally of King Henry. That is all that should concern you.' Agnes's clipped tone brooked no discussion on the matter. 'Trust that your father and I will choose an appropriate man.' She touched Rosamund's hair, adjusting the ribbon. 'My father chose Harold as my husband, and I have never lacked for anything.'

Except love, Rosamund thought.

'Was there never anyone else you wanted to wed?' she asked her mother.

Agnes stiffened at the question before she shielded her response. 'Of course not. I was content to be an obedient daughter. Just like you.'

But she questioned whether her mother had ever held any secret desire of her own. Or whether she had ever loved anyone else.

Rosamund fell silent and walked alongside her mother until they joined the other guests. Lord Montbrooke was seated at the high table upon a dais with his wife beside him. His eldest son Rhys sat with his betrothed wife Lianna MacKinnon, while Warrick sat on the far end, furthest from all of them. Lianna was tall and beautiful, with long red hair that curled to her shoulders. She wore a deep green kirtle and a circlet made of beaten silver. A simple cross hung around her throat. But it was the expression of grief and misery that caught Rosamund's attention. The young woman appeared devastated at the prospect of this marriage, and she would not even look at Rhys.

Heaven help them both.

The thought of her own marriage troubled

her, and she prayed her father would change his mind. She had no wish to marry Alan de Courcy, whether he was wealthy or not. And it felt as if she were becoming a pawn in a game she could not win.

Rosamund joined her parents at the table closest to the dais, fully aware of Warrick's presence. Despite being at the high table, he appeared distracted and separated from all of them. It almost seemed that he would have preferred dining among the soldiers. Even his father never spoke to him at all. It was as if he were invisible.

Strange.

Men and women raised their drinks to toast the health of the betrothed couple, but the veiled enmity between Lianna and Rhys was undeniable. The young woman never spoke to him, only to Lord Montbrooke and his wife.

For a moment, Rosamund let herself imagine what it would be like if she were betrothed to Warrick, sitting in their places. The very thought warmed her, for she liked him very much. Not only was he a strong fighter and handsome, but she would never forget his words—*I like listening to you.*

The feasting continued, and her sister Cecilia

leaned in. 'Let him go, Rosamund. I don't want to see you hurt.'

'Why could they not arrange a betrothal with Warrick?' she whispered. 'He is the son of an earl and from a noble family.'

'But he is the youngest. He will have no property of his own.'

'Surely he has something,' she argued. 'They have vast holdings.'

'*Rhys* has everything,' Cecilia said. 'And their sister Joan has the rest as part of her dowry. His father left him nothing at all.'

It made no sense at all. 'How did you learn this?'

'I eavesdropped when Mother was sewing with Lady Montbrooke. She told her everything. Did you know that Warrick didn't speak for nearly two years, after his baby sister died?'

'No, I didn't.' And yet, it didn't surprise her. A grieving brother would have little to say. But she couldn't understand why his own father had cut him off. When she lifted her gaze to his, Warrick met it with his own intense stare. In that moment, it was as if everything else disappeared and it was only the two of them.

It might only be infatuation, but she could not deny the feelings he conjured within her. She wished that she could sit beside him now and speak with him.

As the meal ended, Lord Montbrooke called for everyone to gather outside for evening stories, contests, and games. Rosamund followed the others and took her place beside her sister when Lady Montbrooke called her forward.

'Will you join the other ladies in a game of stoolball?' she enquired.

She had never played the game, but it sounded intriguing. 'If you wish.'

Several other young ladies were gathered together, along with Lianna MacKinnon. Lady Montbrooke gave each of them a small tansy cake wrapped in linen, explaining, 'I know we usually play this game at Easter, but it's one of Rhys's favourites. These are the prizes.' Then she led them to an open clearing where six wooden stools were placed. On the opposite end, there were several wooden balls and a stick with a paddle on one end.

'Go and choose a stool to stand upon,' she directed the women.

Lianna hung back, unwilling to join them. 'I have no wish to play. Let the others enjoy themselves.' But after Lady Montbrooke spoke with her quietly, Lianna reluctantly chose the stool nearest to the men.

Rosamund didn't understand what they were meant to do, but she followed what the other girls were doing. One of the women nearby was giggling, and Rosamund asked, 'Why are you laughing?'

The girl stepped onto her stool and said, 'Because the men can choose which prize they want. Either the tansy cake or a kiss.'

Rosamund felt her face burn with apprehension at the idea. Especially since Warrick was one of the men competing. Now her mother's earlier warning made sense. She had no desire to be kissed by a stranger. But if Warrick wanted a kiss…she didn't know what she should do.

At the far end, the men lined up for their turn. She soon realised that one man was attempting to throw a ball at the stool Lianna was standing upon. Another man defended her by striking the ball away with the stick. He ran hard around the line of stools, and his ball struck the base of it. After he had scored a point for his team, he returned to stand before one of the maidens. She offered him the cake, but instead, he took her face between his hands and brought her down for a deep kiss.

The men cheered, and the winner escorted the

maiden away from the stools. Another young woman took her place.

Rosamund studied the crowd of men and women and saw Rhys pick up his ball. Warrick took his place with the bat and waited.

'Don't hit it, Brother,' Rhys warned. His betrothed wife, Lianna, stood motionless while he prepared to aim the ball towards her stool. Rosamund almost pitied the woman for if Warrick did nothing, she would certainly be kissed in front of everyone. But Rhys's anger made it an uncomfortable moment. It seemed that he wanted to humiliate Lianna, to force her to accept him.

Rosamund lifted her gaze to Warrick, hoping he would understand her unspoken message. He glanced at her and gave a single nod. The moment Rhys released the ball, Warrick struck it hard with his bat. It bounded across the grass and struck Rosamund's stool hard.

She should have realised he would aim it towards her. It might have been luck that he'd hit it there, but she wasn't certain. But as he ran past all the stools, she glimpsed a hard smile.

Would he try to kiss her in front of everyone? If he tried, her father would be furious. And yet, she wanted nothing more than to feel his mouth upon hers again. Her heart pounded when he approached the stool.

She remained frozen, feeling terrified that he might actually kiss her. But there was a way around this. In the barest whisper, she said, 'At dawn, I will meet you by the stream for the kiss. For now, please accept the tansy cake.'

He made no effort to hide his interest. But when he took the tansy cake, he unwrapped the linen and broke off a piece. In front of everyone, he fed it to her, his thumb brushing against her lips. The gesture startled her, and she tasted the cake.

It was terrible, and she made a face at the herbs. With a laugh, she broke off a piece and fed it to him in return. 'You try it. It's awful.'

But his mouth closed over her thumb, gently kissing it as he ate the cake. There was no doubting that he wanted the kiss. 'Tomorrow, Rosamund.'

She took his arm, and he guided her away from the others. With a soft smile, she answered, 'I promise.'

Chapter Four

Warrick rode towards the forest, but Rosamund was not yet there. He sat upon a rock, waiting for her. Only a few moments later, he heard a rustling noise in the tree beside him. He glanced up and saw her sitting among the branches, a delighted smile upon her face.

'Why are you in the tree, Rosamund?' Though it wasn't high above the ground, it must have been difficult to climb with her skirts. And he saw no sign of her horse anywhere.

'I had to, else someone might find me.' She beckoned for him to climb up with her. 'Will you join me here?'

'It would be easier to kiss you here on the ground,' he pointed out. Her promise had haunted him all the night, as had the fleeting taste of her skin. He could not deny the effect she had on him.

He would have walked through a pillar of fire to kiss her again.

'No one will see us here,' she said. And in that, she had a good point. Warrick wasn't entirely certain how she had managed to get into the tree, but he seized a large branch above his head and swung one leg over. He was upside down for a moment and then righted himself. It was then that he saw her studying a bird's nest between two smaller branches.

'Look at the blue eggs,' she murmured. 'They will hatch any day now.'

'Don't touch the nest,' he warned. 'Else the mother will abandon them.'

She nodded, her face alight with wonder. It was something he would never tire of seeing—her reaction to the world around her. Rosamund saw beauty in the most ordinary things, and it pleased him to see her smile. He had brought her a gift this day, one that he hoped she would like.

'I have something for you,' he said. 'First, the sewing you left on the stairs.'

Her face relaxed into a smile and she accepted the folded linen. 'Thank you. I was hoping you would bring it to me.'

'But I also wanted to give you this.' He pulled out a small pouch and handed it to her. It pleased him to see the delighted expression on her face. But when she opened the pouch and withdrew skeins of dyed thread, her smile faded. Instead, she appeared upset, and he had no notion of what he'd done wrong.

'Don't you like it?'

Her eyes welled up with tears, and she nodded. 'No one has ever given me such a gift. I adore it.' And yet, she appeared miserable.

An awkward silence spread between them. He had thought she would be overjoyed, that she would smile and embrace him. Instead, she appeared devastated by the gift, regardless of her words.

'Why do you weep?' he ventured. He wasn't entirely certain he wanted to know the answer.

Rosamund tucked away the pouch of threads, swiping at the tears. A pained expression came over her face as she gathered her composure. Then she took his hands in hers, swallowing hard. 'Because my mother told me I am to be married to Alan de Courcy. And I would rather be married to a man like you. Someone who understands me.' She lifted her gaze to his, and in her green eyes, he saw the yearning.

In that moment, time seemed to stop moving. He understood that he was not worthy of her, but he needed to show her how much she meant to him. This exquisite woman was so far beyond his reach, but he could not deny the need to touch her. He touched the edge of her cheek with his knuckle, and she covered his hand with her own.

'I want the kiss you promised.' His voice came out ragged, and he wanted to lose himself in that mouth, to show her how much he wanted her.

Rosamund pressed her lips to his hand, kissing it softly. With a wry smile, he remarked, 'That isn't where I wanted you to kiss me, Rosamund.'

Her expression held amusement, and she lifted her face to his. Her lips were soft, moulding against his. Rosamund wound her arms around his neck, and he was careful to keep her safely balanced upon the wide tree branch. He couldn't get enough of her, and the kiss turned wilder, hotter. Warrick felt the primal needs rising, and he moved her so that her back was against the tree trunk. He straddled the branch and brought her close so that her legs were around his waist. Then he wrapped his arms around the tree trunk, nestling their bodies close.

And yet, it wasn't close enough.

She let out a gasp when he slid his tongue inside her mouth. Though she was an innocent, she pressed her hips close so that the ridge of his arousal lay between her legs.

Her eyes widened, and Rosamund pulled back a moment. Her lips were swollen, and she framed his face with her hands. Then she traced a path down to his shoulders. 'I know I should not kiss you like this. But it doesn't feel wrong.'

She moved against him, and he could imagine the sweet wetness between her legs. He wanted to touch her intimately, to move her skirts aside and bury himself within her depths. It took an act of the greatest concentration not to move.

'Do you want me to stop?' he asked. His tone balanced on the razor edge of unfulfilled desire. Did she understand what she was doing to him when she moved against him? He tried to hold her with one arm, to keep her still.

Rosamund shook her head. 'I feel as if you are the only man in the world for me. And it breaks my heart to know that my father chose differently.'

She closed her eyes, and he saw the shadow of pain. Though he wasn't surprised at the betrothal, it was her response that startled him. She genuinely appeared upset.

He held her close, breathing in the scent of this woman. Nothing in the world would please him more than to have Rosamund de Beaufort at his side. He would have slain a thousand demons if it meant awakening beside her each day.

But he lacked everything her father wanted. He was not the heir, and though he was of noble birth, his wealth paled beside a man like Alan de Courcy.

Her green eyes held dismay, but he leaned in and kissed her. 'I would want nothing more than to marry you, Rosamund.'

But both of them knew it was impossible.

He tasted the salt of her tears, and she kissed him as if she never wanted it to end. The embrace shifted until he couldn't stop his own response. He needed to be closer to this woman, and he pulled her onto his lap with her legs around him. She let out a soft moan, trembling in his arms.

'Warrick,' she whispered. And then she moved herself against him, mimicking the sexual act. She let out a soft gasp, and her fingers dug into his arms.

He gritted his teeth, trying to hold back his body's needs. This was about her, about pleasuring this woman and stealing a forbidden moment.

'Do you trust me, Rosamund?' he asked.

Her expression was hazy, and she bit her lip as he continued to move against her. 'Yes.' Her face flushed with embarrassment and her own desire.

Warrick ignored the warnings that plundered his mind. He needed to brand himself upon Rosamund, so that no man could ever take his place.

She was pliant upon his lap, her skirts falling across them. But despite the barrier of fabric, he felt the heated warmth of her womanhood.

'Tell me what you would do if I were your wife,' she breathed. 'I want to hear it.'

He could hardly speak at all from the lust roaring inside him. But he understood that words would have to take the place of touch. He could not claim Rosamund the way he wanted to.

'If you were mine, I would lift your skirts right now,' he murmured. 'I would touch your bare skin.'

In silent answer, Rosamund lifted the edge of her hem and drew his hand to her calf. The invitation was impossible to resist. His hand trailed down until he slipped his hand beneath the kirtle. Against his fingertips, he felt the soft silk of her leg. Gently, he stroked her, his hand rising higher until he cupped her thigh.

Her face tightened with shock, but she didn't pull away. Instead, she lifted her mouth to his, kissing him again. He traced the outline of her hip and then found the curve of her bottom.

Against her lips, he said, 'I want you, Rosamund.' He took her hand and moved it to his heartbeat. 'Do you feel how badly I need you?'

'I do.' Her eyes were hazy with desire, her lips full and red. 'I have never felt this way towards any man.' She lifted her hand to his bristled cheek, and her touch seared him. If he didn't stop now, he would take her at this very moment.

He kissed her palm and gathered the remnants of his control. 'Will you come with me on a ride? I have somewhere else I want to show you.'

She nodded. 'Anywhere.'

Warrick climbed down from the tree first and held out his arms. Rosamund slid down from the branch, and he drew towards him, holding her body against his. She fit perfectly with him, and for a moment, he kept her close, resting his arms beneath her hips. Then he let her body slide down, keeping his arms around her. Rosamund framed his face with her hands and drew him in for another kiss. The moment her mouth met his, he was lost. He pressed her back against the tree, claiming her kiss as his own. She gripped him hard, kissing him as though this day were their last. Their tongues met, and he tightened her body against his, nestling his hard erection against her softness.

'You make me lose myself, Rosamund.'

Her cheeks were flushed, her eyes bright from her own arousal. 'Good.' She laughed a little and took his hand. 'Where are we going?'

'It's about a five-mile ride towards the coast. They are finalising my brother's betrothal contract today, and we have a little time to slip away.' He led her towards his own horse, which was tethered near the stream. 'Where is your mare?

'I didn't bring a horse,' she admitted. 'It would have taken too much time. And it was easier to slip away without one.'

The thought of her walking alone bothered him. 'Don't go anywhere without a guard, Rosamund. It's not safe.'

'I knew you would defend me if I needed help.' She touched his cheek, bringing him down for another kiss. 'And I saw you following me, once I reached the woods.'

It still unnerved him that she had come this far alone. She was so innocent, she didn't fully understand the danger. 'Promise me you won't leave the *donjon* without a guard again.'

She hesitated. 'I didn't want anyone to be punished for helping me.'

He took her hand and squeezed it. 'Take Ademar with you next time. He is only thirteen, but he's strong enough to defend you, despite his youth.'

The lad was often teased by others because of his stammer, but he more than made up for it with his fighting skills. Were he a knight, Warrick would take him as a squire.

Rosamund nodded in agreement. 'If it will make you feel better.'

'It would.' He lifted her onto the saddle and then mounted behind her. The position drew her bottom against his rigid erection, and he gritted his teeth against the sensation. By the time they reached the coast, he knew his body would be craving hers in a way he couldn't control.

Better to ride swiftly then.

'We'll return in the afternoon,' he told her. 'I brought food for us as well.'

He guided the horse out of the woods until they reached the open field. The sun was beginning to rise, and it spread rose-coloured light over the fields. He urged the horse into a canter and then a gallop. Rosamund's hair blew into his face, and he had to push it away.

She laughed. 'Don't spit my hair out!'

'I can hardly see.' But he moved it over one shoulder, pressing his mouth to her nape. She stilled, and he kept one arm around her waist while they rode. It was both torturous and wondrous, having her so near. His mind conjured up arousing images of lifting her skirts and sliding into her wetness, letting her ride him. He let out a hiss, and she tensed against him.

'Is something wrong, Warrick?'

'Only that I want you too badly,' he said. This journey needed to end soon, or else his very skin would ignite into flames.

After riding for several more miles, they reached their destination, and he dismounted, letting the horse graze. He lifted her down, holding her hand as he took her towards the rocky cliffside. The hill rose up from the embankment in a wall of pure rock, giving them numerous places to sit. The sea stretched as far as the horizon in a pool of endless blue.

'It's like the edge of the world, isn't it?' she breathed. 'I've never seen anything like it.' She embraced him, murmuring her thanks. Then he helped her walk through the rocks, letting her choose a place to sit. She selected a ledge nearby that was wide enough for them to be seated.

Warrick leaned back and she sat within his arms, drinking in the landscape. A moment later, she withdrew from the pouch the sewing he had returned to her. Then she took out a needle and the coloured thread that he had given her. 'Where did you get the thread, Warrick?'

'I had one of the maids buy it for me. I know you enjoy sewing.'

She pulled out a length of deep blue thread. 'This is the perfect colour for the sea.' She threaded her needle and began creating a blend of long and short stitches, creating the movement of the waves. Then she switched to a grey colour, blending it into the blue threads to give it depth. He marvelled in her ability to capture the colours of the water.

He sat beside her, watching as she stitched the colours of the sea. Though she was quiet and serious in her work, there was also a sense of her joy.

'You have a gift, of seeing things the way you do. You find beauty where no one else would see it.'

'There is beauty in everything around us.' She turned and caught his gaze. Though she still held the embroidery, he leaned in and stole a swift kiss. Her smile warmed him, though he didn't miss the cast of sadness.

She leaned back against him, continuing her sewing. It contented him just to hold her while he watched her add the colours of green, grey, amber, and light blue, forming dimension within her embroidery. Only when she had completed a small sample of the landscape did she set the sewing aside. 'Thank you for bringing me here, Warrick.'

He stroked her long black hair in answer, drawing her back into his arms. For a time, she lay back against him while the waves coursed over the rocks.

'We will be leaving soon,' she murmured. 'And I do not want to go.' She turned to face him, and he saw the sorrow in her eyes. 'I cannot imagine marrying someone else.'

The force of his own denial was a silent fury. No longer did it matter that both of their families would oppose a match between them. What mattered was this woman and what *she* wanted. He would find a way to provide for her, even if it meant going with Rhys to Scotland.

Warrick tightened his arms around her waist. 'We will find a way to change your father's mind. You will marry no one but me.'

She leaned in and kissed him. 'It's what I want, too. But I don't know how, unless we run away.'

He thought back to her earlier wish, for children of her own. And though it would be a move born of desperation, there was another way to force her father's hand.

'You could wed me, if you were carrying my

child,' he said quietly. 'Your father would have no choice.'

Her face paled at his proposition. There was fear in her eyes, for she understood the consequences well enough. 'I want to be with you, Warrick. But if I act against my father's wishes, I—I'm afraid of what he'll do.'

'I will protect you,' he swore. 'From him and from everyone else.'

She grew silent for a time. The wind blew her hair back from her face, and he supposed he had asked too much of her. Then, from a fold of her cloak, she withdrew another piece of linen she had been embroidering. 'I made this for you.'

He unfolded it and saw the outline of a tall tree beside a stream. She had stitched the water with a light spray of mist over the rocks. Even the leaves of the large tree had shades of green, grey, and blue. It was a scene of the place where he had first kissed her.

'It's beautiful,' he said. But he was looking at her face and not the fabric. Her expression softened and in her eyes, he saw the longing that mirrored his. Yet he understood that she was an innocent, untouched and pure.

'I want you to have it,' she said. 'So you will remember me.'

It was the last thing he'd expected her to say. She acted as if she would never see him again, as if this were a final farewell. And it infuriated him.

'Is that what you want?' he demanded. 'For me to stand aside and let you wed another man? Or do you not believe I am capable of protecting you?'

His mind and body had gone numb. He had wanted so badly to believe that he could change his life, to live with someone who cared for him in the way his father never would. And yet, her hesitance was real.

Her face paled and she shook her head. 'No, that isn't it. It's just that I don't want our two families to war against one another.'

Warrick cupped her face and drew her into a kiss. He poured himself into it, wanting her to know how much he needed her. She responded with her own desires, clinging to him as he showed her without words what she meant to him.

'If you want to wed me, I will take you away from this place,' he said. 'We will be together.' He hardly cared if anyone approved of the match— all that mattered was Rosamund's desires.

'I'm afraid,' she confessed. 'Both of our families will cut us off. We may be outcasts if we dare to defy them.'

'Trust in me,' he ordered. 'I will find a way for

us. I swear it.' He caressed her cheek and added, 'But it is your decision to make.'

Rosamund had spent several restless nights, trying to decide what was right. Warrick had given her distance, not asking her to meet again. And yet, every time she had caught a glimpse of him, she yearned to be in his arms. The thought of marrying another man was simply unthinkable. And though it was dangerous, she knew she had to follow her heart's desires.

'He's w-w-waiting for you outside the g-gates,' Ademar stammered. Despite his difficulty in speaking, he was taller than the other boys his age. He led her down a darkened corridor, carrying the bundle of her belongings. Last night, she and her sister had packed up their trunks, preparing for the journey home at dawn. But Cecelia knew nothing of Rosamund's plan to run away.

She had deliberated upon the decision for days. Her family would be outraged if she defied her father's command. Although the betrothal agreement had not yet been signed, her mother was behaving as if she were already wed.

Which, if everything went to plan, she would be after this night—but to Warrick de Laurent and not Alan de Courcy.

Her nerves were raw as she followed Ademar into the darkness. Inside the bundle he carried, she had packed only a single gown, some jewels she could sell, and a little food. Her heart was racing at the thought of being caught. Her father would punish them both, and she feared for Warrick. Although he was a strong fighter, he would never use his strength against her family.

She would have to defy all of them, even at the risk of her safety. But the thought of wedding Alan de Courcy was far worse. Her heart was already lost to Warrick de Laurent, and she could not imagine being with anyone else.

Rosamund didn't know how Warrick planned for them to run away, but she had prepared herself as best she could. She had chosen a simple dark blue woollen cloak to hide herself at night, but it might not be enough. Now the question was how she and Ademar could sneak past the guards to where Warrick was waiting. The soldiers would undoubtedly see her.

Ademar led her to stand beside the inner bailey wall while his attention was transfixed upon the guards near the gate. Without words, he pressed her back, waiting. The flare of torches illuminated the walls of the fortress, and she held her breath.

Then he seized her wrist and pulled her forward

to run. Rosamund obeyed without question, and once again, he moved her into the shadows. It felt like a game of predator and prey, seeking to elude the men who would capture her and force her back to her father.

Ademar bent to her ear and whispered. 'I will d-draw the guards away from the gate. When I do, you must g-go. You will f-find Warrick waiting for you at the bottom of the hill.' He didn't wait for her to respond, but strode away from her towards the men at the gates. The guards were armed with spears, but they did not appear concerned by Ademar's presence. He spoke to them quietly, and Rosamund was annoyed to hear one of them laughing at the boy's stammer. She inched her way along the wall, waiting until the two guards had their back to her. There was a slight gap where she could slip past the first soldier, and she seized the opportunity.

Her heart hammered with fear as she moved past him, praying to remain soundless. She hurried across the drawbridge into the darkness, fully expecting to hear a warning shout from the guards.

But there came nothing at all. She saw Ademar continuing to distract the guards, and the moment she disappeared into the darkness, she found Warrick waiting. He took her hand in his and kissed her softly before leading her away. She was thankful to have found him, but her fears didn't diminish at all.

They walked in silence through the meadow with no moon to guide them. Only when they reached the sanctuary of the woods did Warrick lift her onto the horse, mounting behind her. She had no idea where he planned to take her, and she didn't care. All she wanted was to be with him, no matter the cost.

He kept their pace slow at first until the castle was well behind them. She was conscious of every line of his body, of the strength and power of his thighs as he guided the horse. And only when more time passed, did some of her fears soften.

They rode through the night, and Rosamund fell asleep in his arms. When dawn came, her body ached with stiffness as he helped her down. He had stopped beside a stream and let the horse drink for a time. Rosamund spied the ruins of a church nearby and she wondered if this was their destination or only a stopping point. Warrick took her by the hand and led her towards the church.

'We'll stop here to rest.' He led her inside the stone ruins, and she stood for a moment, studying the fallen stones. The morning sunlight illuminated the church, bathing the stone fragments with rays of gold and rose. Rosamund moved closer, drawing her hand across the stones, learning the patterns of grey, black, and green within the ruins. She memorised the colours, knowing she could duplicate this with the right threads.

A few moments later, Warrick came up behind her, resting his hands upon her shoulders. 'What are you thinking about, Rosamund?'

'Sewing,' she confessed, turning to smile at him. She drew her arms around his waist, welcoming his embrace. They stood in the early morning light, and she breathed in the scent of his skin. But the longer she remained near him, the more she grew aware of her own feelings. She wanted to lose herself again in his kiss, to feel his skin upon hers. A rush of blood roared through her, and she rested her cheek against his chest.

'I would marry you right now, if I could,' he murmured. 'Before God and all the world.'

'So would I.' She lifted her mouth for his kiss and this time, there was no denying his desires. She tasted the fierce needs, and he devoured her mouth as if he could never get enough.

He broke free, his eyes deadly serious. 'Rosamund de Beaufort, I take you as my wife. I swear to guard you with my body and protect you with all that I have.'

She braved a smile. 'Warrick de Laurent, I take you as my husband. I promise to love you for the rest of my life.'

With the marriage vows spoken, it was as if her very blood had caught fire. Rosamund felt the echoing arousal within her body, and the need to touch this man drowned out the voices of reason.

She reached for his shirt and drew her fingers over the laces. Slowly, she loosened it, staring at him with undisguised need. Warrick's eyes turned heated, and he pulled the shirt over his head, revealing his hardened chest. She traced the lines of his pectoral muscles, marvelling at his strength.

And when he began to undress her, she did not voice a single protest. Layers of linen and silk fell away until she stood in her shift in the morning sunlight. The air was cool, puckering her breasts. Her nipples ached for his touch, and between her legs, she grew moist with desire.

She knew the danger in this, but she understood that it was the only way to force her father's hand. If she surrendered her innocence and there was the possibility of a child, no other man would wed her.

But even through the blurred heat of desire, she

was afraid. Not only of being claimed by this man but of the consequences.

'Lie down,' he murmured, guiding her back upon their discarded clothing. She obeyed, feeling a sudden rush of nervousness. He removed her shoes and woollen stockings, and she inhaled sharply as his hand caressed her calves, moving higher.

He rested his weight upon his arms, staring at her. 'I've never lain with a woman before, Rosamund.'

'It's all right,' she whispered. With a rueful smile, she added, 'I don't know what I'm doing, either.'

His hand moved between her legs to the intimate place where he would enter her body. The touch of his fingers startled her, and she admitted, 'Be gentle with me.'

She opened her legs, expecting him to take her then, but he hesitated. 'I have heard that it may cause you pain if you are not ready.'

Rosamund had heard the same but was trying not to think of it. She knew that this was the surest way to gain a true marriage between them. Consummation was necessary, and she did love Warrick. His quiet strength and thoughtfulness drew her closer to him.

For a moment, she tried to calm the storm of her rising feelings. She knew what would happen between them, and the heat of his skin was a stark contrast against her own. Softly, she touched him, feeling a strange surge of possession as she traced the lines of his muscles. He went motionless as she did and leaned back to let her do as she wished.

There was power in this, and she kissed his skin, hearing the pounding of his heart as she brushed her lips over his chest. And in touching him, she felt her own arousal deepen. This man belonged to her now, and she surrendered to her own desire.

Rosamund kissed him deeply, her body awakening as his tongue slid against hers. Her body grew warmer, and at last she broke away from the kiss. 'I want to see all of you, Warrick.'

He stood from the ground and slowly removed his clothing. There was not a trace of softness upon him, and when he removed his braies, she was caught up in the vision of his erect flesh.

He would slide his shaft inside her, and the thought made her ache between her legs. She hungered for this man, and when she stood up from the ground, he commanded, 'Now you.'

She drew up the hem of her shift, pulling it over

her head until she stood naked before him. His eyes held wonder as he looked upon her.

'You are the most beautiful woman I have ever seen,' he murmured. With his hands and mouth, he touched her, kissing the buds of her breasts and caressing her. She felt herself rising to him, pressing closer as he touched the wetness between her legs. Gently, he slid a finger inside her, and she gasped, startled by the sudden rush of sensation.

But then, she gathered her courage and reached for his hardened length. His skin was so warm, the tip of him smooth with a bead of moisture. He guided her palm around him, and she drew it up over the length.

He inhaled sharply, and slid a second finger within her. His thumb nudged the folds of her flesh, and she felt her own arousal rising.

When she gasped, he ceased his movement and asked, 'Am I hurting you?'

'No…' She sighed, closing her eyes. 'It feels good.' But she was afraid of the strong feelings rising up. His hand was gentle, and yet, she sensed that everything was about to unravel.

'It's all right, Rosamund,' he said, leaning down to soothe her. 'I will stop if you want me to.' He kissed her lightly to underscore his words.

She looked into his eyes and moved her hands

to his shoulders. There was no doubt in her mind that he would not take her against her desires. But she gathered her composure and locked her gaze upon his. In his eyes, she saw a man who wanted to pleasure her, and the knowledge evoked an aching need.

'Don't stop,' she whispered.

His hand was gentle, kindling a fire that burned through her. Her nails dug into his shoulders, and she shuddered at the ripple of delicious sensation. His mouth captured hers, kissing her deeply while his fingers entered and withdrew. She caressed his shaft, and as they touched one another, her yearning grew stronger.

Warrick drew her back down to the ground. This time, he rolled to his back, bringing her to sit astride him. She was startled by the heat of his erection and the way it felt so good to have him nestled beneath her. He raised her hips until he was poised at her entrance. Then he sat up slowly to kiss her again, his shaft slowly penetrating her. The sensation was overwhelming, and she held steady and unmoving as he breached her. There was a slight pain, but she masked it, kissing him.

'You are mine, Rosamund,' he said. 'Now and always.'

'I am yours,' she answered, letting him sheathe

himself fully. The pressure of his thick shaft was unfamiliar, and she wasn't certain what to do. Warrick answered by holding her hips in place, not allowing her to move. He held her there a moment, letting her adjust to his size. Gradually the pain abated, and he began to withdraw from her, only to thrust again and penetrate her body. He entered her smoothly, and she felt a shimmer of desire take hold once more.

Warrick continued kissing her mouth, and then changed their angle to take her nipple in his mouth. Rosamund moaned at the gentle suction that echoed within her womb. Instinct claimed her, and she raised up against him, feeling her body aching with need.

'Does this hurt you?' he asked softly.

'N-no.' But she was afraid even to breathe right now. The gentle thrusting was a give and take, claiming her while he filled her. He reached up to caress her taut nipples, and she felt the tremors gathering deeper. His hands moved away, and she protested, 'Warrick, wait. I—I liked that.'

At her encouragement, he began to stroke her, keeping his thrusts easy while he rubbed his thumbs across her nipples. She found herself riding him slowly, watching as his face grew hooded with passion. She squeezed against him, and he let out a guttural groan. 'Rosamund, my God.'

She quickened her pace, discovering what excited him. There was goodness in this joining, and she felt as if they were learning together.

He rolled her to her back, still embedded within her. This time, he thrust deeply, raising her knees.

She gasped at the sensation, but welcomed the heat and the drowning desire. Though he was careful not to be too rough, she found that each thrust drew her away from clear thinking and towards a more primitive part of herself. She met his invasion with her own pressure, drawing him into her arms.

He gritted his teeth, his body tensing as he continued to make love to her. 'Rosamund, I don't think I can last much longer.'

'It's all right,' she whispered. 'I am ready.'

He quickened the pace, and she answered his call by squeezing him. He balanced his weight upon his forearms, and she raised her bottom so he could thrust deeper. She felt herself growing molten beneath him, crying out when the peak rose into a shattering release. Never in her life had she imagined such pleasure, as if her body had been made to love this man. She clung to him while the surging tide seized her, forcing her to arch hard against him and dig her nails into his backside. A cry escaped her lips, and with a few strokes more, he finished inside her.

She lay with his warm body atop hers, feeling alive and eager. Warrick rolled to his side, a sleepy smile on his face. Her body quaked with a soft shiver of the aftershocks. He traced the outline of her body, and she wound her arms around his neck. Though she was still afraid of what would happen when they were caught, at least they had each other.

Warrick continued to caress her skin, kissing her throat. 'Would that we could stay here for hours.'

She caught her breath when his mouth covered her breast again. A shudder of pleasure rocked through her, and she asked, 'Where will we go?'

'North. Ademar's family lives in Dolwyth, and I believe they will help us.'

'My father won't give up,' she said. 'He likely has men searching at this very moment.'

'But he will not find you for a few weeks,' Warrick countered. 'I know how we will avoid his guards.' She didn't understand, but he helped her don her shift. When she stood up, he pointed towards the north. 'We will take a ship and sail the rest of the way to Dolwyth. I will sell our horse, and your father's men will track that by mistake.'

Rosamund wasn't certain if his plan would work, but it was all they had. She moved towards him, embracing Warrick hard. 'I do not regret a single moment of this day.'

She could only hope that she never would.

Chapter Five

They sailed along the coast for days while the sunlight rimmed the waves with gold. Warrick rowed until his arms were numb, but he wouldn't have traded a moment of this time with Rosamund. Sometimes he would rest, and she would open her arms to him. He made love to her on the open water, and the rocking of the boat mimicked their loving.

He couldn't get enough of her, but he dared not take the time to stop and rest. The days and nights blended together, until he was nearly trembling from lack of sleep. But there was no choice but to continue. Once or twice, he did fall asleep by mistake. He said nothing to her, but he could tell that the waves had taken them off course. They were moving against the tide, and he didn't know how much time they had lost.

Rosamund's father would pursue them, and

Warrick knew his punishment would be worse than anything she could imagine. Like as not, his own father would exile him, leaving him to survive without a home. Until now, Edward de Laurent had ignored his presence, behaving as if Warrick did not exist. Soon there would be a confrontation—and he knew not what his father would do.

But he would face any hell upon this earth for the nights and days he had spent in Rosamund's arms. She sat at the bow of the boat and sewed for hours upon end. Sometimes she would look back and smile at him. And it was enough.

When at last they reached the coast of Dolwyth at sunset, she offered him a weary smile. 'I will be glad to be on land again.' He rowed their tiny boat into shallow waters before he tied the vessel to the wooden pier and helped her out. She smiled at him and held him close. 'We need to find somewhere to stay for the night.'

'I feel as if I could fall asleep right here on the sand.' After so many days without sleep, dizziness washed over him. But Warrick tucked her arm in his and led her across the strand towards the open meadow. Ademar had told him of his father's settlement, a motte and bailey structure that lay a few miles from the coast. The grasses were long and brushed against their knees as he guided her in that direction.

But when they neared Dolwyth, he saw the glow of torches lining the walls. His instincts flared, for there were too many soldiers there.

'Rosamund,' he murmured, tightening his grip upon her hand. 'I don't think we should take shelter there tonight.'

'But why? I thought—' Her words were broken off when she came to the same realisation. 'It isn't possible for them to have found us so soon.'

'Unless they knew where we were going.' He couldn't hide the grimness in his voice. It was entirely possible that they had forced the truth out of Ademar. The lad was young and unable to fend off harsh questioning.

God help them, he didn't know what to do. Dolwyth was a small fortress, with hardly more than fifty men and women. And from the looks of it, there were far more people there now. He drew her to sit down in the grass. In the darkness, he could barely see Rosamund's face, but he sensed the worry in her.

'Even if they knew where we were going, we went by sea,' she insisted. 'It should have been impossible for them to catch up.'

'There was a time when we were blown off course.'

Because he'd been too weak to remain awake each day and night they had sailed. And now they would have to face her father sooner than he wanted to. But he had spoken vows to Rosamund before God and consummated the marriage. Harold de Beaufort would have no choice but to accept their union.

She knelt before him, and Warrick drew his hand into the dark silk of her hair. 'Kiss me,' she pleaded. 'I'm afraid of what will happen in the morning.'

He could make her no promises, but he would not deny her this night. Warrick reached for the laces of her kirtle, loosening her bodice. She guided his hand to her bare breast and lay back in the grass. He stroked her, memorising the curves before he lowered his mouth to suckle her.

They both knew there was hardly any time remaining, and he wanted to claim her swiftly. When Warrick drew his hand between her legs, she was already wet for him. He needed to be inside her, and he fumbled with his clothing, hurrying at her urging.

Then he plunged deep and was rewarded with her shuddering cry. Her hands moved beneath his tunic, raking his back as he thrust. This time, their lovemaking was far different. He wanted to brand himself upon Rosamund, so that no man would ever touch her again.

'I love you,' she blurted out, gripping his hair as he plunged and withdrew. 'Now and always.'

He couldn't say the words, but he swore, 'No one will ever part us, Rosamund.'

She wept as he took her over the edge once more, and finally he emptied himself into her, groaning as their bodies became one. Her breathing was hitched as she lay beneath him. He dried her tears, holding her as the moon rose above them.

'I don't want to lose you,' she whispered.

But he knew the battle for this woman would be hard won. And if her father had indeed come after her, Harold would do anything to separate them.

For this night, they would remain outside the gates. Warrick withdrew from her body and arranged a blanket from his cloak. She lay down upon it, and he enfolded her in the wool, wrapping it around both of them. The night air was crisp, but her body was warm from their lovemaking.

He knew not what the morrow would bring, but for now, he would lie with this woman in his arms.

* * *

Rosamund awakened to the sound of horses approaching. She sat up and saw that Warrick was standing over her, fully armed with a sword and shield in his hands. Though he was only one man, she knew he would let no one harm her.

Her hair was a tousled mess around her shoulders, but she stood up to face the men. As she had feared, her father was leading the group. Harold de Beaufort appeared strangely calm, as if he had been waiting for her. He lifted his hand in a silent signal, and the soldiers surrounded them.

Her father studied her, eyeing her rumpled gown and unkempt appearance. Then he ordered the men, 'Take him.'

'Do not harm my husband,' Rosamund blurted out. She took Warrick's hand in hers, though she suspected it was futile trying to protect him.

'He is not your husband,' Harold said quietly. 'Tell whatever lies you wish, but you are already betrothed to Alan de Courcy.'

Warrick fought against the men closing in. He raised his shield, keeping her behind him. But he murmured in her ear, 'Go with your father, Rosamund. I will be fine.'

She didn't believe that at all. Her father's calm demeanour suggested that he had already decided what to do with Warrick. 'If I go, I don't trust him not to harm you.'

In the end, she had no choice when the men separated them. Rosamund cried out as two soldiers seized her by both arms and jerked her away from him. Warrick fought hard to get to her, but another soldier struck him across the skull with his shield. He lost consciousness, and she screamed when he dropped to the ground.

But the soldiers held her so tightly, she could not go to him. 'What have you done?' she demanded of her father.

'He will be dealt with soon enough,' Harold said. 'You will come with me, and we will discuss what will happen now.' He motioned for her to join him on horseback. The two soldiers forced her onto the saddle, though she fought them.

Warrick still had not regained consciousness, and fear roared through her. She wanted to run to him, to know if he was alive. Was he bleeding?

'I will go nowhere with you,' she shot back. Though she tried to dismount, the men held her there.

'His life depends on your obedience,' her father said quietly. He signalled for his men to pick up Warrick's fallen body, and they placed him face down on horseback. A moment later, he stirred, and she was able to breathe again.

Tears of relief streamed down her face, and she pleaded, 'Let me go to him. I need to know if he will be all right.'

Her father guided his horse alongside hers. He seized her wrist in a firm grip. 'Come with me, Rosamund. I have a great deal to say to you.'

He took the reins of her horse in his other hand and forced her to follow. She looked back at Warrick, and a moment later, her father's soldiers surrounded them. Wildly, she wondered if it was possible to free him somehow. But no, there were too many men. She tried to calm her mind, and she realised that defying her father would only make matters worse. They needed to speak with one another calmly and come to an understanding. Though she doubted if her father would kill Warrick, she did not know how Harold would punish the man she loved.

Her throat closed up at the thought, and she lowered her head. 'I will go with you willingly, as long as your men do not hurt Warrick.'

Harold said nothing but continued riding towards the fortress. 'You have no choice, Rosamund. When you decided to leave with him, you surrendered your free will. Now you will do exactly as I say, or he will suffer for every command you disobey.'

Her heart thundered at the warning, for she knew he spoke the truth. He had absolute power, and Rosamund wept silently. Her only hope was that obedience would pacify him.

Harold led the men into Dolwyth, lifting her down from her horse. To the soldiers he commanded, 'Put our prisoner in chains.'

She forced herself to watch as they dragged Warrick towards a wooden tower. There was a wall beside it with chains and manacles. He regained consciousness at last, and they hammered the pins into the manacles. He was powerless to move, but he straightened and met her gaze. In his eyes, she saw his quiet reassurance.

But she feared the worst.

She loved this man and it hurt so deeply to imagine being parted from him. For that reason, she touched her fingers to her lips and turned back to her father. His life depended upon her decisions, and she would do anything to protect him.

Harold led her inside towards a small chamber with a single chair and a pallet. There were no windows, and she rather thought it was her own prison.

'Did you lie with him?' he asked quietly.

'Yes.' She raised her chin and met his questions with her own stare. 'We spoke vows within a church and consummated our marriage. He is of a noble family, and I love him.'

Her father's expression remained cold. 'You will tell no one what you have done. Or if you do, I will see to it that you are widowed.'

She was horrified that he would threaten Warrick's life. 'You cannot do such a thing.'

'You made a grave mistake when you decided to defy my orders,' her father said. 'And whatever sins you committed with this man, you will not be his wife.'

I am already his wife, she wanted to argue. In the eyes of God she was. But she bit back her words, knowing they would only fuel his anger.

'I have sent for Alan de Courcy. You will return home with me and await him there. You should pray that he will agree to wed you, in spite of what you have done.'

'I cannot wed him.' She met her father's hard stare with one of her own. 'I am already married, and I may be carrying Warrick's child.'

Harold crossed his arms. 'I will not sacrifice the alliances made for our family because of your foolish actions.'

'I have married him, and it is done now. I care not about your alliances.'

Her father crossed the room and seized her wrist. His grip was rough, and she fought to keep from crying out. 'You *should* care. For his life depends upon your agreement.'

'You cannot kill him.' Harold would never strike such a blow against a noble family. It would mean war.

'Think you I would not kill the man who stole my daughter's innocence?' He spoke with such calmness, she knew he meant it. 'You will say nothing of this so-called marriage. Or if you dare to defy my wishes, I will see him struck down.'

Ice ran through her veins at his threat. She had not at all considered her father to be so ruthless. They had been naïve to believe that Harold de Beaufort would allow them to marry without his consent. Without a word, she sank down to the floor, sitting upon the pallet. It felt as if she were breathing underwater, and a rushing sound filled her ears.

'You *will* obey me, Rosamund. You will return home without question and wed Alan de Courcy, if he agrees. And if you speak one word about a so-called marriage to Warrick de Laurent, I will see to it that he breathes his last.'

Harold wanted her to lie to everyone, to pretend as if they had spoken no vows. The Church would have to recognise any marriage where vows were given and the union consummated. But there had been no witnesses that night, and her father knew this.

'Edward de Laurent would not let you threaten his son,' she argued weakly. But in her heart, she knew she was cornered. Her father was furious, and Warrick would suffer the consequences.

'Edward sent his own men to help mine. He has given me full authority to punish his son as I see fit.'

She didn't want to believe such a thing could be true, but she had seen for herself the lack of love between father and son. Something had caused the distance, and whatever the reason, it unnerved her.

Harold's gaze narrowed upon her. 'You will tell Warrick de Laurent that you are going to wed Alan de Courcy. Convince him that you do not want him.'

'He will not believe it. Not after what we endured to travel this far.' She drew her knees up to her chest, feeling numb inside. 'Why does it matter to you who I marry? An alliance with Edward de Laurent has its own worth.'

'You defied me in front of everyone. My daughter ran away with her lover, making a mockery of her family. I will not stand for it.'

She swallowed hard, not knowing how to save herself and Warrick. 'We could both do penance for our disobedience, and then have a proper marriage.'

Her father backhanded her with his fist, and pain radiated through her jaw. She lay face down on the pallet, in shock. Never in her life had he beaten her.

'There will *be* no marriage between you and de Laurent,' he shot back. 'You dared to embarrass our family. If you were not my eldest daughter, I would put you in a nunnery and wash my hands of you.'

Hot tears bled against her cheeks, and she said nothing. Her stomach clenched with fear, and her jaw still ached from his blow.

'Look at me, Rosamund,' he demanded. 'Tell Warrick that you have changed your mind. As long as you do not confess to speaking your own vows, the marriage does not exist.'

But it does, she wanted to say. Their marriage was as real as any other.

In the lines of his face, she saw the unrelenting fury. He would never forgive her for this, and as punishment, he would give her to another man. She didn't know if it was possible to endure such a thing.

'What will happen to Warrick?' she whispered.

There was no sympathy on his face. 'It depends on you. He will be whipped for taking you away. His father ordered twenty lashes.'

'His own father?' She had expected fury from Harold, but she had never imagined it from Warrick's sire.

'Yes. Afterwards, he will be sent away, and you will return with me to wed de Courcy.' He sat down in the chair, and his face hardened. 'Warrick will never touch you again. You will make sure he knows this, or I will double the lashes.'

She could feel the hatred rising within her. 'You want me to lie to him.'

'Would you not do this, to diminish his suffering? If you say you love him.'

She rose from the pallet and faced him with all her anger. 'I do not understand why you are so eager to sell me off into marriage, despite my feelings.'

Her father opened the door. 'I will tell the commander to give forty lashes, then. Would you like to watch?'

She felt sick to her stomach. *Dear God, no.* 'Let him go, Father. I beg you.'

There was no mercy in his eyes. Instead, he turned and shut the door behind him. The moment he was gone, her hands began to tremble. She had never felt so alone or helpless. This was about pride and wielding power, she realised. He cared more about appearances than his own daughter.

Though she had not been close to Harold, never had she seen this side to him. God help her, she didn't know how to stop this nightmare. All of this was her fault. She should have known better than to cross swords with her father. And now, Warrick would bear the scars.

The bleak finality of their situation washed over her. She could not change her father's mind, nor could she force him to accept her marriage.

But she could save the man she loved. Even if it meant slashing her own heart in two. She would do whatever she must to save Warrick's life.

Rosamund pushed the door open and hurried outside. The sky was overcast, holding shadowed clouds. Her father was standing beside Ademar's father, Rourke of Dolwyth. Both men appeared displeased with the sight before them.

The soldiers had chained Warrick with both arms outstretched, while another man held a whip

in his hand. He raised it, and a loud crack re-
sounded as the lash bit through Warrick's back,
drawing blood. He flinched but never uttered a
sound.

Rosamund felt the blow as surely as if it had bit-
ten into her own skin. She choked back a cry and
rushed to her father's side. 'Please don't! I will do
what you ask.'

His face was stony, as if he cared nothing for
her plea for mercy. She didn't know how to make
him stop, and the lash struck over and over. Once,
she heard Warrick let out a harsh grunt, and his
knees sagged. His back was covered in blood, and
she got down on her knees before Harold. 'I beg
of you. Let him go.'

When he would not relent, she stared him in the
eye. 'If you do not release him, I swear, I will go
and take the remainder of his punishment. I will
bear the lash myself.'

Rosamund started to walk towards Warrick, but
her father seized her wrist and squeezed tightly.
'You will stay here.'

She tried to pull back, but his grip intensified
until she feared he would break her hand. The
soldier had struck the twentieth blow, and at last,
Harold raised his hand. 'Go to him. And end it.'

Warrick's head hung low, and he slumped to

his knees. The wounds were deep, and she despised herself for bringing him such pain. She didn't know if she would have the strength to say what her father had ordered. Slowly, she crossed the inner bailey and moved to stand before him. She could not stop her tears, but she bit her lip hard and forced herself to continue.

He didn't raise his head to look at her, and she knew he was in unbearable pain. At last, he spoke. 'I would take every blow three times over for your sake, Rosamund.'

She swiped the tears away and anguish filled her up. 'I am sorry, Warrick. But I cannot be with you any more.'

He stiffened as if her words were another whiplash. 'You are my wife. You belong with me.'

'No,' she whispered. Though she tried to hold them back, her tears escaped. 'I am not.'

'Your father is forcing you to say this,' he accused.

She could not bring herself to lie, and instead she murmured, 'I never wanted this to happen to you. I blame myself. I should not have defied him.'

At last, he raised his head. Deep blue eyes regarded her with disbelief. 'I never took you for a coward.'

She wanted to tell him no, to insist that she loved

him still. But if she dared to voice the words, she believed her father would kill him somehow.

'I am going to marry Alan de Courcy.'

'No. You won't.' His voice held an edge of a man barely containing his fury. 'You are already wedded to me.'

She ignored his statement and continued. 'This is best for both of us. You'll find someone else to marry.' Her voice sounded thick, heavy with her own grief.

'You're speaking the words he told you to say.'

She held his gaze, knowing that he would suffer if she dared to tell him the truth. 'I am sorry,' she repeated.

Then she turned her back and walked away while her heart broke into a thousand pieces.

Chapter Six

One week later

Rosamund needed to be alone. After all that had come to pass, she needed to engage in mindless activity that would take her mind off the tumultuous arrangement Alan wanted.

She knelt down beside the herb garden, hardly caring about the dirt. She pulled weeds, ripping them out by the roots as she attacked the garden with her own private frustration.

I won't do this, she thought to herself. *Alan cannot force me to commit adultery.* The thought lent her comfort as she tore out another handful of weeds.

From behind her, she heard horses approaching. Rosamund stood and brushed off the dirt, wondering who the guards had allowed to enter Pevensham. She strode past the garden and walked into the inner bailey. It was then that she saw Owen de Courcy riding towards the stables, accompanied by half-a-dozen armed men.

No. She nearly groaned aloud. The last thing she wanted was Alan's younger brother intruding right now.

Owen's expression grew sly when he saw her. He dismounted and gave the reins over to a stable lad. Then he motioned for his men to stay back as he walked across the castle grounds, already behaving as if he were Lord of Pevensham. Rosamund remained in place, knowing that it was safer to remain standing here with her guards nearby than to retreat inside the donjon.

'My brother, it is good to see you,' she lied, extending her hands in greeting. She was well aware that it annoyed him to hear her call him that. 'I apologise that you caught me working in the garden.'

'Rosamund,' he said warmly. Owen took her soiled hands and squeezed them. In his smile, she saw a man who believed himself superior to everyone. His gaze lingered too long upon her body, and she pulled her hands free.

'Forgive me, but I should go and tell Cook to prepare more food for you and your men. And I will let Alan know you are here.'

'You needn't bother. I should like to surprise my brother.' His gaze shifted behind her and hardened. A sense of warning crossed over her, and when Rosamund turned, Warrick de Laurent was standing there, his hand upon his sword. His blue eyes narrowed upon Owen, though his expression remained neutral. Even so, she didn't miss the subtle challenge between them.

'And who is this, Rosamund?' Owen behaved as if Warrick were a stranger. 'He appears familiar somehow.'

Such a liar he was, when Warrick had already revealed Owen's intentions. She didn't doubt for a moment that he wanted Alan dead and would use any means necessary to achieve that purpose.

She veiled her thoughts and answered, 'This is Warrick de Laurent. I believe you met him at my wedding. He was one of the guests.'

A thin smile spread over Owen's face. 'You were betrothed to him once, were you not?'

Married, more like. But she refused to play cat and mouse with this man. It was easier to sweep aside his assumptions. 'Alan summoned him to Pevensham.' She dusted off her hands and nodded to the men. 'Now if you will excuse me, I must—'

'Not yet.' Owen blocked her path, probing further. 'Why is he here, Rosamund?'

'That is between my husband and Warrick. I have no part in it.' She forced herself to look up at him.

His expression was knowing, as if he was aware of her deceit. Warrick took a step closer, silently offering his protection. For a moment, the two men locked gazes in a stare.

Then Owen changed tactics, asking, 'How is Alan? I came to see if my brother is improving.'

Which wasn't at all true, but Rosamund let it go. She simply murmured, 'He is the same as ever.' Only God knew how much time her husband had remaining. But every instinct within her warned that Owen was here to hurt Alan. She could never allow that to happen. Warrick ought to guard her husband at all times, for she did trust him as a fighter. Without thinking, she took a step towards de Laurent.

The faint smile upon Owen's face unnerved her. 'Do I frighten you, Rosamund?'

'Of course not.' It was a lie, and he knew it.

He touched her cheek, stroking her chin. Owen's touch made her skin crawl, for it was not at all brotherly in nature. 'Would that I could take away your fear. Perhaps we should go riding, and I could convince you that I am harmless.'

The thought filled her with revulsion. 'I have no time for riding.'

This time, she pushed her way past him, wishing she could run from the man. She had always known he wanted everything that belonged to Alan. And yet, she had not truly understood the depths of his jealousy.

He truly might kill his own brother. And worse, she knew she could do nothing to stop him.

She hurried as far away from the men as she dared, moving towards the kitchens. Only when she was free of both men did she look back.

Warrick's hand was firmly upon the hilt of his sword. He was speaking quietly to Owen, and she had no idea what they were talking about. Was he warning the man to stay away from her? The thought should have been reassuring, but she didn't want Warrick provoking a fight.

It was better to leave now, to ensure that she had no part in this. Just as she was about to retreat inside, her maid, Berta, caught up to her. 'My lady, are you all right?'

She nodded. 'I am.' She knew she ought to reassure her maid that Owen de Courcy would not dare to harm them. But she couldn't quite bring herself to lie. 'We have guests, and we must prepare for them.'

Rosamund entered the kitchen and told the cook of Owen's arrival, instructing the servants to prepare more food. Amid the bustling noise and cooking, she took solace in a corner of the room, breathing in the scent of rosemary and sage.

Warrick claimed that Owen had hired him to kill Alan. She was grateful that he had refused, but her husband was still in danger. It might be best to ask several men to stand guard outside Alan's room. Only then could she be certain he was safe.

All around her, the invisible web seemed to tighten. She no longer knew how she could keep everyone protected within Pevensham—her husband, her people, and especially herself.

But she could not remain passive and allow Owen to take command of Pevensham. Her husband lacked the strength to fight for his estate, so she would have to do so. There was still time to add reinforcements to her soldiers. If she could learn who was loyal to Alan and which men supported Owen, then she could make the right decisions.

Rosamund straightened as she stared outside the window at their property. Why was she allowing others to pull her life in directions she didn't want to go? This was *her* home now, and she was entitled to live here for the rest of her days. She had no desire ever to return home to her parents—not after all that had happened years ago.

But in spite of the inauspicious beginning, Pevensham had become hers. She loved the people who dwelled upon the land, and she felt protective of them. Owen could not be allowed to destroy this place.

He will never leave you alone, a voice inside whispered. *Even if he takes a wife.*

She knew that Owen coveted her, and the thought strengthened her resolve to fight her own battles.

Her husband's solution—to conceive a child—appeared simple upon the surface, but it was fraught with danger. Every memory of the pregnancy was a knife buried into her heart. She had loved her daughter, though the baby had never taken a single breath. She had cradled the cold infant against her breast, shattered by grief.

And Alan wanted her to face that fear once again.

No. She would find another way to protect the estate, even if it meant surrounding herself with guards at all times. Nothing could convince her to attempt another child.

Not even with Warrick, the man who had fathered her daughter and knew nothing of it.

'Will we return to Montbrooke in the morning?' his man-at-arms, Bennett, asked. Both Bennett and Godfrey had been his companions since they'd fought together in Normandy.

Warrick accepted a cup of ale from a serving maid and shook his head. 'Our task here is not yet finished.' He eyed Owen de Courcy, who had seated himself upon the dais beside Rosamund. The man was entirely too comfortable giving orders, and Warrick tensed when he saw Owen touching Rosamund in subtle ways. The man's hand brushed against hers when he reached for salt, and he tried to feed her a portion of cold meat and cheese.

From across the room, Warrick saw her pleading look for help. She was trying to be courteous, but had barely touched her food. He kept eye contact with her and stood from his table among the men. 'This has to stop.'

'Where are you going?' Bennett asked.

'Lady Pevensham summoned me.' He clapped a hand on the man's shoulder. 'She wishes me to escort her to her husband's chamber.'

Godfrey eyed him with a doubtful look. 'She is still eating. Are you certain?'

Warrick took a cloth and wrapped up his own portion of bread and cheese, tucking it away in a fold of his cloak. 'I am.' He nodded to the men and walked away.

He strode across the rows of trestle tables until he reached the dais. Then he bowed before Lady Pevensham, letting Owen believe that he was also paying tribute to him.

'My lady, I received a message that your lord husband desires your presence in his chamber.' When Owen started to rise, Warrick added, 'I will escort you there, for your safety.'

The man stared hard at him, and Warrick kept his hand upon the hilt of his sword. Let him believe that he was trying to infiltrate the castle with the intent of murdering Alan. It was the furthest thing from the truth.

'Shall I come with you, Lady Pevensham?' Owen suggested. His hand moved to her shoulder, and Rosamund stood to extricate herself from his touch.

'That won't be necessary. If my husband wishes to speak with you, I will send word.'

Owen and Alan had already met, following his arrival earlier in the day. Owen had claimed that he only wanted his brother to be well, filling the man's ears with lies. Warrick had remained nearby, though a part of him wondered if he had any right to be here. This was not his battle to fight.

But Rosamund was caught in the middle of the two men, and he had no intention of allowing her to fall prey to Owen's desires, unholy as they were.

He allowed her to leave first, keeping a short distance behind. Before he left, he sent a dark look towards Owen, making it clear that the man should not follow.

Rosamund walked up the spiral stone stairs and Warrick shadowed her. Before she reached her husband's room, he said quietly, 'A moment, if you will.'

She leaned back against the wall. 'What is it?'

'Your husband has said that he does not trust his men to keep you safe after he dies. He fears they will turn against you.' He paused a moment. 'Do you agree with this?'

'They would see no reason to defend Pevensham from a family member. Especially if Owen is the heir.' She lifted her face to meet his gaze. 'They would not see it as being disloyal at all.'

That was the answer he had suspected. In a low

voice, he said, 'You will need to find a sanctuary after Alan is gone. If Owen believes that you are a threat to him—especially if he fears a pregnancy—your life will be endangered. You need an ally who will protect you.'

'There is no child,' she argued. Her face flushed, and she added, 'And even if I did agree to my husband's plan, it might not be possible for me to conceive another.'

'Do you intend to stay here, then? Do you believe Owen would leave you alone?' In the dim light, he saw the fear upon her face.

'No. But there are many of my people who are loyal to me.'

'Owen could send them away.' Warrick nodded towards the bedchamber. 'But more likely, he would try to manipulate you. You are aware that he desires you.'

She nodded. 'He behaves in that way. But it seems more that he covets me as Alan's wife. He treats me like a jewel, an adornment to his rank, not as a person.'

'What about your family? Could you return to your father's house?'

'I could, but I will not.' *Not after everything my father did*, she thought. 'I am entitled to a dower portion, according to the law. Owen cannot take that from me.'

'He is a man who will do as he pleases. And he will take whatever he wants.' He hoped she understood that and would take the necessary precautions. Yet, it seemed that Rosamund was stubborn enough to fight for her own inheritance.

But after he had seen the way Owen stared at her, Warrick wasn't about to walk away. Not now.

Alan wasn't strong enough to protect her—but *he* was. He could also take Rosamund away to Pevensham's property in Ireland. It was far enough away that Owen might not bother pursuing her.

God's blood, why was he allowing himself to become entangled in this? It wasn't his battle to face.

And yet, when he looked at Rosamund, a tightness seized in his gut. Her soft face, framed by silken dark hair, held him spellbound. He wanted to cross the space and wrap her hair around his wrist, bringing her mouth to his in a bruising kiss.

He could do more than that, if he agreed to Alan's bargain. The thought awakened a darkness inside him, for he had desired Rosamund from the first moment he'd seen her. He didn't care if she conceived a child or not. All he wanted was to touch her, to show her what a mistake she had made. He knew he could bring her to fulfilment, making her cry out in ecstasy. And her husband had given full permission for this sin.

'What do you want to do?' he asked quietly.

'I want you to find out which guards are loyal to me, instead of Owen. I am willing to pay you if you will ask your men-at-arms to watch and listen.' She folded her hands in front of her, trying to behave as if she were unafraid. 'I will stay here for whatever time Alan has remaining.' Her expression faltered. 'And when he is gone, I will surround myself with guards.' She hoped to visit the serfs and ensure that they had enough to eat and were content, even when Owen took possession of the land.

Warrick's face twisted with doubt. 'Owen intends to remain at Pevensham until your husband is dead. He will take you prisoner and ensure that you do not have an heir. And after he has claimed Alan's lands, he will claim you.' He studied her closely, adding, 'Unless you want my help.'

'How? There is nothing you can do.'

'After Alan dies, I could bring you to Ireland. I have friends there, one of whom is acquainted with the MacEgan tribe. They could give you sanctuary.' The MacEgan King had four brothers and their family controlled vast lands in the south. There was no safer place for Rosamund.

Rosamund motioned for him to follow her into a smaller chamber. No one was inside, and she closed the door behind them. 'You want me to flee and abandon my responsibilities.'

'Owen will control this land by law. You can do nothing to threaten his inheritance unless you give birth to Alan's heir.'

'I have already said that I will not lie with you, Warrick. I cannot do that to Alan. It's not the sort of woman I am.' She kept her voice hushed, and in the darkness, he could barely see her face.

'You were mine first,' he insisted. 'Or did you forget the vows you spoke?' The words were bitter, despite his efforts to keep them neutral.

'I had no right to make those promises. We were never truly married.' Her voice was flat, as if she hardly believed the words she was speaking.

'Say what you will, we were bound by holy vows and by flesh. The Church would have recognised our marriage.'

'And if I had not obeyed my father, you would be dead.' She stared back at him. 'I did what I had to.'

'Do you love him?' he asked quietly.

'Yes.'

From her tone, he sensed that it was a different love, almost that of a sister towards her brother. And yet, she had given her body to Alan, consummating their marriage. The thought brought about a surge of jealousy. Lord Pevensham had possessed her for nearly three years, and nothing would change that.

Warrick started to turn away, but then she caught the edge of his tunic and pulled him back. In her eyes, he saw the turmoil. She looked torn about whether to speak. He didn't press her for answers but simply waited.

At last, she whispered, 'Alan is a friend, a kind man who did his best to care for me.'

Her hand touched his, and Warrick held it for a moment. Her actions and words warred with one another, as if she didn't know what she wanted.

'You're asking me to walk away and let you be Owen's victim,' Warrick ground out.

'No.' With a shaky sigh, she added, 'I do want you to stay and guard me from him. I trust you more than any other man.'

Even if she had refused, he had no intention of leaving her behind. He reached out and touched her chin, lifting her face to look at him. In her green eyes, he saw fear, determination, and a faint trace of longing.

The years had not destroyed the love that had once been between them. It had only buried it. And when he looked into her eyes, there was no denying his hunger for this woman. He understood her tangled emotions, but he saw the solution, just as Alan did. A child would invalidate Owen's claim to Pevensham, as long as they could keep him safe.

'What if…we allow Alan to believe that we have been intimate, even though both of us know the truth?' she murmured.

He took her hand and brought it to his throat so she would feel the way his pulse had quickened. Her fingers were soft against his skin, and God help him, he wanted this woman. 'Are you afraid of me, Rosamund?'

She closed her eyes and shook her head. 'I know you would never hurt me.'

'But I never promised not to tempt you,' he said quietly. 'I want you still, even after all this time.'

He drew her hand lower to his heartbeat. She didn't even try to pull away, and he unlaced his leather armour and tunic, placing her hand upon his bare skin. 'If you want a child, I will give you one,' he said quietly. The very thought aroused him. Here, in the darkness, he envisioned her lying upon his sheets, her naked body exposed to him. He wanted to taste her skin, to watch the gooseflesh rise as he caressed her breasts. She would moan as he suckled her breasts, arching into him as she grew wet between her thighs. Warrick gritted his teeth, trying to force back the rush of need.

She held her hand against his heart a moment longer before she drew it away. 'No,' she murmured. 'I will not take that risk. Let Alan believe we tried and did not succeed.'

God help him, he wanted more than she would give. With each day he spent at her side, he longed to accept Alan's proposition. Her husband was going to die, and Rosamund would be at the mercy of Owen de Courcy.

He could not stand by and let it happen.

He had been given a chance to reclaim the woman he wanted above all. Alan wanted her to be protected after he was gone, and the man was right—there was no one else who would guard her the way Warrick could.

The more he considered it, the more he saw the sound reasoning behind Lord Pevensham's proposition. All the man lacked was an heir of his own. But Rosamund would not surrender easily. She guarded her body as fiercely as she did her heart.

He followed Rosamund out of the room and into the corridor. 'What will you do about Owen?'

She paled but lifted her chin to face him. 'I am aware of his…eagerness for Alan to die. But Owen would never do anything to endanger himself. Too many would suspect his involvement if Alan died whilst he was here.'

They continued towards her husband's chamber and Rosamund opened the door. The moment they stepped inside, Warrick saw Alan lying prone on the bed. His limp hair was tangled around his face, and his hand hung over the side of the mattress.

Rosamund gasped at the sight and hurried to his side. A moment later, her shoulders relaxed. In a low whisper, she murmured, 'Thanks be to God, he is only sleeping.'

But he understood that this was the burden that hung over her each day. She never knew whether Alan would survive the day and lived in fear of the moment he would die. Worry lined her face, and she chose a stool near the hearth, as if keeping vigil. Warrick took another chair and sat across from her.

'I want Owen to leave,' she admitted beneath her breath. 'But I do not think he will. He is naught but a vulture, circling his brother.'

'I agree—he will not leave until Alan is dead.'

Her face grew pained at the idea. 'My husband is a good man, and he does not deserve any of this. Would that he could live out his days in peace.' In her green eyes, he saw tears welling up. Whether they were tears of grief or of frustration, he could not say. But her shoulders slumped forward, her head bowed.

A few moments later, Alan stirred upon the bed. 'Rosamund, is that you?'

'Yes, my lord.' She moved to his side and helped him to sit up. 'Would you like any food or wine? Berta left you some cheese and bread. Or there is venison, if that would tempt you.'

He gave a weak smile. 'I am not so very hungry, but I would be glad of your company.'

Warrick remained on the far side of the room, leaving the pair of them to share a private moment. Although Rosamund fussed over her husband, Warrick noticed that she treated him like a friend, not a lover. There was no sense of intimacy with the man, but he saw the way Alan doted upon her.

He was about to quietly leave their chamber when Alan called him back. 'Please come and sit beside us, Warrick.'

He crossed the room but did not sit. Instead, he stood behind Rosamund in a respectful distance.

'My brother has come to inspect his inheritance. I told him today that Rosamund is with child.' Alan eyed his wife, who appeared horrified at his proclamation. 'I want everyone to believe this child is legitimate.'

'A child who does not exist,' Rosamund shot back. 'Why would you say this, Alan?'

'I know that you are reluctant, *ma petite*, but I command this of you. This is the best way to ensure the protection of Pevensham and you.'

Although Warrick understood why the man had lied to his brother, Alan's revelation would undoubtedly bring danger to Rosamund.

Then Alan lifted his gaze to Warrick. 'The time has come, de Laurent. What is your answer? Will you sire a child for us?'

A chill of fear rose upon Rosamund's skin, for she did not know the answer he would give. Though Warrick would never take her against her will, she was also well aware that he held the power to seduce her. Her treacherous mind remembered the weight of his body upon hers. He had been a warrior all his life, and she had traced the hardened muscles of his torso beneath her fingertips. Everything about him unnerved her, causing her emotions to fall into chaos.

She didn't trust herself any more.

'I leave the decision to Rosamund,' Warrick answered. 'But if I do this, I have conditions that must be met.'

'As do I,' Alan said. The man's complexion was pale, his hand ice cold when Warrick clasped it in agreement.

Their arrangement shook her to the core. This was about far more than conceiving an heir. Did her husband honestly believe she could simply lie back and let another man join with her, for the sake of a child? Even if it meant protecting Pevensham and herself? No, not at all.

Rosamund had locked away her feelings of the past, obeying her father to save Warrick's life. She could not dare lower the boundaries that shielded her heart.

She backed away from the two men. The need for physical distance overrode all else. It infuriated her that her husband viewed her as a pawn, to be sacrificed for the greater good.

A small voice inside warned, *That is all you have ever been. A pawn, sacrificed for a greater strategy. Not a woman with any strength or will of her own.*

Her father had treated her in this way, and now her husband was behaving in the same manner, for the sake of an heir.

In all honesty, the idea of another pregnancy terrified her. Every time she imagined it, she thought of the terrible labour pains and the lifeless body of her daughter. Rosamund closed her eyes, forcing back the memory.

'I can't,' she whispered. 'I am sorry, but I just… can't.' Not only because of her pregnancy fears, but also because she could no longer allow herself to become a silent shadow. If she let them manipulate her like a lump of clay, she would lose the last pieces of herself.

Her husband turned to stare at her, and for the first time, she saw a darker side to Alan. No longer was he a benevolent nobleman—instead, he was a baron fighting to save his estate from the enemy.

'You will do as I command.' His voice was rigid, emotionless. 'In this Rosamund, I give you no choice. You must conceive a child or all is lost.'

Anger flared up within her. How could he take the choice from her? He was her husband, but she was not a vessel to be impregnated and set aside.

'What of my honour?' Rosamund demanded.

'You expect me to submit to another man, setting aside my marriage vows?'

'Yes,' Alan answered. His voice was like a knife, fiercer that she had ever heard before. 'I have put aside my own personal feelings for the sake of this estate. You must do the same.'

Rebellion brewed within her, and she turned back to Warrick. He said nothing at all, but he made no effort to hide his interest. His searing gaze slid over her like an invisible caress.

When she stared back at her husband, making no effort to hide her wrath, Alan's eyes were frosted. They locked in a silent battle, but her husband's next words stopped her cold.

'I have given you time enough to grow accustomed to the idea. But now, we must act. You will have Berta prepare you this night. I will come to your room and dismiss her. Then de Laurent will enter through the passageway that adjoins our chambers. No one will see him, and no one will know he is there. Everyone will believe that we lay together.'

Her heartbeat quickened at his orders. She had always known of the small passageway that connected their two rooms. When they were first married, Alan had shown it to her, in the event that she ever needed him.

But from what he'd said, she understood that he would not allow her to create a pretence. Dear God, did he intend to witness the joining? Her stomach twisted at the thought. It was bad enough that he had proposed this idea, but did he intend to ensure that the act was carried out?

Saints help her, she couldn't do this.

'How can you simply give me to another man?' she whispered. 'Do I mean so little to you?' The truth was, her fear of lying with Warrick had nothing to do with the sexual act. It was the fear of her own response.

He had the power to make her yield with the softest touch. If she took a single bite from this forbidden apple, it would irrevocably change her marriage.

Though she did not look back at Warrick, she could feel his stare burning into her skin. Awareness rippled over her body, and she wished she held the power to withstand her own unspoken desires.

'You mean far too much to me,' Alan said softly. 'And that is why I brought Warrick here. I know you wanted him years ago, and I believe he will treat you gently.' His eyes hardened into grey steel. 'You will send for a bottle of our best wine from the cellar. And I intend to drink all of it to-night.'

She bit her lip, understanding what he was saying. But even so, she knew there was a little power she could still wield. Right now, she needed every weapon at her disposal to protect her heart from the man standing behind her.

No longer could she stand here and listen to them dictating her life. She gave a single nod and glared at Warrick before striding out of the room. From behind her, she heard her husband say, 'Tell me of your conditions.'

She didn't want to hear them. Right now, she wanted to break something, to rebel against the two men who were trying to control her. It felt rather satisfying to slam the door behind her when she left Alan's chamber.

Rosamund wished she could return to the Great Hall and walk outside, feeling the cool spring air. But if she did, she would only be faced with Owen.

How could Alan have told him she was with child? The lie endangered her very life. Even if her husband remained alive a little longer, Owen would find a way to hurt her.

Or had he said this to ensure that she never

left Warrick's protection? If so, then his ruse had worked.

She stormed back to her room, feeling the satisfaction of another door slamming. Berta's eyes widened, and she asked, 'What has happened, my lady?'

'My husband has decided that he wishes to visit my bed this night.'

Her maid gave a concerned look. 'Is he…able, my lady?'

'He seems to think so,' she snapped. But it burned through her that she was to be the sacrificial lamb, that Alan had no intention of letting her elude his plans. And worse, that Warrick was in agreement.

Was this meant to punish her for her choice? Was he attempting his own form of vengeance?

If so, then he would regret it.

She knew not if Alan intended to witness their joining, but she wouldn't put it past him. Yet, if she was forced into this, she refused to feel anything. She would numb herself to all else, finding a way to guard her traitorous body.

And most of all, her heart.

Rosamund spent the rest of the day staring out of the window. The spring winds had grown cooler, and outside, a bright amber moon rose over their lands. But the beauty of the night did nothing to dispel the fear rising inside.

She wore her shift and Berta had brushed her hair. It fell into dark waves down to her waist after being in braids for most of the day.

Her maid appeared agitated for some reason, and finally Rosamund asked, 'What ails you? You are not yourself today.'

Berta's face tightened, and she hesitated. 'My— my son has been taken by Owen de Courcy. He claims he wishes to train him as a squire.' But there was no happiness in her maid's expression— only fear.

'Do you want me to speak on your behalf?' Rosamund suggested. 'I can tell Owen you do not wish Martin to be fostered with him.' Though the man might not listen, she was willing to try.

Berta appeared dismayed by her offer. 'Oh, no, my lady. It is kind of you, but no.'

She didn't entirely understand why her maid refused, but for now, she would let it be. Berta knew that she would intervene for her, if needed, and that was enough.

When there came a knock at the chamber door, Rosamund stiffened. Every muscle in her body tensed, and she fought to quell her anxiety and frustration. Berta answered it, and Alan stood at the threshold. He was clad in a silk tunic and chausses, and she noticed the lines of pain on his face. The act of walking to her chamber had exhausted him, though he had tried to feign strength. She wanted to help him return to his own room, but she could not shame him in front of her maid.

Rosamund dismissed Berta, and Alan waited a moment before approaching the window.

'Are you ready, *ma petite*?'

'No.' She crossed her arms and glanced outside. 'In truth, I was contemplating whether to throw myself from this window since the pair of you seem intent upon rearranging my life.' She eyed the distance to the ground before turning back. 'You could discuss the plans for my funeral Mass, if you wished.'

A laugh escaped him, and Alan sat upon the bed. 'By God, you are the most stout-hearted woman I have ever known, Rosamund. I do love you.'

'Then don't ask me to do this.' She leaned against the wall, pleading with him.

Alan started to stand, but she raised a hand, motioning him down. He had exerted himself enough by walking this far.

'I know that you were forced into our marriage,

and I am grateful for every moment of it.' His gaze softened upon her. 'I wish I had the means to give you a child, my Rosamund. But God did not grant me that.'

He reached for her hand, and she took it, feeling the shadow of guilt. This man deserved a wife who loved him in truth. Though Rosamund had tried to be the woman he wanted, she had never desired him as much as Warrick. Alan was not at fault for their forced marriage, and she had never blamed him for claiming her. Instead, she had harboured resentment towards her father.

'I know you desire a child,' she answered softly. 'But what if it doesn't happen?'

His palm tightened over hers, and his grey eyes held sadness. 'It happened once before, Rosamund. With him.'

All the blood seemed to freeze within her body, and she paled at his statement. Before she could speak, he touched her lips with a finger. 'Do not deny it. I knew you were already with child when we wed. Your father told me.'

It overwhelmed her to realise that he had known her darkest secret all these years. 'Then why did you wed me?'

'Because I wanted you,' he admitted. 'I was willing to have you in any way I could. And I was willing to pretend that your child was mine.' He caressed her cheek and offered, 'I know Warrick can give you a child because of that. And I would do everything possible to protect this estate and you.'

Rosamund didn't know what to say. For three years, she had kept the secret of the man who had fathered her stillborn child, believing that Alan would be furious to learn of it. But he had known all along. She wasn't certain how she should respond to the knowledge.

'I am sorry,' she said at last.

'You loved him,' he answered. 'And you believed you would marry him.' He shrugged and reached for her shift. 'There is nothing to be done about it now. Except, we know he is capable of giving you a child—and that is what we need most.'

His hands trembled upon her shift, passing over her body before he reached the hem and lifted it away. She stood naked before him, and he leaned forward and kissed her.

'Lie down, Rosamund,' he murmured. He walked with her to the bed and pulled back the coverlet. 'You are the most beautiful woman I have ever seen. I was always proud to call you my wife.'

Her body grew cold, not only from the chill, but from his actions. 'Alan, please. Don't ask this of me.'

He drew her to lie down, his face serious. 'Our time together grows short. Let me die knowing I have done everything I could to take care of you.' He kissed her lips and then moved away from the bed. 'Stay here, and do as I have commanded.'

Her fingers dug into the sheets, but she understood how weak he was and how difficult this short walk had been.

When he walked to the opposite wall, he moved aside a tapestry and found the latch that opened up the passageway. A moment later, Warrick appeared.

'Be gentle with her,' Alan cautioned. And then he disappeared into the passageway, closing the door behind him.

Warrick let the tapestry fall back into place. He wore only his braies, and the moment he arrived, she rolled herself up within the sheets, hiding her body. In the firelight, his body gleamed. He was the most magnificent man she had ever seen, and against her will, a flood of memories washed over her. She could almost feel his hands upon her skin, his breath mingled with hers.

He stood motionless at the entrance, his expression unreadable. Only his eyes revealed a trace of heat. Beneath the coverlet, her skin prickled with sensitivity, her breasts rising as if he had caressed them.

Rosamund looked away, trying to gather her composure. But she was too aware of his gaze upon her. And she knew she had to say something, to remind him that she had no intention of submitting to him.

'I don't want—' Rosamund started to say, but Warrick raised a finger to his lips and pointed towards the wall. Her eyes widened. Did he mean that Alan was hiding himself in the passageway to witness this?

The very thought unnerved her. Why would her husband do such a thing? But then, she supposed he didn't trust her, and with good reason. She might have obeyed him in the preparations, but she was not going to go through with this.

Warrick crossed the room with slow steps and stood in front of the bed. She had wrapped herself up so tightly in the sheets, she was helpless to move.

He sat down, his weight pressing against the mattress. She didn't know what his intentions were, but he leaned in. His voice was a silken whisper against her ear. 'Do you want to know the conditions I forced Alan to accept?'

Her mouth went dry with anxious fear, and she didn't answer him. Her heart pounded within her chest, her pulse racing.

Warrick drew his hand over her hair, smoothing the length of it. The light touch evoked a longing she couldn't deny. His blue eyes were searing in his desire, and he murmured, 'I asked for three nights with you.' He leaned in and brushed his mouth against hers.

The light kiss seared her skin, and she turned her face. 'I have already told you that I do not want to lie with you.'

He nodded. 'So you did. And I have sworn to Alan that I will not claim you unless you ask it of me.'

Her shoulders relaxed slightly at that. 'Then… you are wasting your time here. For I will not change my mind.'

His thumb moved down her face to her lips. 'Perhaps not. But if you do not obey Alan, he has said he will find another man to take my place.'

'No,' she blurted out. She didn't believe her husband would do such a thing. 'I would never allow that.'

He loosened the sheet and untucked it from beneath her, allowing her more freedom of motion. 'If he believes that you are willing to let me touch you, it is enough for now. He agreed that we need not consummate anything for the first two nights.'

'Or any night thereafter,' she shot back. With the sheets fully covering her body, she sat up and swung her legs over the side. 'I told him I would obey, but we both know it was a lie.'

He reached out to the nape of her neck, his strong fingers threaded in her hair. 'Was it?'

She was startled when he kissed her again with no warning at all. At first, she kept her mouth firmly closed, but he tilted his mouth, nipping at her lips in an invitation. His hand began to massage the base of her neck, finding the tightness and tension. She wanted to moan in thanksgiving, it felt so good. And God above, she'd forgotten what it was like to kiss this man.

He knew how to take her lips, how to use his mouth to awaken her desires. Her mind was spinning, her emotions in turmoil—especially with the question of whether Alan was still watching them.

Warrick continued to kiss her, with lazy effort, as if he had all the time in the world. Her mouth grew swollen as it went on and on. Then he slid his tongue inside her mouth, and her skin grew heated. It was as if she could feel his hands upon her skin, even though it was only his kiss.

He moved his mouth to her throat, and her skin erupted in gooseflesh. For a moment, she managed to collect herself, and she murmured, 'It doesn't matter whether you kiss me or not. I will not change my mind about this.'

She had to fight him with all her resolve. The sleekness of his tongue was like the echo of his body moving inside hers. She couldn't stop the rush of feelings, nor her body's desires. Though they had only lain together a few times, she had never forgotten the way he had made her feel.

And he *had* been her first husband. Regardless of what her father had done to drive them apart, Warrick had spoken vows and consummated the marriage. There was no denying it.

Not once in three years of marriage had Alan awakened her to such sensations. Her eyes welled up with tears, for she hated herself for feeling anything at all. She wanted to remain closed off to this man, as if she were enclosed within stone.

But his hand moved beneath the bedsheet, caressing the lines of her bare flesh. The moment he did, she shivered from the heat.

Warrick never stopped kissing her, and after a time, she felt herself falling back into the girl she had once been. She had loved this man then and had desperately wanted to stay married to him.

A heaviness closed over her, tears burning in her eyes as she began to kiss him back. Never had she imagined it would come to this. With all her heart, she wished she could turn back the years and make different choices.

Chapter Seven

Warrick waited until he heard the faint click of the door to the passageway before he broke away from Rosamund. Beneath his breath, he murmured, 'He's gone now.'

Her cheeks were rosy, her lips swollen, and she didn't seem to understand what was happening. He picked up her fallen shift and tossed it to her. Then he turned his back and walked towards the table and two chairs on the far side of the room. 'Clothe yourself.'

There was a moment of silence as if she were still uncertain of what to do. His abrupt departure seemed to leave her confused. She didn't know that Alan had sworn he would witness the first joining. Warrick had suspected her husband would leave when he believed they were obeying his command, for no man was self-sacrificing enough to witness his wife with another man.

The kiss had been a distraction, but Warrick wasn't a saint. This woman had haunted him for three years, and he had no qualms about taking anything she offered.

The soft rustle of fabric and sheets told him she had put on her shift once more. Then came her footsteps approaching. Rosamund moved towards the fire and sat down in a chair, staring at him. Her expression held wariness. 'You made me believe I would have to...' Her words drifted away, but he shook his head.

'Alan was watching.' For a time, he studied the glowing hearth, wondering what to do now. They had to delay for a length of time, making her husband believe that they were complying with his wishes. It was an elaborate ruse, but a necessary one.

More than that, he wanted to regain Rosamund's trust. Alan wanted him to marry her upon his death, to keep her protected. The man's health waned with each day, and it was certain he could not last through the end of the year. If Warrick accepted Lord Pevensham's proposition that he wed Rosamund, he had a chance to gain the land he'd always wanted.

But only if there was an heir.

He sat in silence beside her, letting his mind

drift as he tried to find a solution. Rosamund was a woman of honour and would not stray from her vows, no matter what Alan wanted. And yet, Warrick could not deny the temptation before him. Her kiss had pushed back the years of anger and regret, making him crave even more. He wanted this woman, wanted to give her a child and live beside her in this place. He had not lied about the three days Alan had granted them…and yet, she might despise him if he did seduce her.

They were damned, no matter which path they chose.

He looked around Rosamund's bedchamber, searching for some way they could occupy the time. 'Have you any dice or a game?' he suggested. 'Or is there some other way we could pass the time?'

She appeared puzzled a moment. 'Do you mean to say that you didn't intend to…to…claim me?'

He sat back in his chair, his gaze fixed upon her. 'I wouldn't refuse if that was what you wanted, Rosamund.' He did desire this woman, and he had never forgotten what it was like to touch her. Even the stolen moment tonight had brought back the fire between them.

She crossed her arms, suddenly appearing vulnerable. 'No. It's not what I want.' Her voice was the barest whisper, but her downcast gaze suggested something else. She tucked her knees beneath the hem of her shift, hiding her body as best she could. But he knew she had not been indifferent to his kiss, despite her protests.

Warrick stood and walked towards the opposite side of the room. Rosamund pointed towards a low table. 'There may be dice inside there.'

It was a welcome distraction. He did not know how he would pass the time with her wearing so little and his body craving her touch. But he kept his yearnings under tight command.

Upon the table, he saw an iron box just larger than both of his hands. The metal held intricate carvings, and he couldn't resist tracing the edge.

'Alan bought it from a crusader,' she said. 'I sometimes wonder how old it is.'

Inside the box, he saw a set of bone dice and other objects from Jerusalem. A small pouch held sand, and he spied a dried olive branch beside it.

He tested the weight of the dice and brought them over. 'We will cast lots for different wagers. That will pass the time quickly enough.'

And God willing, he would get through this night.

'What do you want to wager?' she asked with a raised eyebrow.

He could have told her higher stakes, demanding a kiss or an intimate touch. Instead, he offered, 'Answers. Whoever wins has to answer a question with only honesty.'

Rosamund seemed to consider it for a moment, and then nodded. 'So be it.' She stood from her chair and joined him on the floor beside the hearth. The firelight revealed the thin material of her shift, and beneath the linen, he saw the rosy outline of her nipples. He forced his attention back to the dice, and said, 'We will roll to see who goes first.' They both took a turn, and Rosamund won the round. She gathered up the dice and studied him a moment, a slight smile on her face.

'Ask me a question,' he said.

She thought a moment and then asked, 'Why did you come to Pevensham and answer Alan's summons?'

He took the dice from her, wondering how honest he should be. It had nothing to do with either Alan or Owen...only Rosamund.

'Because I was angry,' he admitted. 'I hated you for leaving me to marry him. And I wanted to see if Alan had made you as miserable as I was.' He rolled the dice between his fingertips. 'But he didn't, did he?'

'My father forced me to marry a man who was

in love with me,' she said quietly. 'Alan did everything he could to make me happy. And in time, it was enough.' Her expression held a trace of sadness. It did seem that, although Alan had given her a home and wealth, it wasn't the same. Warrick took a small measure of satisfaction from that.

He rolled the dice and then passed them over. Rosamund picked them up and tossed the bone dice, winning a second time. 'What is it you truly want from all of this, Warrick? Is it land?'

He shrugged. 'I would like a place of my own, yes.' One where he could be apart from his father and live in peace. The idea of Ireland was appealing, but it was far more than that. Even if there was no heir, this felt like a second chance at the life he'd wanted.

'Pevensham would give you that status, wouldn't it?'

'It would.' Warrick let her believe this was about land, not wanting to reveal too much. Then he rolled the bone dice a third time. When she took her turn and won again, he detected a faint note of amusement in her eyes. His suspicion grew, and he took the dice from her. 'These are weighted, aren't they?'

Her smile widened. 'Of course they are.'

'You cheated.'

But he wasn't entirely angry with her. He might have done the same thing, truth to tell. Her hair had fallen across her shoulders, and in her state of undress, it reminded him of the fragile moments when she had belonged to him. Right now, he wanted to claim her lips again, to lay her back and surrender to the heated desire rising within.

Rosamund's expression faltered as if she could read his thoughts. 'Y-you owe me the answer to another question.'

'I owe you nothing.' He tossed the dice aside and rested his hands on either side of her. 'You, my lady, deserve a penalty for what you did.'

He kept his tone teasing, so as not to frighten her. She softened and smiled again. 'You should know better than to wager with me, Warrick.' Her eyes were bright, and she narrowed her gaze at him. 'There will be no penalty.'

He ignored her and claimed, 'On the morrow, you will ride with me,' he said. 'Just as we did when we were young.'

Her face faltered at that. 'The people will talk, if I do this. I cannot.'

'Then you will ride alone, and I will come as your guard. I will wait for you near the stables.'

She rested her hands upon his shoulders. 'For what purpose, Warrick?'

He drew his knuckles over the curve of her cheek. 'Because I'm going to marry you again, after he's dead. And you need time to know me once again.'

She didn't move, didn't flinch at his words. 'Why do you think I will wed you?'

'Because Alan commanded you to. And because this time, I won't let you go.' With that, he leaned in and kissed her hard.

Rosamund lay awake in bed for most of the night. Her thoughts were tangled up like knotted threads, and she felt torn between two men. On one hand, Warrick was right. Alan's days were numbered, and she feared falling beneath Owen's control. Marriage would indeed keep her protected, and it was what Alan wanted.

And yet, she did not want to bear another child. The thought chilled her to the bone, for in her heart, she feared she could never give birth to a living son. She closed her eyes for a moment, trying to push back the darkness.

With a heavy heart, she dressed herself in the darkness. Outside her window, she saw traces of the morning sky battling against the shadowed clouds. The need to escape this place was too much to overcome, so she reached for a familiar bundle and tied it at her waist. Her maid awakened, and she bid Berta return to sleep.

She tiptoed down the stone staircase, the restlessness rising in her blood. Men were sleeping upon the floor in the Great Hall, and she crept around them, hoping no one would see her. One soldier emerged, and she motioned him back, not wanting anyone to follow. He must have come recently from sentry duty, for he wore full armour and a conical helm that obscured his face.

She was not strong enough to open the heavy doors of the main entrance. Before she could try again, the soldier moved in front of her and pulled the door open. He remained silent, and she nodded her thanks.

With her cloak around her, she savoured the morning stillness. This was the time of day that she loved the most, for many of the castle folk were still abed. She could take solace in being alone.

Rosamund awakened one of the stable boys and ordered her horse to be saddled. The same soldier who had opened the door stepped forward once again. He signalled for the stable boy to bring his own horse, and now, she recognised him and understood why he had followed her. Warrick had kept his identity shielded, and he meant to guard her, as he had promised last night. So be it.

When the horses were ready, she took the lead, and he followed. She rode across her lands, skirting the village and keeping to the open meadow. Nearby, she saw the fields of barley swaying in the morning breeze. She kept her pace steady, feeling her apprehension slowly beginning to lift.

The morning dawn transformed the sky from grey to shades of rose. The light eased her mood, softening the hard edges of sleeplessness. When she reached the edge of her lands, she was slightly out of breath but felt better. She dismounted and led her horse towards the banks of a large lake, letting him drink. Warrick kept his distance, for which she was grateful. She understood why he had accompanied her, but she had no desire to speak to him at this moment.

She chose a flat rock near the edge of the water, spreading her skirts around her. From inside the bundle at her waist, she pulled out her embroidery and several lengths of thread. He remained behind her, but she was fully conscious of his presence.

There was now enough light to see the design she had begun. Blue, brown, and grey threads intertwined to form the pattern of water. Upon the surface of it, she began stitching small threads of gold. She drank in the sight of the sunrise, adding threads of pink and soft grey as she recreated the sunrise before her.

Only in this did she possess the power to form beauty. Though her life was a tangled snarl of threads, some nearly ready to break, it was in her work that she found peace. She gave herself up to the artistry, feeling the rest of the world slip away.

Warrick did not interrupt, but stood behind her, a quiet sentry. Only after she had finished did she turn back to him. He had already removed his helm, revealing his face.

She was grateful that he had not asked her to speak, nor had he revealed his identity to anyone else.

'Thank you for watching over me,' she said quietly. 'I needed this moment.'

He gave a single nod. Though he was armed only with a sword, she felt entirely safe with him.

'Did you sleep at all last night?' she asked. He shook his head, but she saw the faint upward turn of his mouth.

'Neither did I.' She stood up from the large stone and removed her shoes. Then she tucked up her skirts and stepped into the cool water. 'I suppose you think I am mad to go riding at a time like this, only to sit and sew.'

'It's what you've always done when you are troubled,' he said quietly.

'I fear for what lies ahead,' she said. 'I don't want Alan to die. And I'm afraid of what Owen will do when he does.' She walked along the water's edge, wishing she could tell him everything. But he would not understand the guilt she held in her heart. Every time she had made her own choices, defying the commands of others, it had resulted in tragedy.

'I will not let anyone harm you,' he stated. And she knew he meant it. This fierce warrior would guard her from any foe, no matter how many enemies might threaten her.

'You cannot guard me from myself.' She would not look at him now. 'If I were a different woman, perhaps I could put aside my feelings, obey my husband's wishes and conceive a child to save Pevensham. But I can't. I won't.'

'Are you afraid of me?' he asked quietly.

'I am afraid of the way I feel when you kiss me.' But more than that, she was afraid to become pregnant again. Deep inside, she believed that any child she conceived would not live. Many women miscarried, time after time. And what reason was there to betray her honour for the sake of a child who might die? 'You made me remember.'

And God help her, it had hurt her deeply. Warrick had always known how to touch her, how to tempt her. No longer did she trust herself. This time, she did turn to face him. She stared into his deep blue eyes. 'I need you to leave Pevensham. Go back to your family, go back to your home. I beg this of you.'

'Why?' He spoke the words with a gruffness that revealed his own frustration.

'Because my husband deserves a better death than this. How can I betray him and then watch him die? It's not right.'

'No, it isn't. But he wants to know that you will be protected after he is gone. Were I in his place, I would want the same.'

'Alan is a good man,' she admitted, her eyes filling up with tears. 'He deserved a wife so much better than me. I wish, sometimes, that I could have been the woman he wanted.'

'You are that woman.'

He didn't seem to understand what she meant. Rosamund stepped out of the shallow water. Her bare feet were cool against the flat stone, but she faced him. 'I cannot simply stand back and let others command my life. With or without Alan.' Pevensham would fall into Owen's hands by right of succession, but she would still have her dower portion, according to the law. The only question was whether Owen would leave her alone.

She could ask to live in Ireland, but it would mean leaving behind the people of Pevensham.

'What do you want to do?' Warrick asked.

She sat down upon the rock, folded up her sewing, and put it away. 'I will need someone to protect me from Owen after Alan is gone.'

He adjusted his sword belt and sat down beside her. There was tension in his shoulders as he stared at the water. 'And you want me to be your hired sword.'

'I would pay you,' she started to say, but he stared hard at her.

'I don't want your silver, Rosamund. And I won't be under your command, to go or stay as it pleases you.'

The stone beneath her palms felt cold and damp from the water, but the chill inside her went deeper. 'What is it you want?'

'I want you as my wife, just as you were before.' He reached out to trace the curve of her cheek. 'I want your bare skin beneath me when I bury myself inside you. I want to touch you until you cry out with mindless need. The way it was, years ago.'

Her body seemed to come alive at his words.

She bit her lip, trying to push away the unwanted feelings.

'I won't stand by and let another man take you from me again, Rosamund. When Alan dies, I intend to claim you.'

He spoke like a barbaric conqueror, bent upon taking her captive. And despite her attempt to remain calm, her heart beat faster.

'And what if I refuse?' she whispered.

'You won't want to.' His hand moved lower, down her throat. She was intensely aware of his masculine scent, and he slid his fingers beneath the chain of her necklace. It hung above her bodice, and he leaned in to steal a kiss.

She tried not to move, tried not to respond to him. But his hand moved lower still, to the soft curve of her breast. He kissed her deeply, his tongue sliding within her mouth as his thumbs found her erect nipples.

She gasped when he stroked her aroused breasts, and the sensation echoed between her thighs. She understood what he was doing, that he was still angry about her refusal to wed him. This was his vengeance, and by making her feel desire, it was an invisible weapon.

'You still have feelings for me,' he said darkly, moving his hands down to her waist. 'And I won't let any man touch you ever again. You are still my wife in the eyes of God, Rosamund, just as you have always been.'

She touched her bruised lips, feeling the shame wash over her. Alan had never made her feel this way, and her treacherous body craved more of Warrick's touch.

'Why would you do this?' she demanded. 'You know this isn't honourable.' She stared back into his blue eyes and read the jealousy there. This man had claimed her innocence and now, he wanted her back.

'It was a mistake to wed him, and you know this. He commanded you to wed me after he dies. And you will.'

Warrick took her back to the castle later that morning, and spent the remainder of the time watching Owen de Courcy. He let himself slip into the role of a silent soldier, listening for any threats towards Rosamund and ordered his friends to do the same. No one spoke of her or of Alan, but he sensed the vultures' circling presence.

When he hung behind the group of men, Owen spied him at last. He walked alongside him, keeping his face neutral.

'I saw you escort Lady Pevensham earlier. My

brother tells me she is with child.' He spoke with an air of indifference, but Warrick sensed the sharp edge beneath his words.

'I do not know if she is or not.'

Owen slowed his pace until the soldiers were further away. Then he dropped his voice to the barest whisper. 'Why is my brother still alive?'

'I told you I would not be your assassin. I came at his summons.'

'And what did he want from you?'

Warrick paused a moment and then said, 'He wanted protection for his wife after he dies. He wants me to marry Rosamund.'

Owen shrugged. 'Pevensham will belong to me, soon enough. And if you prove your loyalty, I have no objection to your marriage.' He stopped walking and regarded him. 'But I will not allow an infant to threaten what is rightfully mine. She lost her first child, and she will lose this one, too. I promise you that.'

A sudden flare of rage washed over him at the words. Warrick took a step closer and met the man's threat with one of his own. 'You will not lay a hand upon her.'

Owen only smiled. 'You can do nothing, de Laurent. For if you try to interfere, I will see to it that you are blamed for my brother's death.'

Warrick remained motionless after the man left, his mind seething with rage. The snare of Owen's plans was tightening all around them, and he needed to free Rosamund and himself. She could not remain here with such a ruthless man.

The urge came over him, to take her away and flee to Ireland. But if he abducted her—even willingly—he had nothing to offer, not even a home. And she would come to despise him for it.

He decided to speak with Alan. Although the man believed himself to be safe, nothing could be further from the truth.

As he crossed the courtyard, he saw Rosamund's maid pass by. The young woman looked as if she had been weeping, and her expression held worry. He wondered if Alan de Courcy's condition had worsened, and he stopped her.

'How is Lord Pevensham?'

The maid paled and shook her head. 'He is gravely weak, but still living.' With that, she excused herself and hurried away.

Warrick's instincts rose on alert. Something had happened, and though he suspected Alan's death was imminent, he could not stand back and do nothing. He entered the donjon and went up the spiral stairs leading to de Courcy's bedchamber. Two guards stood outside the man's door, and

Warrick said, 'Let me pass. I must speak with Lord Pevensham.'

'We have our orders not to let anyone pass,' the first guard said. 'Our lord is resting.' He wore chainmail armour and held a spear. The other guard was heavier, and his grim expression revealed a trace of concern.

'And who gave these orders?'

'Owen de Courcy,' the first said.

It didn't surprise him to hear it. But it did seem that Owen was intensifying his efforts to ensure his inheritance. For all he knew, Alan could be alone and suffering.

'Let me pass,' he insisted. Before he could force his way through, another voice interrupted.

'Step aside.' It was Rosamund approaching, and her voice was soft and commanding. 'My lord husband summoned this man.' She stepped forward, and her presence seemed to confuse the men. 'I am the Lady of Pevensham. Put your weapons away.'

The soldiers did not obey her orders. 'My lady, we were given the command that Lord Pevensham should not be disturbed.'

Rosamund's expression grew strained. 'My husband is alive, and so am I. You obey orders from us, not from any other man.' Her tone was firm and icy. 'Now let me pass.' She stepped between them and Warrick pushed their spears aside.

Inside, Alan was lying upon the bed, coughing. His shoulders shook with exertion, and Rosamund fetched a cup of wine. 'My lord, drink this. It may help.' She tilted the goblet and held it to his lips.

Warrick hung back, studying the room. Upon a low table rested the contents of Alan's meal. The bread and cheese didn't surprise him, but when he drew closer, he saw that there was a fine grain sprinkled over the plate. It appeared to be a powder of some kind, though he could not say what it was. While Rosamund tended to her husband, Warrick touched a damp fingertip to the granules and tasted them. The bitterness was faint, and his suspicions darkened as he poured wine into a glass. He rinsed his mouth and spat it out.

He wouldn't put it past Owen to attempt poison. Perhaps one of the soldiers had put it there. And more and more, he was convinced that Owen would accuse anyone of Alan's death, including Rosamund. While she had done everything to extend her husband's life, she was not safe here any longer.

When Alan had fallen back asleep, Warrick beckoned for Rosamund to come closer. 'For the next few weeks, watch his food and drink. Be certain that he eats only what you have prepared for him.'

She paled. 'You think someone is poisoning him, then.'

'Possibly. Or trying to hasten his death.' There was no way to know for certain. Then he said quietly, 'Rosamund, it is not safe for you here. Owen will find a way to harm you.'

'Don't ask me to leave my husband when he is dying. Alan needs me.'

He understood her wishes, but this was about her protection, not her husband's. 'I fear for your safety.' He took her hand in his, gripping her palm. 'Rosamund, Owen has threatened to hurt you and any unborn child you might bear.'

'I will not run away like a frightened deer,' she argued back. 'I am lady of this castle, and I see no reason to leave my home.'

Her voice had grown louder, and Alan stirred. The man shifted against his bed, and in a weak voice, he added, 'I may be weak, but I have not lost my hearing.'

Rosamund stood and returned to his bedside. Warrick remained back, keeping his distance. 'Do you need anything, my lord?'

'Is it true what he says, that Owen is threatening you?'

'Not directly, no.'

'He threatened to ensure that she never bore any child,' Warrick interrupted. 'And he is giving orders to your men, trying to undermine her.'

Alan's fists gripped the sheets. 'Then you are right. Rosamund must leave Pevensham, in order to keep her and the child safe.'

'And how will that look to our people?' Rosamund demanded. 'If I go with Warrick, they will believe that I have abandoned you.'

'He will not go with you. Instead, he will remain here, as one of my guards.'

Warrick detected a faint note of disapproval in Alan's tone. But he couldn't imagine leaving Rosamund among other soldiers who might be loyal to Owen. He far preferred to protect her himself.

Alan reached out his hand, and she took it. 'Once we believe you are with child, I will send you to Ireland. You will remain there until the child is born. I will ensure that your son's inheritance is protected.'

Dismay creased Rosamund's face. 'You ask me to leave whilst you are dying. It's not right.'

Alan brought her hand to his lips. 'I have ordered Father Francis to write down my orders upon my death. All will believe that this child is legitimate, and you will be safe.'

Rosamund looked as if she wanted to protest but held her tongue instead. But her husband did not miss her reluctance.

'If you hold any affection towards me at all, then you will wed Warrick, as I have commanded. It is best for you, and you know this.' Alan studied her a moment, then said, 'Tonight, you must lie with him again and conceive. There can be no further delay.'

She said nothing, and guilt was written upon her face. Warrick came forward and added, 'And then you must send her away where she will be safe.' His expression hardened into stone. 'I will wait a day or two and then follow her. I do not trust your men.'

Alan met his gaze and then inclined his head in silent agreement. He studied his wife, and in his eyes, Warrick saw the rigid jealousy.

He could not have done the same, were he in Alan's place. Heir or not, he would flay any man alive who dared to touch Rosamund.

It was dangerous to think of her in this way. The years were falling away, and it was as if Fate had given him a second chance with this woman. He knew her all too well, and he craved the joining she was avoiding.

'I can feel my strength waning,' Alan said. 'I

know not how much time God will grant me, but I *will* have an heir.'

Rosamund's eyes turned the colour of storm clouds. 'And what if God grants me a daughter again? She cannot inherit, and I will have betrayed you for naught.'

'It is a chance we must take.'

She stood, her face bright with anger. He could tell she was itching to lash back at her husband, but she bit back the words. Instead, she turned her back on both of them and fled.

'Go through the passageway between our chambers and follow her,' Alan commanded him. 'No one will see you.'

But Warrick's own anger tightened beneath his skin. Despite his desire, Rosamund did not deserve to be treated like this. It was clear that Alan had made her into a pawn, manipulating her into a game she did not wish to play.

'She said no. Does that not mean anything to you?' His voice held a feral edge, and he held himself back from the violence rising.

'No,' Alan said quietly. 'It doesn't. She will do as I command, or I will find someone else.'

Warrick seized the man by his shoulders, hardly caring that de Courcy was so weakened. 'She is not your brood mare. She is a good woman, and

I'm damned if I will stand back and let you hurt her in any way.'

'You still love her,' Alan accused. The words sliced through him, for Warrick had vowed that he would never let himself fall prey to that emotion again. He started to shake his head, but de Courcy was not finished. 'It matters not that you care for my wife. She married *me*, not you, and I have been patient enough with her. Time has run out, and she must obey. She will, if I have to witness the consummation myself.'

'You care more about Pevensham than her,' Warrick shot back. 'You would throw her to the wolves if it meant saving your estate.'

A strange expression passed over Alan's face. 'You don't know what it has been like these past three years. To love a woman and know that she wept at the thought of marrying you. To claim her body and know that she loathed the very act.' There was weariness in his tone. 'I love her nearly as much as I despise her.'

Warrick took a step back from the man. There was no mistaking the resentment in Alan's words or the hatred towards him.

'I will go to her after midnight, when it is too dark to see. She will think it is me touching her.

And you will do what is necessary to help her conceive an heir.'

Warrick wanted to say no, for Rosamund would immediately know the difference between them. But he could not deny that he hungered for the woman he'd wanted to wed. Though it was a sin, he craved the silken touch of her skin. He wanted to kiss her, to pleasure her in the darkness until she could not refuse him.

Without a word, he left de Courcy's chambers and didn't look back.

Chapter Eight

It was dark within her bedchamber when she heard the passageway open. Immediately, Rosamund froze in her bed.

'It is I,' she heard Alan say. His voice was a relief, and she started to sit up when he refused. 'No. Lie back upon the bed.'

She heard him approach, but for some reason, her instincts were raised. She felt him reach towards her in the darkness, pushing back the coverlet.

'Remove your shift,' he commanded. 'I am going to lie with you.'

She hesitated, for she was not eager for his touch. And yet, she understood his desperate need for an heir.

It is your duty, her conscience reminded her. It didn't matter that she did not want her husband to join with her.

'Are you…well enough for this?' she asked him, feeling awkward about the question. He had grown weaker each day, so much that the very idea of lovemaking seemed impossible.

It will not take long, she told herself. If she lay still and did not argue, it would be over soon.

'Do not ask questions,' he rebuked her. 'Take off your shift and lie naked upon the bed. I want you on your stomach with your legs spread apart.'

Rosamund flushed at his blatant request. But then, the position was likely easier for him to manage in his condition. In the darkness, she could not see his face, but she heard his footsteps drawing nearer.

Dear God, she didn't want this. The idea of lying still while he drove himself inside her was not at all appealing. But she gritted her teeth and removed her shift. Slowly, she rolled over to her stomach and did as he asked, spreading her legs apart.

She closed her eyes tight, hoping that somehow he would be unable to perform. That he would be overtired and would give up.

But then, she felt a warm hand upon her bottom, and she jolted at the sensation. It was not Alan's hand. She knew it from the moment she felt Warrick's caress upon her. She was shocked to realise what her husband planned.

'Alan, wait.'

'Be silent.' His voice was sharp, and he ordered, 'You will not speak. You will not move. You will obey me, for you are my wife, and I may do with you as I wish.'

The hand upon her bottom moved lower, and she felt her body respond to the wicked touch. It was sinful, so very wrong. But when Warrick's fingers moved lower between her thighs, a surge of aching wetness dampened her intimate flesh. Pleasure and need coursed through her body, and he began to stroke her.

He was relentless, circling his thumb against her hooded flesh. Warrick knew exactly how to draw out her response, and she understood what this was.

Revenge.

His fingers dipped inside her wetness, filling her. He didn't plunge hard, but instead played with her body, tantalising her with a gentle surge and withdrawal. She moaned, her breathing growing more excited as he led her closer and closer to the edge.

It had been three years since she had felt like this. Her mind knew it was wrong, and yet, her body could not stop responding to him. His other hand touched her bottom, and she could not stop pressing back against his fingers inside her. She was losing control of herself, unable to grasp a single thought.

'Alan?' she pleaded, praying her husband would put an end to this wickedness. Was he still here?

'Lie still and I will see this done.' There was rage within his voice, the hateful anger of a man who wanted an heir so badly, he would stop at nothing.

But it was not Alan's hands upon her. She knew it with every breath she took, with every shocking pulse of pleasure rising inside. Her husband wanted her to take Warrick within her body, and Alan was past the point of reason—especially if he had taken matters this far.

The hands touching her were not demanding, nor were they threatening in any way. Instead, Warrick was doing exactly what he had promised. He was showing her all that she had missed during these three years. His thumb began to circle her intimate flesh with a different pressure, and he stilled the thrust of his fingers. Now, she felt a different sort of deepening quiver within her womb. He rolled her to her back, still rubbing her intimately.

Warrick continued his onslaught while his left hand reached higher towards her naked breast. Rosamund cried out when he touched her erect nipple, gently twisting it as he thrust with his other hand. She could not stop the moan from escaping her, and she desperately tried not to take pleasure from this.

She heard the soft click of the passageway closing and knew that Alan had left. He would not witness the rest. *Thank God.*

His departure marked her own decision. If she wanted to stop now, she could. Alan would never know what happened between them.

She was torn apart by what was right and what was not. Was it a mistake to give Alan what he wanted and join with the man who had been her first husband? God help her, she was so confused. She *had* spoken vows to Warrick, binding him as her husband. And then her father had forced her to marry Alan, abandoning her first marriage. She had obeyed his orders to save Warrick's life.

But what if she *was* still married to Warrick? What if this marriage to Alan had been invalid all along?

Or was it only her mind trying to justify the sin?

Warrick's mouth lowered to her breast, and a dark spear of lust drove straight through her. Her hands gripped the edges of the sheets, and she was barely able to breathe. He took her to the edge, and then slowed his caress, pushing her back again.

Her body was pulsing like a living heartbeat, and she wanted him so badly, she wanted to weep.

'Please,' she begged. His tongue slid over her nipple, suckling and pulling at her until she was writhing against him. Then she heard a rustling noise, and she felt his shaft at her wet entrance. She tried to guide him, but his strong arms held her fast.

He was teasing her again, showing her what she had been missing.

She wanted to tell him that she knew what was happening, that it was not Alan touching her. But another part of her was furious with her husband for treating her like this—for his deception and his own part in this night. She wanted to lash back at him, for he saw her as nothing more than a vessel for his heir. Alan cared about none of her feelings or her sense of honour.

He had begun this night, wanting her to believe that she was giving her body to him.

But she was not stupid. She knew Warrick was touching her, and she wanted her own vengeance against her powerless state.

And so, she gave in to the rush of sensation, arching her hips until the suffocating pleasure rose into a shimmering peak. She squeezed the inner muscles of her womanhood until she broke apart, shattering as Warrick gave her the release she'd sought. A cry of ecstasy escaped her lips, and she wanted to weep from it.

Warrick was poised at her entrance, his thick erection barely inside her. And before she could change her mind, Rosamund reached for his hips and pulled him inside her, their bodies joining together.

Warrick did not take her roughly, as he could have. Instead, he slowed his pace, sliding within so that she felt every inch of his shaft. There was tenderness and she met his thrusts while he claimed her. The heaviness of desire gathered inside, pushing her back towards the edge. She lost sight of everything, save the sharp pleasure that heightened within. He took her breast in his mouth again, and the hot pressure was enough to drive her over the brink. She allowed the blissful tide to carry her under, squeezing him tightly as he pulled back and penetrated her again.

Rosamund let him ride her, arching and meeting him as he plunged. He was starting to lose his own control, and she wanted that from him. She heard him hiss as she crossed her ankles beneath him, giving him an added pressure as he entered and withdrew. It forced him to give more shallow penetrations, but she could tell that it was driving him into madness. Over and over he pumped into her, and she came apart once again, the heat of her body erupting and seizing all around him.

Warrick withdrew from her and pushed her back to her stomach, this time invading her flesh with more speed. His pace was gruelling, and she heard a cry tear from her lips as he slammed against her in a reckless plunder of aching flesh. With each thrust, she took her own revenge against her husband's wicked orders.

And she felt the moment Warrick tensed, his body rigid with iron need. He grunted and thrust, pouring himself into her. She quaked beneath him, feeling his hard release as she accepted his seed.

For a moment, he lay atop her, his rigid body embedded within. Rosamund said nothing at all, but her body continued to shudder with the aftershocks. Her emotions were battered, and she felt the terrible guilt shadowing her when he withdrew from her body.

Warrick said nothing at all, but pulled the sheet over her and left.

And when she was alone, she closed her eyes and damned them both for what they had done.

In the morning, Rosamund awakened alone. Memories of last night washed over her, and she had never felt more ashamed and angry in her life.

You could have said no, her conscience chided. *You knew what was happening, and you allowed it. The sin is yours to bear.*

And there could be a child now.

She tore the sheets off her bed, tangling them into a ball and throwing them across the room. Damn them both for this. She hated being so powerless, unable to make decisions in her own life.

She put on her shift and kirtle, struggling with the laces. She didn't know where Berta was, but she was glad that her maid had been elsewhere last night. Rosamund strode towards the fireplace, and her footing slipped upon something small and hard. She went reeling and struck the floor. Too late, she realised it was a weighted gaming die she had played with Warrick the other night. She winced and sat up on the floor, reaching for the die. It was made of bone and filled on one side just enough to land on the side she wanted it to.

Would that she could arrange her own life to fall into the pattern she desired. She remained on the floor with her kirtle tangled in her legs, hardly caring.

Her husband had never been this demanding before, not once in the three years of their marriage. Now, he had revealed another side of himself, a ruthless side that she didn't like. Did he honestly believe she wouldn't know when another man touched her? Frustration seethed within her, and Rosamund finally stood up from the floor, picking up the small gaming die as she did. A knock sounded at her door, and she suspected it must be Warrick, sent by her husband.

She jerked the door open and was startled to see Owen de Courcy standing on the other side. He was dressed in travelling clothes with no armour, but a light sword hung at his waist.

He moved into her bedchamber without a word, adding, 'Close the door, Rosamund.'

Her nerves tightened at the sight of this man. There was no denying the threat he posed, though she tried to calm her beating heart.

Rosamund didn't move, but instead wondered if she could escape his presence instead. When she stepped towards the door, intending to flee, he closed the distance and shut it behind him. 'Never mind, then.'

'You should not be within my chamber,' she argued. 'If you wish to speak to me, we will do so elsewhere. In my husband's room or in the Great Hall.'

'Too many would overhear our conversation,' he said smoothly.

An icy coldness slid over her skin, for she knew he had come to threaten her. She had no weapons in her chamber, no means of defending herself.

'I have placed a guard outside the door to keep us safe,' Owen continued.

In other words, there was no escaping him. Her pulse raced within her veins, and she questioned whether to move away from this man or stay close to the door.

'What do you want?' But even as she voiced the question, she knew.

'Your husband tells me you are with child. But you are not, are you?' His tone held a darkness that frightened her.

Rosamund didn't know how to answer him, for after last night, she could be. She didn't know if Alan had already made provisions for an unborn heir or whether to tell him the truth.

'I believe so,' she hedged. 'But it is very soon.'

Owen's gaze passed over her, lingering upon her breasts and hips. 'Or perhaps you bear a bastard child, conceived with Warrick de Laurent.

And you think to pass him off as Alan's heir.' He circled her, effectively cornering her against the door.

Her heart beat faster at his insinuation, but she refused to cower before him.

'Leave my chamber,' she shot back. She poured all her fury into her words, and tried to reach for the door handle. But Owen blocked her and pressed her against the wall. His body was upon hers, and he leaned in to whisper in her ear. 'The only bastard I will allow you to bear is mine.'

She could feel the hard ridge of his arousal, and it repulsed her. With all her strength, she tried to shove him back. But he seized her waist, imprisoning her in his arms. 'I have wanted you from the first moment I saw you, Rosamund. And I swore that one day you would be mine.'

'It would be incest,' she gritted out. 'We are related by marriage.'

He laughed softly. 'Oh, I don't intend to wed you, Rosamund. You will receive your dower portion, as promised. And I will come to you at night to share your bed.' His hand passed over her breast, and she drew her knee up between his legs. But he twisted to avoid her blow, keeping her trapped against the wall.

'Don't touch me!' she warned.

Owen moved back swiftly, and spun her away from the wall. His fist smashed against her jaw, and she dropped to the ground, pain flooding through her.

Dimly, she was aware of her door opening, and men's voices arguing. She was barely conscious, but she heard Warrick speak.

'If you ever touch her again, I will tie your entrails around your throat,' he swore.

She raised her head and saw Warrick's fist strike Owen across the face. The man crumpled, but Warrick continued to beat him until his fists were bloody.

One of the guards came into the room and tried to intervene. Warrick disarmed him in seconds and threw the weapon across the room. Then he unsheathed his blade, his eyes burning with hatred towards the soldier. 'You call yourself loyal to my lady? Or were you hoping to raise yourself up with de Courcy?'

The guard backed away slowly and left the door open.

'Are you all right?' Warrick asked her. Rosamund couldn't answer, but her cheek and jaw were already swelling up. He lifted her into his arms and carried her into the hallway towards her husband's chamber.

It was the safest place for her, she knew, but right now, she was trembling from fear. She had mistakenly believed she could shut out Owen de Courcy and live her life without any danger from him. Why had she believed it was only Pevensham he'd wanted? Now, it was clear that he had coveted *all* of his brother's property, even his wife.

Warrick lowered her to sit upon a chair, but her husband was sleeping and did not awaken. He must have taken a sleeping potion to not notice them.

A moment later, Warrick brought a linen cloth soaked in cool water. 'Put this against your cheek, Rosamund.'

She did, and the cold water eased the pain slightly. 'Thank you.'

But even as she rested the cool cloth against her face, another yearning rose within her. She needed Warrick to hold her in his arms, to comfort her and keep her safe.

God help her, he had crumpled her defences. And she did not know what would happen between them now.

Her cheeks were blazing, but she forced herself to look at him. In a low voice, she murmured, 'I know what happened last night. And it was a mistake.'

His expression was stone, revealing none of his thoughts. Instead, he commanded, 'Stay here and bolt the door.'

In other words, he held no regrets. His gaze fixed upon her for a moment, and then drifted over her body in an invisible caress. Her breasts tightened in memory of his mouth suckling them, and heat pooled between her legs. Warrick was merciless in his silent perusal, and it was an invisible weapon against her defences.

'I will return soon.' His voice was calm, but she detected a merciless air within it.

'Where are you going?'

He didn't answer, but repeated, 'Bolt the door.' Then he slid his hand over her hair in a caress and departed.

She obeyed him, feeling abandoned and alone after she closed the door. But then, she should have known she was not safe. She'd wanted to believe that her own people would defend her... but they, too, were afraid of Owen.

It was now clear that she could not stay, and Alan could no longer protect her. Owen would find a way to hurt her, even if she imprisoned herself within her chamber.

She stood from her chair and went to sit at her husband's bedside. Alan was deathly pale, so weakened, it was a wonder he could draw breath. She had believed it was her duty to stay with him until the end, to hold vigil with every hour that passed.

But now, she no longer knew what was right. It felt as if God were punishing her for falling in love with the wrong man. Alan had given her a life of comfort and kindness thus far, but she had been unable to give him more than friendship. And right now, she was frustrated and angry with him for what he had done.

Did he truly need a child so badly that he would deceive her in that way? And when she had tried to protest, he had demanded her silence. She didn't know how he had found the strength to come to her chamber last night and stay long enough to ensure that the deed was done. A weariness passed over her, and she didn't know what to say to him.

'Rosamund,' he murmured, reaching a hand towards her. She couldn't bring herself to take it… not just yet.

'I am here.' A restlessness brewed inside her, and she felt the tide of anger building up. Her jaw throbbed from Owen's blow, and a part of her was resentful that she was caught in a war between brothers.

'I am sorry for this,' Alan murmured. 'But I do

not regret what had to be done.' His voice was slurred, and he closed his eyes once again.

She gripped her hands together, feeling lost and alone. It became clear that she had truly misunderstood her marriage to Alan. She had believed that he loved her, but she couldn't imagine how he could give her over to another man if that were true. Her heart was bruised at the thought.

Rosamund watched over him for a moment, and it suddenly occurred to her that there was a reason why some of the soldiers had turned their fealty towards Owen. She had remained at her husband's bedside for so long, the people hardly knew who to turn to. She had believed it was the right thing to do, to watch over a dying man.

But by doing so, she had left their people without a leader. They needed someone strong to handle disputes and to ensure that they were protected from enemies.

Yet she had hidden herself away instead of taking her husband's place.

The realisation startled her, for she had allowed herself to become complacent, remaining in Alan's shadow. It was no wonder Owen had tried to claim Pevensham. She could not merely stand aside and let him take command of this estate or their soldiers.

'I will leave you to sleep,' she told Alan, as she rose to go. Her cheek and jaw were aching, but she used the passageway between their rooms to go back to her chamber. There was no sign of her maid, Berta, but she washed her face and re-braided her hair. It was the best she could do for now.

She straightened and eyed the fallen spear from the soldier who had entered her chamber earlier. Though she had never wielded such a weapon before, she picked it up and gripped the shaft.

No longer would she be Owen's victim. She refused to let him dictate her life or her husband's. He had no right to be here, and she wanted him gone.

Warrick carried Owen's unconscious form down the stone stairs and outside to the inner bailey. Several soldiers came forward, but backed down when they saw his expression. He did nothing to hide the raw hatred he felt towards de Courcy. The man had dared to attack Rosamund, and he would not allow Owen to remain at Pevensham.

The possessive bearing Warrick felt towards Rosamund went beyond all else. His intention last night was to punish her with searing pleasure and damn the consequences. But she had known it was him from the first. She had every opportunity to refuse, but she had not denied him. Instead, she had welcomed him into her body—something he had never expected. She had met his thrusts with her hips, squeezing him so tightly, the intensity had shaken him to his very soul.

He didn't know what to think of it any more. Alan was dying, and he'd all but given Rosamund up, insisting that he take care of her.

And so he would. No man would ever touch her again. Somehow, he would find a way to give her the life she deserved, even if it meant hiring his sword as a mercenary. Her father might intervene again, but Warrick would not lose her a second time. He would do all that was needed to be her husband once again and be worthy of her.

Warrick strode across the space with Owen slung over one shoulder, and when they spied him, the men began to gather together. He ordered a horse for Owen, and then faced the soldiers. A dozen of Owen's own men held spears and swords, encircling him.

'Your lord attacked Lady Pevensham,' he said quietly. 'She has ordered him to leave the estate. I will leave you to take him back to Northleigh.'

But the men never moved. Instead, Lord Pevensham's commander said quietly, 'Seize him.'

When the men closed in, Warrick had no choice but to grip de Courcy's unconscious body and raise a blade to the man's throat. 'Stand down.' He couldn't believe that the leader of Alan's men would turn against them.

Owen stirred when his feet touched the ground, and he blinked. Warrick kept the weapon steady, but then he felt the pressure of a spear against his back. It was a silent warning to release his prisoner.

But if he did, they would surely kill him where he stood. He pressed the blade until a thin line of blood welled up on Owen de Courcy's throat. It was a silent message that he meant what he'd said. He would have no qualms about killing the man who had hurt Rosamund—and they knew it.

'Tell them to back away,' he ordered Owen. The man was now standing on his own, though weakened from the beating.

'Stop this, all of you,' called out a woman's voice. Warrick turned and saw Rosamund approaching. She carried herself like a queen and moved across the space. In one hand, she carried a spear, and she reminded him of a female warrior, despite her bruised and swollen jaw.

The soldiers on sentry duty appeared surprised to see her. Several of them approached at her signal to come forward. When fifteen men gathered, she said, 'My husband may be dying, but he is still alive. As Lady of Pevensham, I hold the right to command our soldiers in his stead.'

She walked forward until she stood nearer to Owen's men. 'Lower your weapons.'

The soldier whose spear rested at Warrick's back did not move. 'My lady, this man—'

'Warrick de Laurent witnessed Owen de Courcy strike me within my own home. I will not tolerate such disrespect.' At that, she beckoned to her own soldiers, who outnumbered Owen's forces. The men stood in front of the soldiers who surrounded Warrick, making their silent threat known. 'I command you to take Owen de Courcy back to Northleigh,' she continued. Then to her own soldiers she added, 'I want every last one of his men gone from Pevensham. And if your loyalty lies with him, you are free to go. But if you leave, you will never hold a place here, so long as I am Lady.'

She turned her attention to Warrick at last. In her eyes, he saw a fierce strength and determination. Her shoulders were squared back, and she ordered, 'Let him go so that his own men can escort him back home.'

To her soldiers she commanded, 'See to it that they leave with their horses. And then I want all of you to gather here in the bailey. I have a great deal to say to you.'

Warrick waited until Owen's men dropped back, before he lowered his blade. But when he sensed a sudden movement, he spun and deflected the spear shaft with his arm, seizing it and jerking it away from the man who had tried to kill him. He knocked the soldier hard across the head, and the man sank to the ground, blood pooling beneath him.

After that, the others obeyed Rosamund's command and stepped back. She remained standing with her own spear, until they mounted their horses. Warrick dragged Owen atop a horse and gave him back to his own men. Then he stood guard until all the men were gone.

They would come back, he knew. But for now, Rosamund had regained control of Pevensham. He remained a short distance behind her for her own protection. She distanced herself from him, moving towards the stairs. When the soldiers had gathered around her, she regarded each one of them.

'My husband, Lord Pevensham, is your overlord, just as I am your Lady. Your fealty belongs to us, not to his younger brother.' Her eyes were icy cool as she stared back at the soldiers. 'I do not care if he is the heir to Pevensham and his brother's estates. He has no right to strike me—not in my own home.'

She raised her voice and in it, there was a quiet power. 'Any man among you who does not honour his oath to my husband will face punishment or be forced to leave.'

There was an uneasy silence that descended over the men. There was a gleam of defiance in the commander's eyes and Warrick answered it with a warning look. Then he picked up a spear and began to pound it against the ground in a gesture of respect. One by one, the others did the same, until the entire bailey was filled with soldiers offering up their support.

Rosamund stared at the faces of each man, her expression hard like an iron blade. Then she turned her back and returned to the steps of the *donjon*. No longer was she a fearful young woman in her husband's shadow. Instead, she reminded him of a fierce warrior maiden who had faced her battle and won.

He waited until the men returned to their duties before he mounted the stairs and followed. Inside the Great Hall, Rosamund had claimed her place at the dais. She dined at the high table, and Warrick moved to the closer end of the room, keeping beside the wall to watch over her. Though she ate in silence, when he studied her closely, he saw that her hands were shaking. He doubted if she had ever addressed her soldiers before.

Owen was gone for now, but he would return. And when he did, Rosamund would have to fight back to protect herself and those she loved.

Rosamund forced herself to dine in front of her people, but every bite was like dirt within her mouth. Never before had she confronted so many men, and it took great effort to appear calm and composed before them.

For now, she was safe. She had given orders that Owen de Courcy not be allowed within the gates, as long as Alan was alive. It was enough for now. But her fears had multiplied inside her, and she knew that safety at Pevensham was only an illusion.

Her maid Berta walked past her table, carrying a tray of food for Alan, but Rosamund stopped her. 'My husband is resting now. I will take the food to him.'

She studied her maid closely, remembering Warrick's warning about the food. Berta had been her maid for so long, she trusted the woman with her own life. Surely she was no threat to Alan.

But Rosamund had to be certain.

She gestured for the maid to come forward with the tray. Berta obeyed, but Rosamund spied a trace of fear. It might be because of Owen, but she wondered if aught was amiss.

'Is something wrong?' she asked the maid.

'No, my lady.'

Rosamund lifted her gaze to the men and saw Warrick rise from his place, bringing his own two men with him. They walked towards the dais, surrounding Berta.

Warrick moved to stand beside the woman. 'You have been a trusted servant for years. And you have been bringing your lord his food and drink, have you not?'

The maid nodded, her expression stricken. But the fear in her eyes suggested something worse.

'Eat the food upon the tray,' Warrick ordered. 'If you are loyal, as you say, then prove it to your lady.'

The woman's face whitened. 'I am not hungry.'

Dear God, Rosamund thought. It suddenly became clear that Warrick's suspicions had merit. She stood from her seat, an icy fury pouring through her. 'I care not if you are hungry. You must eat everything you intended to serve to my husband.'

The maid dropped the tray, sobbing. 'I am sorry, my lady. Owen de Courcy forced me. He said he would kill my son if I did not do as he commanded.'

Her anger deepened at the maid's betrayal. 'And you never thought to come to me for help? After all the years you served us, you never once spoke to Alan or to me.'

The maid only continued sobbing her apologies. Deep inside, Rosamund felt her emotions grow numb. Berta had tried to kill her overlord, and there was only one consequence for such a deed.

She knew it—and yet, she also knew Berta could have killed Alan with a single dose of poison. Why had she delayed it for so long?

'Force her to eat the food!' one of the soldiers urged. The crowd was growing angry on behalf of their lord, and she knew they would tear Berta apart if she did not intervene.

'Seize her and bring her to me in the solar,' Rosamund commanded. Then she strode away from the others. She kept her posture rigid and tried to keep all emotion from her face. But inwardly, she wanted to weep at the thought of her maid's treachery. And how many other men and women in this castle were under orders from Owen?

Rosamund chose foods from her own plate and

took them with her above stairs as she walked to the solar.

Why are you hesitating? her brain demanded. *She is guilty of poisoning Alan.*

But she didn't kill him, another voice reasoned.

And therein lay her doubts. Berta had admitted that Owen had taken her son. No one had seen Martin in days, and undoubtedly Owen was using the boy to control his mother.

I should have her killed, she thought to herself. *She deserves no mercy.*

She sat down, trying to govern her own emotions and think clearly. There was hardly any time, for when Warrick brought her maid to the solar, Berta was weeping uncontrollably. She threw herself at Rosamund's feet, begging, 'Forgive me, my lady. I never meant to harm my lord. But Martin is just a boy. He's only nine, and Owen swore he would slit his throat if I didn't obey. What could I do?'

It took effort to remain cool and poised, but Rosamund refused to let her own emotions interfere. 'When did you begin poisoning Alan?'

Berta sank to her knees. 'Only a few months ago. I never meant for my lord to die. I thought if he grew a little sick, it would protect my boy and convince Owen de Courcy that I was doing as he bade me.' Her maid covered her face with her hands. 'I knew Lord Pevensham would get well, the moment I stopped.'

'How can I ease his pain?'

'Give him milk,' the maid said. 'It will stop the effects of the poison.'

Rosamund eyed Warrick, wondering what to do. If she ordered Berta killed, Owen would learn of it and would murder her child. He met her gaze steadily, letting her know the decision was hers to make.

'I do not deserve your mercy, Lady Pevensham.' Berta was weeping. 'But I beg you to find my son and take him away from Owen. He is an innocent.'

There were no clear answers to this dilemma. Rosamund's stomach clenched with guilt and a sense of helplessness. She simply didn't know what was right.

But the fact remained, Berta could easily have killed Alan at any moment during these past few months, and no one would have known differently. She had given him a thread of mercy. Perhaps she deserved the same.

To Warrick, she ordered, 'Have your men take Berta a few miles outside Northleigh and leave her there.' To her maid, she said in a dark tone,

'We both know I should have you slain right now. But you did not take Alan's life when you had the chance. For that reason, I will have you brought to Northleigh where you may attempt to take your son back from Owen. If you fail and die in the effort, your blood will not be on my hands. But you must never show your face at Pevensham again.'

At that, Berta cried harder. 'God bless you, my lady, for your mercy.'

It was hardly any mercy at all, she knew. It was unlikely that Berta would save her son or even find a way to survive.

But it was a chance.

Rosamund entered Alan's chamber and found him awake. He frowned the moment he saw her. 'What happened to your face? Did someone strike you?'

She explained everything, ending with Berta's role in attempting to poison him. Alan's expression held rage, followed by a sudden transformation of his thoughts. 'Then this illness may lift from my shoulders. I may grow stronger and live.'

There was a glimmer of hope in his tone, but Rosamund could not share in his joy. If Alan recovered and reclaimed his place as Lord Pevensham, Warrick would have no choice but to leave. She could not go with him and bear his child.

Once again, she would be alone, trapped in a marriage she had never wanted. Colour had returned to her husband's face, as if the knowledge had renewed his desire to survive.

'I am glad for your sake, Alan,' she murmured. But the words were a lie. Tears burned in her eyes with the knowledge that she would never see Warrick again. God help her, it seemed they were destined to remain apart for always. Perhaps this was her punishment for daring to betray her vows. The wrenching pain broke her heart at the thought of losing Warrick.

Her husband's mouth tightened, as if he could read her thoughts. But he only said, 'Banishment is too good for Berta. You should have allowed me to pass judgement. It was not your place to decide.'

His chastisement caught her unawares. 'And why not? I am Lady of Pevensham.' She could see no reason why she should not be allowed to decide her maid's fate.

'Your duties are to oversee the household, not to dispense justice. And furthermore, you were not to give commands to my soldiers regarding Owen.'

She stared at him in disbelief. 'If our own guards allow Owen to strike me within these castle grounds, why should I permit that? I am tired of standing aside and letting our men do as they wish.' The soldiers owed *her* their loyalty, as well as Alan. If she allowed disrespect among them, their conduct would only worsen.

'It is not your place to interfere, Rosamund.'

'Do you expect me to sit and sew or weave tapestries while our household crumbles around us? I will not.'

He reached for the food she had brought him and ate while speaking to her. 'You enjoy sewing. I see no reason why you should not continue. I will speak to Warrick and ask him to command our forces. He will find those who are loyal and rid us of those who are not. And when we have only our most trusted men, I will give him leave to return to his family.'

He intended to use Warrick for his own means before sending him away. She did not think she could bear it. But she bit her tongue and offered, 'I will send him to you.'

She left the room, feeling the rise of frustration. Her emotions were a tangled mess right now. Rosamund longed to escape, even if only for a moment. She walked down a narrow hallway to a door that led to the battlements.

The evening air was cool against her cheeks, and she let her thoughts drift as she stared across the grounds. The soldiers stood guard at regular intervals, and another man began lighting torches, setting them into iron sconces around the walls.

The door opened behind her, and she saw Warrick approach. He wore chainmail armour, and he held his helm beneath one arm.

'You're troubled,' he said. 'Is it only your maid or something more?'

It was indeed something far more. Not only Berta's betrayal but also Rosamund's feelings of uncertainty about the future. If Alan lived, then she had to return to the lonely marriage she had endured for three years.

And now that Warrick had loved her once again, she did not know if she could return quietly into the shadow of that life. His very presence ignited a desire within her veins until she wanted to feel his touch once again. But she could never admit it.

'I feel so powerless in my own home,' she said at last. The weight of guilt burdened her spirit.

'And then Alan told me it was not my place to give orders to our men.'

'If he is too weak to lead them, then who will?'

She retreated into the shadow of the battlements, feeling restless. 'It has to be me. But he thinks you should lead our men until he gets better.'

Warrick's expression remained stoic. He leaned against the stone wall and predicted, 'You do not want me to take command, do you?'

Rosamund couldn't find the right words to speak. She was frustrated with her husband and with herself. 'I know he is trying to put you in a position of power.'

'I am not undermining either of you.' He set down his helm. 'But it would allow me to offer my protection. I know how to train the men, and I know how to ensure your safety.'

She saw the sincerity in his eyes and acceded, 'I suppose I have little choice. My own men do not obey me, and my husband believes I am incapable of leading them.' She leaned against the stone beside him. 'He was angry with me for punishing Berta. But he would have done the same in my place.'

'Likely worse,' Warrick agreed. He eyed her a moment and lowered his voice. 'Has Alan mistreated you?'

She shook her head. 'But he was angry with me. I have not seen him that way for a long time.' It occurred to her that Alan was behaving like a jealous husband. But it was his fault. He had forced her into this situation by summoning Warrick. And now, they could not undo what had happened between them.

'I should go,' she told Warrick. 'I just needed a moment to clear my head. Go and speak to our men if you wish.'

He caught her hand and held it lightly. 'I care not if Alan is your husband, Rosamund. I will never let him harm you.'

'He wouldn't.' But she understood his meaning. With a sigh, she squeezed his hand in return. 'Thank you for helping us.'

The gesture was meant in friendship, but he would not release her hand. She grew conscious of the heat of his palm, the strength of his fingers. And she remembered how gently he had touched her, and the shocking sensation of his caress inside her.

His eyes burned into hers, but neither spoke of last night. It was as if their silent refusal to speak of it was a means of pushing back the terrible guilt. But he had played his part, and so had she. They could not undo that forbidden night.

And she didn't want to.

'I'm not here for Alan's sake, Rosamund.' Then he leaned in and kissed her forehead. 'I am here for you.'

Chapter Nine

Warrick asked his own soldiers to accompany him, for their loyalty was unquestioned. 'Guard my back,' he murmured to Godfrey and Bennett under his breath. Although it was doubtful that the commander would initiate an attack, neither would the man welcome the changes he was about to impose.

He approached a tall stocky man with a brown beard, the same commander who had ordered Owen's men to surround him. Warrick kept his hand upon his sword and began with, 'I understand you are the commander of Lord Pevensham's troops.'

'I am.' The man tried to straighten, but he saw eye to eye with Warrick and lacked a height advantage. 'Aldred Fitzwarren is my name.'

'You are relieved of your duties, Fitzwarren.' Warrick regarded him and added, 'I have replaced you, by order of Lord Pevensham. I was asked to oversee the troops and ensure that his men are loyal only to him.'

At that, Aldred unsheathed his sword. 'You have no right to usurp my place.'

'When you allow Lady Pevensham to be attacked within her own home and prevent her from visiting her husband, you lack the leadership to ensure that your men obey commands.' Warrick unsheathed his own weapon. 'There will be no men at Pevensham who are loyal to Owen de Courcy. Only those who have sworn fealty to Lord Pevensham will remain.'

'I must speak with him,' Fitzwarren demanded. 'I will not believe this until I have heard it for myself.'

Of course the man wouldn't believe it. Warrick hardly expected otherwise. 'I will escort you to Lord Pevensham's chamber. But first, sheathe your sword.'

Fitzwarren behaved as if he had not heard him. In a curt voice, he ordered, 'Warrick de Laurent, take your men and go. Before I have you removed by Lord Pevensham's soldiers.'

'It appears he wants to do this the hard way,' Warrick muttered to his men. He detected a smirk from his man-at-arms. 'I think we should go and speak to Pevensham,' he offered quietly to Fitz-warren. 'It is not my wish to humiliate you before your own men.'

'You couldn't if you wanted to, de Laurent. I have trained for over ten years, and I—'

Warrick seized a shield from Bennett and back-handed the commander's face with it. The man went reeling, and three soldiers charged forward.

Warrick held out his sword. 'No. This is between us. I am obeying orders from Alan de Courcy. Go and ask him yourself.' He nodded towards the castle and one of the men departed, likely intending to find out the truth. So be it.

He kept his sword extended as the commander staggered to his feet. Blood dripped from the corner of his lip, and fury blazed in his eyes. He let out a battle roar and charged with his sword. War-rick faced him and deflected the blow with his shield. His shoulder flexed, and he held steady while the man wielded his sword. He was well aware that every man was watching this battle.

He had spent three years training among the strongest of the king's fighters in Normandy, and while Fitzwarren might have experience, Warrick had learned how to break the rules. He toyed with the commander, deflecting each blow and caus-ing the man to become tired. Every move was defensive, but he did nothing to end the fight. He needed to gain the respect of every soldier, and that could only happen if it was a sound defeat.

Sweat poured down the commander's face, and he grunted as he swung his sword. Warrick raised his shield and used his strength to push back against the Fitzwarren. With his full body weight, he pressed the man back and saw him struggle to hold up the sword.

Time to end the fight. Warrick spun abruptly, causing his opponent to stumble forward. He tripped the man hard and then drove him to the ground, his sword pointed against the man's throat.

'Yield,' he said quietly.

The commander's expression held regret, but he muttered, 'I yield.'

Warrick kept his sword blade in place while one of the soldiers hurried down the steps leading from the *donjon.* When he reached the men, he was out of breath. 'It is as he says. Lord Pevensham has placed de Laurent in command of our forces.'

Warrick met their gazes and one by one, he saw the grudging respect in their eyes. Then he sheathed his sword and helped the commander up from the ground.

Three days later

Rosamund waited until early evening to return to Alan's chamber. With each day, he seemed to grow stronger and more alert. He sat up when she arrived and remarked, 'I heard that Warrick has done well commanding my soldiers.'

'He has, my lord. And I believe he spent most of the day overseeing them train.' She kept her attention fixed upon her hands, so as not to betray her thoughts. She had distanced herself from Warrick, but she would not easily forget his strength and power while fighting. It had never been an even match, and every man here now knew that he was in command.

Memory flooded through her, of Warrick's mouth upon her skin. The vision slid deep inside, heating the very blood within her veins. God help her, she yearned for this man. The walls of honour had fallen, breaking apart her willpower.

'Good.' Alan studied her for a time, and said at last, 'I am feeling better now. I intend to leave this bed to regain the rest of my health.'

She managed to nod and smile. 'It pleases me to hear it.'

'Does it?' There was a hard tone in his voice, as if he didn't quite believe her. 'I suppose when a man is being poisoned within his own home, it would be difficult to recover. Were it not for your maid, I would never have fallen ill.'

There was an invisible finger of accusation pointed at her, and it took Rosamund aback. 'I never had any idea Berta would do such a thing. I trusted her.'

Alan's gaze held little trust at all. 'And yet, you allowed her to live.'

The bitterness in his voice bothered her. 'Do you truly believe Owen will let her son live?' She shook her head. 'I could have ordered her slain, but there is no greater punishment for her than to lose her only child. All I did was give her a chance, because of the woman she used to be. I have known her all my life.'

He sobered at that. 'I suppose we all trusted her.'

His words were likely meant as a slight apology, but she stared him in the eyes. 'Believe me when I say that I do not think she meant for you to die. She was trying to save her son.'

'And by poisoning me for so long, she made us all believe that I was dying. She took away my strength so I could not sire a child.' Alan moved closer, sitting beside her on the bed. Rosamund felt the urge to move away but forced herself to remain. He reached out to touch her cheek, but the coolness of his fingers kindled no desire whatsoever. Instead, she wanted to flinch.

You are his wife, she reminded herself. *He has every right to touch you.*

But the thought of returning to her old life, sending Warrick away, was like drowning. She closed her eyes, trying to force away the guilt.

And yet, he saw it on her face.

'You did what I asked, didn't you?' he murmured. 'You let him claim you that night.'

She said nothing at all, for they both knew the truth. And yet, she could not understand the expression upon his face. It almost seemed like… jealousy. A flash of annoyance struck her, for this had been his idea. She had never intended to be unfaithful to Alan. But now, he appeared angry at his own scheme.

'You may be with child, as I demanded of you,' he continued.

She could not give an answer, for she did not trust herself to speak. Alan touched her chin, and he leaned in to kiss her lips in his own mark of ownership.

Once again, she felt nothing. She told herself that she ought to be thankful that her husband was feeling better. But she could not bring herself to kiss him back. Instead, she wanted it to be Warrick's mouth upon hers, not Alan's. God help her, what had she done?

A deep emptiness seemed to fill up her spirit, pushing away the companionship she had once shared with her husband. Now, she resented him for forcing the temptation of Warrick's touch upon her, rekindling the forbidden feelings she had silenced for three years.

'Go to your chamber,' he commanded. 'And later this night, I will come to you. We will try again for a child.'

Alan's demand startled her, and he must have recognised the shock on her face. Rosamund blinked and asked, 'Are you…well enough for that?'

'I am, now that I am no longer being poisoned.' His expression turned grim, and he added, 'If you do bear a son, I want to imagine that I was the one who fathered him.'

She forced herself to nod, but she could not suppress the coldness that encircled her heart or the tears that rose up. Once again, he wanted her to lie with him, as if the physical act meant nothing at all. He wanted her to go from Warrick's bed back into his.

No. She could not do it.

She turned her back and departed his chamber,

closing the door softly behind her. Her mind was torn apart with fear and guilt between the two men…one she desired with her heart and body… and another who was bound to her by the Church and her own vows. She refused to think of another set of vows, made to Warrick, on holy ground.

God help her, Alan was going to recover. He would resume his leadership of Pevensham and believe that everything would go back to the way it was. Why shouldn't he?

Her sin weighed heavily upon her spirits. This was her punishment, to have her heart's desire and then let it be taken away as soon as she surrendered to temptation. Her eyes burned with unshed tears as she tried to gather control of her emotions.

Rosamund walked slowly down the hall, letting her thoughts wander. She tried to tell herself that it was an answered prayer that Alan's illness was gone. It didn't matter what she wanted any more. Marriage was a sacrament she would have to endure, for she had spoken the vows.

She had tried to protect her heart from feelings of the past, but it was no use. The man she wanted was Warrick de Laurent, but Fate had decreed otherwise.

Rosamund stopped walking and leaned against the stone wall inside the hallway, allowing herself to weep for what would never be. The knowledge blistered within her heart that she was trapped within a loveless marriage and would not see Warrick again, once Alan sent him away. The sobs choked up within her, and she doubled over in physical anguish. Why did it have to be this way? Why did she have to fall in love again, and yet be left feeling so alone?

She had tried so hard to shield herself from any feelings at all, but the night with Warrick had only reminded her that she was living within the shell of a marriage. And now that his illness had receded, Alan wanted her back.

She was so blinded by her tears, she never saw the man who seized her waist. His hand clamped over her mouth, and he murmured in her ear, 'Alan de Courcy will not live beyond this month, Lady Pevensham.'

Rosamund froze in shock, struggling to escape his grip. She now recognised the man as their former commander, Aldred Fitzwarren. The man's face was rigid with fury. 'Owen de Courcy is the rightful leader of Pevensham. Warrick de Laurent will never claim what belongs to my lord. I'll see him dead first.'

She fought to free herself from his grasp, but Fitzwarren tightened his grip. 'The men will stay loyal to me. Remember that, my lady. De Laurent may have taken my place, but I am still their leader.'

With that, his fist struck a hard blow against her temple, and she saw nothing more.

Warrick found Rosamund lying motionless in the hall, and his heart nearly stopped. He rushed towards her and turned her over, thankful to see that she was still breathing.

'Rosamund,' he said, touching her cheek. He saw the swollen place upon her temple where she'd been struck, and she moaned as she began to regain consciousness. He was going to kill whoever had done this to her.

Swiftly, Warrick lifted her into his arms and brought her back to her chamber, laying her down upon her bed. Then he bolted the door and went to pour cool water into a basin. He dipped a piece of linen into the water and wrung it out, bringing it to her. The moment he touched the cool cloth to her forehead, she started to awaken.

'Who did this to you?' he demanded. Then he softened his voice, realising that it sounded as if he were blaming her for the attack. 'Are you all right?'

She winced and managed a nod. 'I seem to be in

the habit of men striking me down, as of late. Fitz-warren did this. He said that Pevensham belongs to Owen, and that Alan would not live through the end of the month.'

An iron rage burned through Warrick that the soldiers had not done their duty and escorted the former commander outside the gates. Fitzwarren should never have been permitted to escape. But Bennett and Godfrey had warned him that most of Alan's soldiers had been threatened by Owen. They were too afraid to act against him, knowing that he would one day take command of Pevensham.

They might have driven Owen out temporarily, but the man would return. And when he did, the danger would intensify until fighting would break out among the soldiers. He needed to get Rosamund away from Pevensham before that happened.

'I'm going to take you some place safe,' he said. 'Somewhere Owen can never touch you.'

She sat up, holding the linen to her swollen temple. 'Would that were possible. But I cannot go with you, Warrick. My place is here.'

He was about to argue with her, but something stopped him. There was a deep sadness within her eyes, and it raised up a warning inside. 'What has happened?'

'Alan is getting stronger. I know I should be glad of it, but—' A tear escaped her, and he brushed it away. She covered his hand with her own and whispered, 'He wants to come to me tonight. To try again for a child.'

'No.' The very thought was a dagger within his heart. He cared nothing for Alan de Courcy—but Rosamund belonged to him. Warrick drew his arms around her waist. 'I will not allow it.'

'He is my husband,' she murmured. 'It is his right.'

His anger and jealousy seared him to the bone. 'Do you expect me to stand back and let you go from my arms back into his? I let you go once before, Rosamund. It won't happen again.' He leaned down and captured her mouth, kissing her hard. He needed her to understand that this went beyond honour and vows. They were meant to be together, and he would die before letting her return to Alan's bed.

He realised that he no longer cared if he lacked wealth or status. His father would never accept him, and there was little point in seeking the man's approval. The only person whose approval mattered was Rosamund.

Her hands were trembling, but she kissed him back. He tasted the salt of her tears and leaned her back against her pillow. 'You never should have married Alan, Rosamund. We belong together.'

He lowered his mouth to her throat, and her hands gripped his hair. Her green eyes filled up with sorrow and guilt. 'I believed my father would have killed you. And I would have wed Lucifer himself if it meant saving your life.'

'I survived the punishment.' He sat back and removed his tunic. Then he took her hands and drew them over the scars on his back. 'I will bear these marks for the rest of my life. And I would suffer them twice over for you.'

She traced the scars with her fingertips, and the softness of her touch aroused him deeply. He burned for this woman, and he loosened the laces of her gown, needing her to feel what he was feeling. Without asking permission, he slid his hand beneath her bodice and touched her breast. He caressed her nipple, feeling it harden against his thumb. 'You knew it was me that night, didn't you?'

'I knew.' She closed her eyes, her face holding weariness. 'I should not have allowed it. But I was so angry with Alan, I could not think clearly.'

Her face flushed as he exposed her bare breast.

The white globe was soft within his hand, and he leaned down to kiss her nipple. A gasp escaped her, and she arched against him.

'Warrick, no. I can't.'

But he was beyond any protests. He wanted her to regret leaving him, to know what he had suffered every hour without her. His hand moved beneath her skirts, to the warm wetness between her thighs. And when he touched her intimately, she cried out at the invasion of his fingers.

'I was inside you, just like this.' He moved his hand in soft strokes, while he licked her nipple and suckled her hungrily. 'We were joined together, as God meant us to be. You are my wife in soul, Rosamund, and always have been.' He found the nodule above her entrance and stroked the wet pearl of her. 'I will never let any man touch you again, save me. Remember this.'

With that, he rubbed her, forcing her to ride the crest of pleasure until she bucked in his arms. He felt the moment she came apart, her body squeezing tightly against his fingers. She was trembling violently, and he kissed her again, revelling as she rode the aftershocks.

When he withdrew his hands from her, she lay back against the pillow, her mouth swollen, her hair tousled.

'I am taking you away from Pevensham,' he said. 'And away from Alan. He will not touch you again.'

Rosamund could hardly breathe after Warrick left. Her body was pliant and softened by the pleasure he had given her. And God help her, she wanted to weep. Though she had tried to bury her feelings over the past three years, his very presence had brought them to the surface. He reminded her of the marriage she had yearned for and how much she had loved him.

Marrying Alan had been a mistake, just as he'd said. And now, her spirit was broken in pieces. Though she wanted to believe that Warrick had touched her without permission, in her heart, she knew the truth. He had known what she wanted. And if she had truly wanted him to stop, he would have.

Now, she had betrayed her vows and her honour. She had no idea what to do next, for she could not imagine letting Alan touch her again. But neither did she have the right to reach towards Warrick.

She felt the urge to leave this room, to avoid her husband. But where could she go? Not within the castle grounds or even to the Great Hall where everyone was sleeping.

Rosamund took a warm woollen cloak and slipped it over her shoulders, lifting the hood over her head. Then she stepped outside. One of the guards was in the hallway, and he inclined his head to her. 'My lady, is aught amiss?'

Yes, she wanted to say. *Everything in my life is amiss.* But instead she murmured, 'I am going to the chapel. You may escort me there if you wish.' It would be a good place to kneel and let her mind sift through everything that was happening.

He followed her down the stairs and outside. It was late, and a full amber moon glowed over Pevensham. She took a moment to breathe in the air, to calm her beating heart. And when she finally reached the stone chapel that stood within their walls at the far end of the estate, she inhaled the scent of incense. It was cold inside, and she was glad of the warm cloak. The soldier stepped back, allowing her to enter unaccompanied.

To her surprise, she found that she was not alone in the chapel. Father Francis was kneeling before the altar. His brown robes were wrinkled beneath him and he rested his hands upon the stone floor. Rosamund tiptoed inside, not wanting to disturb him. She found a place further away to kneel, and though it was uncomfortable, there was a sense of peace within the space.

When she was a young maiden, she had obeyed her father blindly. Despite her anguish at losing Warrick, she had never dared to stand up to Harold. And she had not spoken with him since her wedding day.

Duty demanded that she send Warrick away and honour her vows with Alan. But a rebellious part of her wanted to seize command of her own life and go with the man she loved. She had given up three years of her life to a man she had never wanted. How could she surrender the rest of her days now?

The priest rose from prayer and came to stand beside her. He made the sign of the cross and said, 'May God bless you, my lady.'

She murmured a reply, 'Thank you, Father. I am sorry if I disturbed you.'

'All are welcome here.' He offered a warm smile, and in the moonlight, his beard appeared almost silver. 'I find that God hears every one of our prayers—even the ones we cannot speak but hold in our hearts.'

Right now, she needed a confessor, someone to advise her. But she had never sought the counsel of the priest, and she already suspected he would counsel her to do penance and stay with Alan.

The heaviness of her heart made it impossible to speak.

But he offered her a kindly smile and knelt beside her. 'I suppose you are troubled because of the babe you carry.'

She could not bring herself to say anything, for it was clear that Alan had confided already in the priest. Although it was too soon to know if there was any child, it seemed that her husband was doing everything possible to protect Pevensham… even speaking lies to a man of God. And if she revealed her own secrets by confessing her sins, she risked exposing her husband's falsehoods.

Father Francis was waiting for her to speak, so she chose carefully what truths she dared to voice. 'I am afraid of what lies ahead. I do not know what to do, especially when it comes to Alan's brother. He is a threat to us.'

The priest sobered. 'I imagine you are afraid for the child, because Owen de Courcy will lose his place as the heir, if you bear a son. But you must trust that God will protect your family and watch over you.'

She sighed, wishing it were so easy to have faith. 'I want to do what is right,' she told him. 'And I do not know what is best.' It was the only truth she could give. Honour demanded that she seek forgiveness for her sins and return to her husband. Her heart demanded that she go with Warrick and live out the rest of her life with the man she loved.

And neither choice was the right one.

The priest's expression held no judgement, but he said, 'My Lord Pevensham spoke with me as well, though I cannot share with you his confession. I can say only that he has made arrangements so that you will always be protected. He does care deeply for you, though you may not realise it.'

His words were kind, but she felt the heaviness of guilt in her heart. She was no closer to making a decision this night than she was before, but she prayed with the priest before rising from the stone floor and returning outside.

The soldier was waiting to escort her back, but as she crossed the inner bailey, something made her stop. The sentries stood at intervals along the top of the wall, with torches lit. But there were parts of the wall left unguarded. She frowned and turned back to her escort. 'Should there not be someone standing guard atop that wall?'

The soldier shrugged. 'It is common for the guards to change their posts during the night.' He appeared utterly unconcerned.

But Rosamund's suspicions went on alert. She knew that Warrick would never allow such a thing. And yet, she could not bring herself to approach him—not after what had happened between them.

His men-at-arms might be able to help. She ordered the soldier, 'I want to speak with Bennett and Godfrey. Send them to me now.'

The soldier hesitated. 'They are not on duty, my lady.'

'Then wake them up.' She revealed her impatience with the man, but something else was happening.

'I do not know where they are, Lady Pevensham. But perhaps you could return to the Great Hall and find them there.'

His behaviour was unsettling, and she strongly suspected the man was lying to her. Despite her hesitancy to confront Warrick, it seemed she had no choice now. Something was wrong, not only with the gate, but also with his own men.

She softened her face and sent him a serene smile as he escorted her back to the stairs that led to the *donjon*. 'I bid you goodnight.'

But she would not rest until she discovered exactly what was happening inside these walls.

* * *

Warrick awakened when a hand shook him. He jolted upright and saw Rosamund standing before him. She wore a woollen cloak, and her hood rested upon her shoulders. Her dark hair was braided back from her face, revealing a worried expression.

'Come with me.' She didn't wait for him to respond, but he rose and buckled his sword belt. It was the middle of the night, and he recognised the traces of fear in her posture. Outside, nothing appeared out of the ordinary, but she led him towards one of the walls.

'Earlier there was no one guarding this wall. I asked one of the soldiers why, and he made excuses.'

But there were two guards patrolling now. Warrick didn't dismiss her fears, however. 'I will find out what happened.'

'There's more. Bennett and Godfrey are missing.'

His men would never desert their posts, and he understood the unspoken danger. Warrick took her by the hand. 'Go back to your chamber and bolt the door.' If his men were gone, then she had reason to be afraid.

'What will you do?' She squeezed his hand tightly.

'I'll find out what is happening. And if Owen or Fitzwarren are involved, I will put a stop to it.'

Her face paled, but she nodded. She was about to obey him, but he held her fingers a moment longer. 'Are you all right, Rosamund?' He had not intended to touch her so intimately, but he had been so angry at the thought of Alan reclaiming her, he had lost control of himself.

She flushed as she took his meaning. 'Yes,' she whispered. 'Just a little shaken.' Her lips parted, and if he could have, he would have kissed her right now, to reassure her.

'Go to your chamber. I will come to you soon.' He knew it was safer for her there, though he didn't like leaving her. She nodded in assent and turned away, walking towards the stairs.

Even after she had gone, he could still smell the delicate fragrance of her skin. It allured him, making him wish she belonged to him in truth.

Warrick strode across the inner bailey, searching for his men. He let his instincts command him, and although there were sentries upon the wall, he trusted Rosamund's suspicions. Even if men were changing positions, the post would never be left unguarded.

As she had confided, there was no sign of his men. Which was wrong, for he had commanded one of them to be on duty at all times. He surveyed each and every guard, noting which ones stiffened at his presence and which seemed unaffected.

One of the torches was out at the bottom of the wall Rosamund had shown him. Warrick took another torch and brought it over to light the extinguished one. And when it caught the flames, he saw footsteps in the mud. Near the top of the wall, he spied the end of a rope.

Someone had been allowed inside the gates. And he suspected it was Fitzwarren, as Rosamund had told him. But there could be others as well.

A sudden thumping noise caught his attention. It was rhythmic, like someone pounding against a door. He followed the source of the sound to one of the towers used for prisoners. The narrow entrance was hardly large enough for two men to stand inside, but there was a pit below ground. On the opposite wall was a wooden ladder. Warrick entered the space and called out into the darkness, 'Bennett!'

'I am here. And Godfrey as well.'

Warrick cursed and unbolted the heavy grate, lifting it up. He started to lower a ladder into the pit, when a sudden motion caught his eye. He rushed towards the door and threw himself at it, preventing the soldier from closing it.

The man was not one of the soldiers he recognised, and Warrick shoved the door open again. He seized his enemy by the chainmail hauberk and shoved him back against the outer wall. 'Who are you?'

The soldier didn't answer but struggled against his grip. Warrick pressed the man back, resting his hand upon the soldier's throat. 'Who else came over the wall with you?'

'Aldred Fitzwarren,' the man uttered. Which was no surprise at all, given the attack against Rosamund. But where was the man now?

'How many others are here?' Warrick demanded.

The soldier grimaced. 'I could tell you only two or I could tell you ten. You would not believe whatever I say.'

The man was right about that. There was no way to know how many men remained loyal to Lord Pevensham. He turned to Bennett and Godfrey. 'Throw him in the pit and keep him there for questioning.'

There was no sign of what had happened to the

former commander. And right now, the man in the most danger was Alan de Courcy.

His men obeyed his command, taking their prisoner back while Warrick hurried towards the *donjon*. Though Rosamund had done as he'd asked, locking herself in her chamber, he had no way of knowing whether she was safe.

He took the stairs two at a time, shoving open the heavy oak door. At the back of the Great Hall, he saw a shadowed form moving towards the stairs.

His heartbeat quickened as he followed the man.

Rosamund nearly shrieked when the connecting door opened on the opposite wall. Alan was standing there, and she covered her heart with her hand. 'Dear God, you frightened me.'

'Were you expecting someone else? Warrick, perhaps?'

She felt the blush rise over her cheeks, but she denied it. 'No.'

He eyed her closely as if he didn't believe a word she had spoken. 'Then why are you wearing a cloak, Rosamund? Where have you been?' His voice held a jealous tone she didn't like. Especially when it had been his idea from the start, for her to conceive a child with Warrick.

'I came to you earlier,' Alan said, 'but you were gone.'

'I went to the chapel to pray,' she said. 'I was just returning now. Ask Father Francis if you don't believe me.' She removed her cloak, wondering if she should say anything about the unguarded wall. Her husband was behaving in an unpredictable manner, and she told him, 'It's late, and we should both go back to sleep.'

She started to walk towards her bed but soon realised he had no intention of leaving. An uneasiness slid into her veins while he stood on the far end of the room and watched her. 'I am weary, Alan.'

He crossed the room and from the heated look in his eyes, she knew why he was here. But she did not want to lie with him, not now.

Perhaps not ever.

'Go back to your own chamber and rest,' she urged him. 'It has been a trying day.'

He didn't listen but continued walking until he stood before her. Without asking permission, he reached for the laces of her bodice. Though he said nothing, he loosened them, until the gown hung against her shoulders, exposing her shift. His touch made her grow cold inside, and she longed to cover herself.

'Lie down on the bed,' he commanded.

She didn't move. Her mind was spiralling with fear, and all she knew was that she did not want Alan to share her bed. Instead, she reached for her gown and pulled it upright again. 'Please go.'

His response was to seize her and pull her close. He reached for the edge of her gown, pulling it lower. Rosamund let out a cry of shock. 'What are you doing, Alan?'

He turned her body so her back was to his chest. Against her backside, she felt the ridge of his erection. 'You are still my wife, Rosamund. If I want to lie with you, I will.'

She fought to free herself from him, but he had regained some of his strength. Though he was not as tall as Warrick, and had been bedridden until a few days ago, he was not a weak man. Against her ear, he gritted out, 'Perhaps you were not here because you went to *his* bed. You wanted to be with your lover.'

Fury raged through her, and she finally found the strength to break free of him. 'It was you who brought this upon us. I sat by your side, day after day, praying for your recovery. *You* were the one who sent for Warrick. *You* were the one who demanded that I lie with him, and you cared nothing at all about my feelings.'

Rosamund straightened her bodice and glared at him. 'How dare you demand that I give myself to you now, after all that you did? Why would I want you to touch me?' She was beyond fury, and when he tried to seize her again, she picked up her eating knife from a nearby table. 'Go back to your chamber and leave me alone, Alan.'

His eyes glittered as he stared back at her. 'I am sending him away. You will not see him again.'

She met his anger with rage of her own. For all her life, she had been obedient and demure. She had accepted the orders of men, she had done first her father's bidding and then her husband's. But she was finished with all of it.

'Go,' she repeated softly.

His glare held hatred, but there must have been a shred of honour remaining, for he did leave at last. When the passageway closed behind him, she shoved a heavy table in front of the entrance so he would not return.

Then she sat down on her bed and wept. She cried for three years of marriage to a man she had never loved, a man who had wanted her desperately. And now she was trapped with him, unless she abandoned all honour and fled with Warrick. Owen would surely murder his brother, and with no heir for Alan, Owen would inherit everything.

The heaviness of her pain weighed down upon her, and she did not know if she dared to reach for a different life. It defied the vows of marriage she had spoken, and she hardly knew what to do any more.

A knock sounded upon her door, but she didn't move from her bed. The last thing she wanted was another confrontation with her husband. But the knocking was louder this time, and she heard Warrick call out, 'Rosamund! Are you unharmed?'

She dried her tears and rose from the bed, not knowing how to answer him. At last, she crossed the room and murmured. 'I am all right.'

'Open the door,' he commanded.

She did, and the moment he saw her, his face transformed. 'What happened? Tell me.'

Her hands were shaking, but he closed the door behind him. He was still wearing his armour, but his blue eyes turned grim.

'Alan came to my chamber,' she managed to answer. Her voice held a tremor, and Warrick's hands clenched.

'I am going to kill him.'

'Don't.' She touched her palm to his chest. 'I—I made him leave me alone.'

But his gaze settled upon her shaking hands,

and his jaw tightened. 'What did he do, Rosamund?'

'Nothing,' she said dully. Her stomach twisted, and she admitted, 'He tried to touch me, but I sent him away.'

Warrick pulled her into his arms, resting his chin upon her hair. She took comfort from his strong presence, trying not to think about what would happen now. Instead, she simply breathed in his masculine scent, closing her eyes.

He stroked her hair back and held her. 'You were right about the wall. It was Fitzwarren who broke through, and he brought men with him who are loyal to Owen. They imprisoned Bennett and Godfrey.'

She tensed within his arms. 'What will you do now?'

He pulled back and regarded her. 'I will do what is necessary to protect Pevensham. And you.'

She held on to his hands, suddenly afraid. There was no way to know how many men would fight alongside Warrick or how many would try to betray him. 'Be careful.'

From nearby, there was a sudden noise, like a table falling over. She tightened her hands upon his, and Warrick assured her, 'I will go and see what it is.'

She suspected that her husband was angry with her, and hesitated. 'If you do, Alan may attack. He is…not himself right now.'

'We have an intruder among us,' he cautioned. 'I will ensure that there is no threat to you or to him.'

She inclined her head, even though she had no wish for him to go. 'So be it.'

He departed her room, and she grew aware of the silence all around her. She sat down upon her bed, drawing her knees up. A strange coldness washed over her, a chill she could not dispel. She couldn't understand where it had come from or why, but her hands would not stop shaking.

From deep within, came the undeniable urge to go to her husband's chamber. Something was wrong—she knew it in her bones. Although Rosamund told herself it was foolish to feel this way, she picked up her cloak and covered herself before opening her door and walking out into the hallway.

The door to Alan's bedchamber was open. As if under a spell, she crossed the threshold and saw Warrick kneeling upon the floor beside Alan's fallen body.

'Someone strangled him,' he said at last. 'Your husband is dead.'

Chapter Ten

For a moment, she didn't seem to have heard him. Her face had gone deathly pale, and Rosamund took a tentative step into the bedchamber.

'H-how did this happen?' she managed. Her hands were shaking, but she continued towards Alan's body lying upon the bed. His throat was reddened and bruised, with the tell-tale mark of a knotted rope. Alan had clawed at his neck with his fingernails, and now he lay motionless on the bed.

Warrick kept his distance, knowing she needed to see it for herself. 'I assume Fitzwarren was responsible. Or another assassin hired by Owen, possibly. But I promise you, we will find the man who did this.'

It infuriated him that their own soldiers had failed to protect their overlord. Were this his estate, he would have removed most of the soldiers and brought in his own men. There was no loyalty to Rosamund, only fealty to a murderer. For that was what Owen de Courcy was.

It was not safe here any more. Rosamund needed to leave immediately, else she risked being imprisoned by Owen. His mind spun off with a thousand things that needed to be done. A Mass would have to be said for Alan and his body buried. Warrick needed to marry Rosamund to bring her under his protection.

And it was still possible for a pregnancy to happen and complete Alan's plan, if she had not yet conceived.

But the greatest problem was that he trusted no one at Pevensham. At any moment, the men and women could turn on them. He had originally thought about taking Rosamund to Ireland, but now he needed to take her somewhere closer, perhaps to her father's estate. He doubted she would want to go, but Harold de Beaufort would not allow his daughter's future to be threatened.

She was kneeling beside Alan now, straightening his hair and adjusting his clothing. 'Send for Father Francis. He will know what to do now.'

He could see the fear and devastation upon her face. Whatever marriage she had made with Alan, she would grieve his death.

'I will command him to come,' he answered her.

With the intruder still on the grounds of Pevensham, he would not leave Rosamund alone for a single moment. Her life was in danger, whether she knew it or not.

Warrick summoned one of the servants and gave orders for the priest to be brought to Alan's chamber. He said nothing about Lord Pevensham's death. For now, he intended to keep this a secret until they learned who the intruder was.

Rosamund was pacing within the chamber, her hands tightly squeezed together. 'I don't know what to do, Warrick. I feel responsible for this. I should have been with him.'

'You would be dead, if you were.'

'Even so, I cannot believe this has happened. I am certain that Owen is involved in his death. But I worry that someone will think *I* wanted Alan dead.' She paused in her walking and met his gaze. 'No matter what my feelings are for you, I never wanted him to die like this.'

Neither did he. The assailant had slipped past their defences while he had been distracted with Rosamund. He blamed himself for Alan's death, though he had done nothing wrong. A hollow emptiness filled him, along with the sense that he should have been more alert towards danger.

Rosamund was trembling, her arms crossed

over her body. Warrick crossed the bedchamber and took her into his arms. 'We cannot stay at Pevensham. It's not safe for either of us.'

'I know. But I am afraid if we leave, it makes us look responsible for what happened.'

Warrick cared not what others thought—for now, he wanted Rosamund away from the danger. He would sort out the rest, even if it meant involving the king.

'You did nothing wrong.' He held her tightly and stroked her hair. 'But we are leaving as soon as the priest arrives. There is no other choice.'

She gripped him in an embrace. 'And what if Owen arrives? Please do not let him enter the gates, I beg of you.'

He agreed with her silent belief that Owen de Courcy was somehow responsible for his brother's death. And yet, they both knew that the man was now the heir to Pevensham. They had no choice but to allow him to enter.

'I will delay it for as long as possible.' It was the only promise he could make. He drew back from her, and she went to sit beside her husband's body.

Within the hour, Father Francis arrived. He crossed himself when he saw Alan de Courcy and murmured a cry of dismay.

'I feared the worst when you sent for me, my lady.' He bowed and withdrew a small vial of chrism. 'I thought I might have to administer Last Rites. But now I see I was too late. I will pray for the soul of Lord Pevensham.'

Rosamund rose from her husband's side, and tears streamed down her face. 'Father, I do not know what to do. I heard a noise and came to see what had happened. When I arrived, I saw this.' She revealed Alan's bruised throat. 'My husband was murdered.'

Father Francis's glance flickered towards Warrick, and he moved forward. The priest wore a rosary around one wrist, and Warrick knelt down before him. He took the cross and kissed it. 'I swear by the Blood of Christ that I had nothing to do with Alan de Courcy's death. I came when my lady summoned me, and we found him like this.' He explained their suspicions about an intruder and finished with, 'She is not safe here.'

The priest was silent for a time. 'I agree with you. Though I do not wish to imagine why this happened, Lord Pevensham gave orders that her unborn child must be protected at all costs. He told me he wanted you to take Lady Pevensham away for her protection.'

Warrick stilled, and Rosamund lifted her gaze

to his. 'I agree. If Rosamund stays here, the intruder will find a way to get to her. And I cannot stand aside and let that happen.'

The priest paused for a moment and thought. 'It was Lord Pevensham's wish that his wife should marry you upon his death, for that very purpose of protection. He spoke with me about it already.'

Rosamund's expression was stricken, as if she could not believe what was happening. 'Do you honestly expect me to marry when my husband was alive, just an hour ago?'

The priest hesitated. 'Were this an ordinary situation, I would say no. We would want to say a Mass for your husband's soul and honour his life. But Lord Pevensham was quite clear that he did not want you to remain here when Owen takes possession of this estate. He insisted that you marry Warrick de Laurent as soon as possible. That is, if you give your consent.'

Warrick saw the knotted emotions on her face. She closed her eyes as if trying to shut out the world and all that had happened. 'And do you agree with this, Father?'

The priest's face was grim. 'If Lord Pevensham's brother was involved in this murder, I believe you should obey your husband's command and marry swiftly.'

'Not like this,' she whispered. And on that point, Warrick agreed. No woman should be expected to remarry with her former husband's body still in the room. He would take her away from here first. Arrangements needed to be made, and there were only two men he trusted within the walls of this estate.

'Stay here with Father Francis,' Warrick told Rosamund. 'Let no one enter until I return.' To the priest, he added, 'You may administer the final rites for Lord Pevensham and pray for his soul, while I summon my men and make arrangements for our departure.' He studied Rosamund and added, 'I will ensure that they pack up your belongings. And when I return, we will leave this place.'

Rosamund felt like an autumn leaf, torn from its branch and battered by the winds in every direction. She was numb to Alan's death, and the longer she sat beside his body, the guiltier she felt.

The priest prayed in Latin, his voice soothing her wounded spirits. She let the tears fall freely, for she had never wanted it to end like this. Alan's sickness had prepared her for the possibility of his death but not his murder.

You tried to make our marriage a good one, she

thought inwardly. *I am sorry that I could not be the wife you needed.*

Her sadness held regret, more than grief. She understood now that earlier, Alan had been angry with himself and jealous of Warrick. And once he believed he would live again, he could not forgive either of them for what had happened, or himself for what he had brought about. Her emotions were battered by the storm of the past few days, and worst of all was the guilt assailing her conscience. It almost felt as if she had no right to reach for her own happiness—not now.

The candles burned lower, and at last Warrick returned, accompanied by Godfrey and Bennett. He pulled Rosamund aside and murmured, 'Fitzwarren was caught trying to flee the castle. He confessed to the murder, and our men killed him.'

She could hardly grasp any of it, but she didn't delude herself into believing she was safe now. Fitzwarren had been hired by Owen, and her brother-in-law was the greater danger. One murderer was dead, but another still lived.

Father Francis stood up from Alan's body and approached them. 'I will remain in prayer for Lord Pevensham throughout the night, and you must take Lady Pevensham with you. He was most insistent that she be guarded and kept from Owen de Courcy until her child is born.'

Rosamund said nothing, for she understood that the priest was only following her husband's orders. Alan had known of the danger and had prepared them for this. She was grateful for his forethought, and she spoke a silent prayer of thanks in her heart.

'I will take her to her father's house,' Warrick said. 'She will be safe there.'

She did not want to seek sanctuary with her father, not after all that had happened. Even after these past few years, she had not forgiven him for his interference.

'Not there,' she said quietly, raising her eyes to Warrick's.

But he met her gaze and admitted, 'It's closer than Ireland. And I have no doubt your father will keep you safe. Especially if you are carrying an heir.'

His words were meant for the benefit of the priest, but she could not suppress the shudder that rolled over her. There was no denying that there needed to be a child, but in her heart, she did not believe she was pregnant. Father Francis trusted in Alan's confession, however, and he would do everything possible to protect her. Despite the lies, she needed that.

She took a deep breath and nodded. 'I suppose I must do whatever is necessary to protect Alan's heir.' With a rueful look, she added, 'Since I hold little faith in my own soldiers, it seems I have no choice but to leave.'

'Only for a short while,' Warrick reassured her. 'We will return to Pevensham, in time.'

He held out his hand to escort her from the room, but she hesitated. Slowly, Rosamund walked towards her husband's body. Despite all that had happened between them, she wanted to look upon him one last time.

His face held the startled expression of a man who had not anticipated death. And although they had planned for it, neither had expected it to end this way. She reached down and touched his cold hand. 'Farewell, Alan.'

Forgive me.

Her heart was heavy as she left him behind. Warrick waited for her near the door and gave her a dark cloak to wear. She couldn't seem to gather her thoughts together, but followed him silently into the hall. Bennett and Godfrey accompanied them, and she tiptoed down the spiral steps. A sinking feeling caught her heart, and she feared that all their plans would come to naught.

Warrick moved silently among the sleeping men and women, leading her towards the heavy oak doors. Their horses were waiting, and she saw bundles of her belongings tied to the saddle. Warrick helped her onto the mare before mounting his own destrier.

Rosamund approached the main gates with Warrick following behind. She recognised the two men guarding their post and motioned for them to step aside. When they did not, she commanded, 'Let us pass.'

Neither moved until Warrick repeated her order. 'Lady Pevensham has commanded you to move.'

The soldier hesitated, but recognised that he could not possibly defend against a mounted warrior. He stepped aside, still keeping his spear raised. The other guard did the same, and Rosamund urged her horse faster into the darkness. She had no idea where Warrick intended for them to stay the night, but for now, she knew the necessity of fleeing Pevensham.

He had spoken of taking her to her father's holdings, but she doubted if Harold de Beaufort would be a true ally, after all that had happened. She had not seen her father or spoken to him since her wedding day.

She knew she ought to be glad of this escape and grateful to Warrick. But it did feel as if her life had been shifted once again, giving her no control over what would happen now. Was it wrong to wish that she could make her own decisions instead of being forced to stay with her father? She didn't know any more.

But for now, they would ride through the night and pray that Owen de Courcy would not find them.

When dawn rose above the edge of the horizon with the faint traces of gold, Warrick slowed their horses. He saw that Rosamund was so tired, she could barely hold on to her mare. Exhaustion weighed upon her, and he knew she needed rest.

Warrick could not resist the need to take care of her, but he was aware that this was hardly the time for a wedding between them. She had remained pensive, almost numb during their journey. He longed to comfort her, to hold her close and assure her that all would be well. And yet, he had been startled by her response when he'd mentioned Alan's heir. She had visibly shuddered, as if the idea bothered her deeply.

He didn't know what to think of that. A child would protect her and ensure that Owen would never inherit her lands or control her. Was this not what she had longed for?

He told himself that she was upset about all that had happened, particularly her husband's death. In time, she would accept the new circumstances. But a part of him wondered if it was *his* baby that she did not want. He pushed the thought away, unwilling to consider it.

They were near Kingsmere, holdings that belonged to his friend David. The fortress was not nearly as large as Pevensham, but it was a motte and bailey structure. A large stone wall with a single square tower encircled it for defence, and the village stood outside the walls. Warrick trusted David to grant them sanctuary until he could marry Rosamund.

Though he'd wanted to marry her before they left, he knew it was too much to ask. She was in shock from Alan's unexpected death, and he didn't want memories of their wedding tainted by sorrow. But neither could he bring her to her father's estate until they were already wed, since Harold de Beaufort would do anything to prevent their union. He had decided to travel east, to Kingsmere, where they could be wed quietly.

He dismounted and gave orders to his men to make the necessary arrangements. Bennett and Godfrey rode towards the village, leaving him alone with Rosamund.

'Where are we?' she asked, dismounting from her mare. She winced as she walked towards him, holding her horse's reins. Warrick took her hand in his and led his stallion alongside her mare.

'This is Kingsmere,' he said. 'I have a friend who lives here. We will be safe for a time.'

She walked beside him with her mare, staring up at the fortress. Her hair had come free of its braid and hung about her shoulders in long waves. It occurred to him that, for the first time in their lives, they would belong to each other. There was still danger, but for a few days, they could be together.

'Are you all right?' he asked.

She braved a wry smile and admitted, 'All I want right now is a pallet with a blanket and hours to sleep.'

Warrick stopped walking and let the reins drop. For a moment, he caressed her face, tracing the outline of her jaw. Then he leaned in and kissed her, trying to reassure her without words. He wanted her to know that he would take care of her and protect her from all harm.

She kissed him back, but her response was not as impassioned as he had hoped. There was a reluctant quality to her embrace, as if she were shy. He hungered for this woman, as he had for three years…but he was uncertain of the look in her eyes or the worry. No woman wanted to wed under these circumstances of danger and loss.

He had ordered his men to fetch a priest and to prepare for the wedding. And yet, he knew not if this was what she wanted.

'I will take you inside and give you a place where you can rest.' He tucked her hand in his. 'But tonight, I want to wed you.'

As soon as he spoke the words, he amended, 'That is, I think it would be best if we married quickly. For your protection.'

Her expression grew hesitant, but she said nothing. It wasn't clear whether she would agree, but she did not refuse. Instead, she avoided looking at him.

Warrick did not prompt her for an answer, but her silence bothered him a great deal. He guided her inside the gates and sent word to David, in the hopes that his friend would give Rosamund a place to stay.

When they entered the fortress, he was less certain that this was a good place for her. Although it was well defended, the interior held signs of neglect. And there didn't appear to be many women anywhere nearby.

He gave their horses over to a stable lad and kept Rosamund at his side. Another soldier guided them inside where he found David passed out upon a trestle table. His friend had lost weight, and his hair was unkempt. An empty pitcher and a fallen wooden goblet revealed that the man had drunken himself into a stupor.

He shook David's shoulder, and when his friend would not awaken, he seized another pitcher of water and dumped it upon the man's head. David came up sputtering, and demanded, 'Why would you interrupt a sleeping man?'

'You were drunk,' Warrick said. 'Hardly sleeping.' He set down the pitcher and added, 'I came to ask if we could stay here for the night before we continue our journey.'

His friend rubbed the water from his hair and glared at him. 'I ought to throw you out for waking me up.' But his gaze narrowed upon Rosamund. 'And who is this?'

'This is Lady Rosamund of Pevensham. We intend to marry this night before we continue to her father's house.'

David's expression turned grim. 'You could

have chosen a better place than this for a wedding, de Laurent.' To Rosamund, he apologised, 'I fear Kingsmere has not been the same since my wife died.'

Warrick had not heard of Catherine's death, but it must have been recent, to see his friend still caught up in grief. He could understand the man's desire to remain drunk.

'I am sorry to hear of it,' he said. 'And I hope we are not burdening you with our visit.'

David shrugged. 'I will give you both a place to sleep, and our priest can hear your vows.'

Rosamund drew nearer and said, 'I thank you for your kindness, Lord Kingsmere.'

He waved a hand and sighed. 'I apologise that we were unprepared for guests, but I will help you as I am able.' He thought a moment and said, 'There may be a gown you could wear. You can look among Catherine's belongings. I know she would not have minded.'

Warrick echoed Rosamund's murmured thanks, and David staggered to his feet. He led them towards a wooden partition at the back of the space, and there was a single narrow bed there. 'It's not much, but it's all I have to offer.'

Rosamund eyed it with gratefulness, and Warrick offered, 'Why don't you sleep for a time, and I will awaken you later?'

She lay down upon the bed and collapsed with exhaustion. Though Warrick wished he could join her, he intended to use this opportunity for wedding preparations. It would take a great deal of time to arrange it all, but he wanted this marriage to be better than their first union.

He walked alongside David, back to the gathering space. In a low voice, he added, 'We are not safe here, my friend.' He explained their circumstances, adding, 'Rosamund must be protected at all times. Owen de Courcy will want her dead, along with her unborn child.'

Although the lie had slipped from him as a means of protecting her, a part of him wondered if it could be true. They had only spent the one night together, but it was possible. And if she were, then the child was his.

An aching emotion caught up within him, though Rosamund might not want it to be so. He had never let himself imagine the idea of having a family. After he had lost Rosamund three years ago, he had given up any thought of it, for she was the only woman who had ever seemed to look beyond his lowly circumstances. He would never be the son his father wanted, nor could Edward ever see the truth and forgive him.

A voice inside him warned that she was reluctant to marry and even more wary of bearing a child.

David's gaze narrowed, and he asked, 'Are Owen de Courcy's men in pursuit?'

'I have no doubt of it.' He followed David outside the dwelling and into the courtyard. 'But we will not stay long enough to endanger you. Only long enough to be wedded, before I take her on to safety.'

As Warrick approached the other soldiers, he could only hope that Rosamund would be contented with the life he could give her.

Chapter Eleven

Rosamund walked towards the stone chapel, feeling the rise of nerves under her skin. David had given her a gown that had once belonged to his wife, and the emerald silk bliaud fitted her perfectly. The long sleeves were tight against her arms, and the skirts brushed the ground. Her dark hair was braided back beneath a white veil, and she walked alongside Bennett and Godfrey. It was unusual to marry at night, for normally people were supposed to wed in the morning and hold a feast afterwards. But she understood the necessity of wedding Warrick as soon as possible.

Her heart was pounding, and her fingers were cold as she approached the chapel. A part of her wanted to feel overcome by joy. But she couldn't help but sense the shadow of uncertainty and danger—almost as if she didn't deserve to be happy.

Warrick was waiting for her with the priest outside the chapel, along with David and the other villagers. He was holding a lit candle in one hand, and he reached over to light the candle of one of the wedding guests. She realised, then, that each of the people held a candle. One by one, they lit the flames, until the gathering space was filled with candlelight.

Rosamund couldn't imagine how much he had spent on the candles, but it transformed the courtyard into a sea of lights. She stared in wonder, realising that he had done this for her, to make this evening beautiful.

The gesture warmed her, reminding her that, although she'd had no choice in this wedding either, Warrick wanted her to be happy. And she smiled at him, feeling more at ease.

As the priest began the wedding with words of Latin, she took Warrick's hands and realised they were as cold as her own. He, too, seemed somewhat nervous, though his expression remained steady.

This time, there were no tears as she spoke the vows binding him to her. This was the marriage she had longed for, years ago. No matter what lay ahead, they would be together.

Warrick spoke his own vows, and his hands tightened upon hers as he promised to take her as his wife. And when he gave her the kiss of peace, its warmth filled up the emptiness inside her.

The priest blessed their union, and then gave a short Mass within the chapel. Afterwards, they joined the villagers in celebrating the marriage. Warrick remained standing among the men, but he encouraged her to dance with the others and enjoy the night. But she was well aware that he was guarding her, keeping an eye out for their enemies.

She went to stand at his side and took his hand in hers. 'Are you worried that they'll find us?'

'I know they will. The only question is when.' His grim expression was not reassuring, and it cast a shadow over the wedding celebration.

Rosamund didn't want to think of it this night. For now, she wanted to push aside the danger and look towards a different future. She took Warrick by the hand and led him towards the dancing. 'Come and dance with me.'

'I don't dance.' He eyed the villagers as if he would rather have knives thrown at him than join the circle.

'It's not so bad. The steps are easy enough.' She tried to show him, but he glowered at her. In response, she sent him a blinding smile. 'If you dance with me, I will kiss you.'

His mood softened somewhat, though he still didn't try the steps. 'You've kissed me already.'

She stood on tiptoe to whisper in his ear. 'I didn't say *where* I would kiss you.'

His eyes flared at her promise. Without another word, Warrick lifted her into his arms and began to carry her away amid the cheers of the wedding guests.

She couldn't help but smile at his ardour. His long strides covered the distance of the courtyard, and Rosamund started laughing at him. 'What are you doing, Warrick?'

His expression held unveiled desire. 'You don't say something like that to me and expect me to remain with the guests, do you?'

She leaned down and kissed him upon the cheek. 'There. You've had your kiss.'

He lowered her to stand, keeping his arms locked around her waist. 'Was that where you planned to kiss me? Upon my cheek?'

She nodded, still amused by his assumption. 'Or I might kiss you here.' She drew his mouth down to hers, savouring the warmth of his lips. His tongue slipped inside, and she opened to him, feeling the rush of need swirling inside her.

He ended the kiss and sent her a wicked smile. 'There are other places you could kiss me.'

With that, she raised his hand to her lips. 'Surely you meant here.'

'Lower,' he murmured. And his deep voice sent a thrill of anticipation through her. 'Wherever you kiss me, I will do the same, Rosamund.' He lifted her wrist to his mouth and she felt the warmth of his breath within the kiss. Her imagination was caught up with the idea of his mouth upon her, and her skin tightened with her own desire.

Warrick lifted her back into his arms and took her across the threshold into the hall. The partition stood at the back of the space, and furs rested upon the small bed. It was a tiny space, but she supposed that didn't matter.

Rosamund was torn between wanting to enjoy this night, for all the years they had endured apart…and the memory of Alan's death. The guilt pushed down on her, for what right did she have to remarry so swiftly and to be glad of it?

'Are you afraid of me?' he asked quietly.

'No.' But she was afraid of the buried feelings that threatened to overwhelm her. She could not deny her own desire to be with this man, to touch him and take him inside her body. Their marriage would not be valid until that happened. And yet, the shadow of danger lingered here.

Warrick removed his tunic, letting his clothing

fall to the ground. His bare chest gleamed in the dim light of the torches set within the space. She reached out to touch his warm flesh and his hardened muscles were like stone beneath her fingers. Then she traced a path around to his back where she touched the lines of his scars. 'I wish this had never happened to you.'

'There was a time when I cursed you for them,' he admitted. 'For you married Alan in spite of the whipping.'

'My father was not going to stop. He would have killed you and forced me to watch.' She let her hand slide down his spine, wrapping her arms around his waist. 'I could not let that happen.'

'He only said that to bend you to his will.'

Rosamund lifted her chin to meet his gaze. 'He said that your own father gave him permission to have you flogged.' He stiffened at that. But she needed him to understand just how grave the threat had been. 'I could not bear to watch you die.'

She reached up and touched his face, drawing him down to her. 'Kiss me, Warrick. And let us forget the years when we were apart.'

His mouth lowered to hers, and he ignited the fire between them. His tongue mingled with hers, and he held her so close, she could feel the rise of his shaft. The pressure between her hips made her ache, and she grew wet between her legs. He began unlacing the gown, lowering it from her shoulders along with her shift until her breasts were bare. The sleeves were so tight, they held her arms pinned at her sides.

Warrick eyed her with open hunger. 'You are the most beautiful woman I've ever seen, Rosamund.'

She felt his needs echoed in her own. 'Touch me,' she begged.

'Where?' His voice was dark and husky, and she could hardly stand the waiting. In the cool night air, her nipples puckered.

'On my breasts,' she whispered. 'Use your hands and mouth.'

He obeyed her, cupping one breast and stroking the erect tip. The sudden rush of desire flooded through her body, echoing between her legs. He took both breasts in his palms, and then bent to suckle one. The heat of his mouth nearly made her knees tremble, but he caught her, holding her upright.

He drew back and helped her remove the rest of her gown, setting it aside. Then he skimmed his hands down her body, forcing the shift away. She stood naked before him, and he took off his braies and chausses, revealing his body.

It had been a long time since she had seen him in the light. And although he had made love to her in the darkness, she now admired every hardened plane, every part of him. She loved this man now, just as she had three years ago.

Rosamund touched his chest, letting her hands move lower. She cupped the curve of his backside, feeling his hard shaft against her stomach. He mimicked her actions, stroking her bottom. She explored his body, moving her hands down to his length. Slowly, she circled him with her palm, and he slid his hand to her cleft at the same time. A shocking tremor of pleasure rocked through her, and she inhaled sharply at his touch. When she moved her hand over the length of him, squeezing gently, he penetrated her wetness with two fingers.

The sensation was almost her undoing. He mimicked her motions, his thumb keeping a light pressure above her opening. As she stroked him, he did the same, matching her rhythm.

'I am yours,' he said quietly. 'Whatever you do to me, I will do the same for you.' The very thought aroused her deeply. And she wanted to touch this man intimately, to make him feel the same rush of need that he had kindled within her.

'Lie down on the furs,' she commanded, pulling her hand away. If he continued, she would no longer be able to stand. And he had piqued her curiosity, making her wonder if she could push him over the edge, just as he had done to her.

Warrick obeyed, leaning back upon the small bed. Rosamund was intrigued by the power he had given her, and knelt with her legs straddling his waist. She moved her hands over him once again, wanting to explore his body. She touched his chest, and he lifted his palms to her breasts, stroking her nipples until she felt another surge of heat between her legs. And when she started to move lower, his manhood nudged her cheek.

'Face the other way, Rosamund,' he said. His tone was imperious, and she didn't understand what he meant until he guided her so that she knelt with her legs straddling his face. She could feel his very breath against her womanhood.

By all the Saints, was this what he wanted? The very thought sent her needs spiralling out of her control. She lowered her mouth to the tip of his shaft, while he slid his tongue against her cleft.

'Warrick,' she cried out, feeling completely exposed to him.

But the sensation was so heady, she could not resist it. She leaned down again, licking the length of him, and he did the same to her until she shuddered. This time, she took him into her mouth, and he began teasing her nodule with his tongue. The fist of desire squeezed hard inside her, and she felt herself rising to his call. Her folds were swollen, her body so ready for him, she could hardly bear it.

She teased him again, swirling her tongue over the head of him, and he began to flick his own tongue over her until a sudden release broke through, her body seizing up while she arched hard and the pleasure crashed over her.

She could not continue like this, and she moved forward away from his mouth. She reached for his shaft and he sat up to give her better access to him. When she mounted him, he slid inside easily. The pressure of being filled by this man was such a delicious friction, she almost wanted to remain motionless.

But he lifted his hips and began stroking her with his erection. She could feel him filling her and withdrawing, and the reverse position bumped him against her sensitive hooded flesh. It was as if he were caressing her from deep inside, and he ordered, 'Move on me, Rosamund.'

She did, rising up on her knees and sitting down again. He rewarded her by palming both of her breasts, gently pinching them as she rode his shaft.

God help her, she had never felt like this before, even when he had lain with her in the past. She hastened her tempo, and he grasped her waist, pumping into her as she strained against him. His hand moved down from one breast, down to her intimate flesh. He kept a slight pressure of his fingers against her nodule, and the sensation seemed to heighten his strokes. She began to tremble, her body quaking at the onslaught of sensation. Another peak was rising inside, and she reached for it, arching hard as he entered and withdrew. She begged him, 'Warrick, faster. I need you.'

And he gave her what she was craving. With his arm around her waist, he began plunging harder, slamming her body against his until she shattered in his arms. She cried out his name, coming apart as the sensations flooded through her.

When she grew pliant in his arms, he withdrew and rolled her to her back. 'You are mine,' he commanded, driving his erection inside. 'Now and always, Rosamund.'

'I am yours,' she agreed, wrapping her legs around him as he drove inside her. She gripped his hair, meeting each thrust until she felt him grow harder inside her. He let out a gritted sigh and emptied himself into her flesh, sealing their marriage with his seed.

They were joined now as man and wife, and her body still trembled with aftershocks of their lovemaking. He remained buried inside her, cradling her body against his. 'No matter what happens with Pevensham, I hold hope that one day we will have a child of our own.'

His words brought about an unexpected wave of grief. Tears welled up in her eyes at the memory of her daughter. She had held this secret inside her for so long, never intending to tell Warrick. But he deserved to know the truth—especially now.

She took a deep breath, gathering her courage. Her heart pounded in her chest, her nerves tightening. 'We did conceive a child.' Her voice came out softer than she had intended, out of fear of what he might say.

Warrick moved her to her side, his body still joined with hers. 'It's too soon to know that, Rosamund. It will be weeks yet.'

He didn't understand. The brittle sadness swelled inside her, and Rosamund forced herself to say the words she had held back for so long. 'Our daughter would have been nearly three years old, had she lived.'

There was a sudden tension in him as he grasped what she had said. For a moment, Warrick's blue eyes stared into hers, and she sensed his anger.

'Do you mean to say that you were pregnant with my child when you married Alan?'

She hesitated, but gave a nod. 'I was.'

For a long moment, he said nothing, but when he withdrew from her body, there was a sudden coldness emanating from his mood. He sat on the bed, staring at the partition. Then at last, he said, 'Did you know it on the day of your wedding?'

She forced herself to face him. 'I had missed my courses, but I did not know for certain until later.'

Warrick's body held tension, and she wanted to say something to ease the strain between them. She had known he would be angry, but she had not expected this emotionless response. When his silence continued, she said, 'My father found out I was not a virgin. He told Alan this before he wedded me. He was willing to accept me as his wife, despite the risk of a child.'

'Because he hoped to pass it off as his heir.' The ice in Warrick's tone bothered her, and she was uncertain of how to ease his anger.

'I suppose he did, yes.'

'Why did you never tell me?' he demanded. 'Did you think I was incapable of taking care of you and the babe? Were you so bothered by my lack of status that you felt the need to wed a wealthy man?'

'We have been over this. I was afraid,' she snapped back. 'I wanted you to survive, and I made the choices I did because I could not bear to see you die. I would have wedded any man to keep you safe.'

'But you never told me about our child. Not once did you send word.' His tone was rigid with undisguised anger. 'Why would you keep this from me?'

She swallowed hard and admitted the truth. 'Because you would not have stayed away. You would have come to take me from Pevensham.'

'I would have, yes.' He donned his braies and sat away from her. There was a hardened cast to his face, of a man who held resentment for what had happened. And she deserved that.

'There is nothing I can say to change what happened,' she said quietly. 'I was wrong to keep it from you.'

He kept his back to her, his head lowered. Now, she wished she had not spoken of it at all. It had cast despair over a night that should have been meant for loving. And yet, she had wanted no more secrets between them.

'I lost the child,' she said quietly. 'I suppose it was God's punishment for what we did.'

'What we did?' he repeated, staring back at her.

'We spoke vows to one another and consummated our marriage. How was that deserving of punishment?' Warrick leaned in closer and added, 'God does not punish infants. More likely it was Berta who poisoned you and forced you to lose our child.'

She paled, and it felt as if ice now ran through her veins. Dear Heaven, she had never thought of that. Her maid had begun poisoning her husband in the last year. Was it possible that Owen had ordered Berta to prevent any children from being conceived? She had never detected anything out of the ordinary, but the day she had lost her daughter, she had bled and had terrible cramps. The thought was devastating.

'You may be right,' she said at last. 'But no matter the cause of it, she is lost to us. And I am not eager to bear another child, if the truth be known.' She pulled one of the furs over her naked body, even knowing that it was too late to prevent conception. 'It frightens me.'

He said nothing, but there was no denying the dark edge of anger that filled his bearing. He rose from the pallet and went to stand at the far end of the space. 'You should have told me about our daughter. I had the right to know.'

'You did,' Rosamund whispered. She had kept

the secret from him, when he deserved to know that he had fathered a child. 'I am sorry for it.'

His demeanour remained distant, and she knew he was still furious with her. She clutched the furs to her body, wishing she could mend the rift between them. But it would take time for him to trust her again.

'Sleep now. We will leave at dawn.' Warrick finished donning his clothes and left her alone. It seemed that he could not bear to spend the night with her now.

After he had gone, Rosamund let go of the tears and wept. She curled up in the furs, wondering if she could ever bring back the goodness between them.

Or if Warrick would ever forgive her.

Chapter Twelve

As he had promised, Warrick took Rosamund away from Kingsmere at dawn. His men, Bennett and Godfrey, kept a slight distance, riding behind them. Although there was no sign of Owen's men, there was still the chance of pursuit.

Warrick kept his mount alongside hers but found it difficult to look at his wife. Rosamund's revelation that they had conceived a child three years ago had shaken him to the core. It haunted him to imagine her pregnant and frightened, wedded to another man. And worst of all, a child of his blood had died.

It struck him harder than he'd imagined. Though he had never known of the babe, there was a part of him buried in the church graveyard. He imagined a laughing young girl with Rosamund's eyes, running towards him. He would have swept her up in his arms, tossing her into the air until she giggled.

But that child was gone. A heaviness weighed down upon his heart, though he tried to push it away. How could Rosamund have kept such a secret over these years? An invisible wall seemed to rise between them, though he held his silence.

'Do you still intend to take me to my father's house?' Rosamund asked him.

'I do.' Harold was the only man who dwelled close enough to protect Rosamund while he faced Owen. Warrick saw no other choice.

But Rosamund slowed the pace of her horse. 'I would rather not see him again. He was the one who forced me to marry Alan. I blame my father for what happened to us.' She drew her horse to a stop and regarded him. 'You plan to leave me behind, don't you?'

He inclined his head. After last night, some distance would be good. It bothered him that she was afraid of bearing another child and did not believe him capable of taking care of them. She had already given up on the idea of Pevensham, and he possessed no lands and no estate.

He was exactly the sort of man her father despised. And he knew that Harold de Beaufort would grant sanctuary to his daughter...but not to him.

Warrick drew his horse to a stop and met her gaze. 'I will leave you in your father's care until I have settled the matter of Pevensham. I must go to the king.' He motioned for his men to stay back, to give them privacy to speak freely.

'Why would you leave me behind?' she demanded. 'Especially now?'

'Your father will guard you.'

She gave him an incredulous look. 'I have hated my father since the day he gave me to Alan. He tried to kill you, or have you forgotten?'

'It was my own father who gave the order for me to be struck down. And no, I have not forgotten.' The scars of the whip remained upon his back, and he would never forgive his father for them.

She paled and closed her eyes for a moment. 'I thought it would be different this time, Warrick. I thought you would fight for us.'

'That is precisely what I'm doing,' he said coolly. He drew his horse alongside hers and said, 'I have nowhere to give you shelter, don't you understand? I cannot take you to my father's lands, and if I travel to Scotland to my brother's estate, Owen's men will seize you.'

'He cares nothing for me.' Her green eyes swelled with tears, and it bothered him to see this.

'He cares a great deal for any child you might bear. And I will not put you at risk.' A darkness slid through his veins at the thought of the daughter he had never held.

'Do you think so little of yourself that we cannot remain together?' Rosamund demanded. 'Why would you turn from me again?'

'I have only two men!' he shot back. 'Owen has an army. And if you think I would dare to risk your life and the life of an unborn child, you are mistaken.' He knew too well the dangers they faced. He wanted Rosamund safely guarded behind stone walls, with dozens of men to defend her.

She paled and closed her eyes for a moment. 'This isn't only about protecting me, is it? It's about our daughter. You're angry with me after what I told you.'

It did fester inside him, and he would not deny it. 'You should never have kept such a secret from me.' He could not hide the cold anger from his tone and made no effort to do so.

She brought the mare closer to him, forcing him to stop riding. 'Warrick, I cannot change the mistakes I made. All I can do is try to make amends for the past.'

He saw the pain in her expression and the sadness. There was no question that she regretted what she had done, but he needed time.

'Stay with your father until I return for you,' he said softly.

Rosamund reached out to his hand, tracing the edge of his thumb. Her touch seared him, and then she threaded her fingers with his. 'I am your wife, Warrick. And whatever happens, we will make a life together—one we should have had three years ago.'

He was weary from a night of no sleep, but he gave a nod of acknowledgement. 'We should reach your father's holdings by nightfall.'

Rosamund didn't know how to lift her husband's mood. The closer they rode towards her father's lands, the more tension rose between them. He ordered her to remain with his men while he rode ahead. She obeyed but didn't like the idea.

'For a man newly wedded, he seems on edge,' Bennett remarked. The soldier eyed her and added, 'I suppose he's been too long without a woman. Last night wasn't nearly enough.' His teasing smile made her blush.

'He is concerned about Pevensham,' she admitted. 'I think he intends to leave me here.' And despite his insistence that it would keep her safe, she didn't want to be abandoned.

'You could sweeten his mood,' Godfrey added. 'A man is easily led by his pr—'

'Quiet,' Bennett interrupted. 'She's a lady, not a serving wench.'

Godfrey shrugged in mock innocence. 'Be that as it may, there's no doubting that the man could use a good romp or two.'

Rosamund clamped her hands over her ears. 'Enough of this.' Though she supposed the men were trying to be helpful, it was not a subject she wanted to discuss.

But she understood their meaning. Warrick was angry with her, and his mood was still simmering, despite his shielded expression. This was not finished yet, and she needed to confront him.

The men guarded her as they followed where Warrick had gone. Rosamund studied her surroundings, recognising many of the people as she entered her childhood home. She had once loved this estate, especially the climbing roses her mother had planted in the garden.

She wondered if her parents would accept Warrick as her new husband, especially after all that had happened. Though she wanted to see her mother, she didn't care if she ever set eyes on her father. The hatred she'd kept in her heart still burned brightly. She could never forgive him for manipulating her and harming the man she loved.

But Harold de Beaufort stood at the top of the stairs, his expression neutral. He wore a burgundy silk tunic, trimmed with squirrel fur. There were no words of welcome to her, nor did he smile. She kept her own face calm, betraying none of her thoughts.

Bennett held her horse and helped her to dismount. She went to stand beside her husband and didn't miss the distaste on her father's face.

'I heard that Alan de Courcy is dead,' Harold said to her. 'And now I learn that you married this man hardly more than a day later.'

'I wedded Rosamund at Alan's command,' Warrick responded. 'He feared for her safety and demanded it of me, upon his death.'

'So you say.' His gaze flickered over them. 'What do you want of me?'

'Rosamund is carrying Alan's heir, and if she bears a son, he will inherit Pevensham. But we have reason to believe that Owen ordered his brother's death. Rosamund could not remain at Pevensham, or he would threaten her unborn child.'

The lies flowed easily from him, but Rosamund could not deny the possibility of another pregnancy. It had happened once before with Warrick. Alan had done all that he could to protect her, but she understood that it might not be enough.

Her father's expression remained cold. 'Now that you have married her, others will believe that any child she bears is yours.' His unspoken message was that he believed it, too.

'Alan had already spoken of it to other witnesses. Even his own brother and the family priest knew,' Warrick responded. 'For now, Rosamund needs a safe place to stay until her child is born.'

'And what of your own property? Have you no place to provide for a wife?'

Her father's remark was a deliberate weapon aimed at Warrick's pride. She saw the flicker of unrest in her husband's eyes before he answered, 'My father's lands are farther away, and I intend to confront Owen over his brother's death. I need someone to protect Rosamund while I am gone. Your lands were closer.'

Though she had known he intended to leave, a sudden icy portent of sadness washed over her. She had the terrible fear that something would happen to Warrick, leaving her a widow once more. And she did not want him to go—not until she had soothed his anger and he had forgiven her.

'May we come inside, Father?' she asked.

Harold moved sideways, gesturing for them to join him. She could not tell what he thought of their circumstances, for he hid his thoughts, as always.

When she drew nearer, she saw that his hair was rimmed with silver, his beard tinged with grey. His eyes held wariness, which was not surprising. She had brought danger among them, for she had no doubt Owen would try to pursue them.

He led them both inside and gave orders for bread and ale. 'You have not eaten, I suppose?'

'No. Only travelling food, earlier this morning,' Rosamund answered. 'I would be grateful for a hot meal.'

She walked through the Great Hall, searching for a glimpse of her mother, but there was no sign of Agnes. Instead, she spied her sister standing near the far end. Cecilia's eyes widened, but she stepped forward to greet them with her hands outstretched. 'Rosamund. I never thought to see you here again.'

'I didn't expect to be here myself.'

Her sister's gaze drifted to Warrick with a questioning look. Rosamund introduced him as her new husband. Though Cecilia greeted him with politeness, there was a strained tone in her voice.

When there was still no sign of Agnes, Rosamund asked, 'Where is Mother?' She had not seen her in such a long time. Although she was prepared to receive a lecture on the hasty wedding, she had missed her overbearing presence. Beneath her mother's criticism lay a woman who truly did care about her.

Cecilia spared a stricken look at their father and then admitted, 'She died last winter.'

Rosamund's heart sank at the news, followed by a rush of anger. 'And no one thought to send word?' Although Agnes had been a chiding mother who had always found fault with every little thing, Rosamund would have come to her funeral Mass. 'You should have told me.'

'Father forbade it,' Cecilia answered. Then she squeezed her hand and leaned forward. 'We will speak of this later.'

It seemed that her father had not changed at all. Rosamund realised that if she remained here, he would, no doubt, find a reason to imprison her in her rooms. Or prevent her from seeing Warrick again.

She didn't know how to manage the tangle of emotions within her. But she knew better than to lash out at her father. He would only lash back at her. Better to be subtle and calm, using her own invisible weapons.

She joined her father at the high table with Warrick at her side. Harold barely acknowledged her husband, and Rosamund decided to confront him. 'I wish you had told me of Mother's death.'

'Why would you care?' he retorted. 'You never bothered to visit since your marriage. In three years, we heard nothing from you.'

She met his gaze evenly, her voice quiet. 'You know why.' But she guessed it was his own petty vengeance for her silence.

Harold shrugged and lifted his cup of wine. 'Agnes grew ill from a coughing sickness and did not recover.'

She tore off a piece of bread. 'I would have come if you had sent word.'

'But now you come seeking my help?' Her father poured another cup of wine. A hard edge lined his face, as if he resented her very presence.

'Do you truly wish to remain enemies?' she asked softly. 'After all this time?'

Harold drained the second cup of wine and said nothing. So be it. Rosamund finished her food and wine and then turned to Warrick. 'I am going up to the solar with my sister. I will join you later.'

She leaned in and kissed his cheek, making it clear to her father that this marriage had been her choice. Warrick held her hand for a brief moment, and she squeezed it with a silent promise.

Cecilia stood from her place and guided her up the stairs. Rosamund walked into the solar and saw a basket near a stool. She recognised it as her mother's embroidery and picked it up to examine the work. It was a simple pattern of pink roses, and Agnes had begun stitching the greenery. The sight of the linen made her eyes well up with tears. Although she had not been very close to her mother, both of them had loved to sit in the solar and sew. It was a piece of Agnes left behind, and it bruised her heart to see it.

Rosamund held the linen for a moment and asked her sister, 'May I take this? So that I may finish her work?'

Cecilia nodded. 'She would have wanted that.' Her sister went to stand by the window. 'Whether he admits it or not, Father did miss you. We all did. Mother tried to convince him to go and visit, but he said he would never ride to Pevensham until you invited him.'

Because he had known how deeply she had hated him. Her heart hardened at the invisible wall of bitterness that had kept them apart over the years. Turning the subject, Rosamund ventured, 'I thought you would have been married by now with a household of your own.'

Her sister's expression turned wry. 'No one wanted to marry me.'

'But that's foolish. You are a beautiful woman, one any man would be proud to wed.'

Cecilia smiled, and she sighed. 'They call me a shrew and sing songs about me because I refused to wed the man Father chose.'

Rosamund blinked at that, but her sister admitted, 'He was a terrible suitor—a cruel man who starved his hounds and beat them. I would never want a man like that to sire children…especially with me.' Cecilia shrugged. 'Father swore that if I did not marry Gerard, I would have to stay at home and wed no one. Or perhaps I could join a convent.' With a wry expression, she finished, 'You can see what my choice was.'

'Do you want to be married?' Rosamund asked, sitting down and picking up a needle. She chose a lighter shade of green for the embroidery, wanting to add depth to her mother's stitching.

'I might. But only if he is a good man.' Cecilia pulled up a stool and sat across from her. 'I overheard them say you are expecting Alan's child. When will you give birth?'

Rosamund lowered her gaze to the stitching. 'In the winter.' She was deliberately vague, not wanting to reveal anything.

Her sister nodded, resting her hands upon her lap. 'I bid you good fortune with your child.' She waited a moment and asked, 'Is it so terrible to lie with a man? The very thought sounds awful.'

A slight motion caught her attention, and Rosamund saw Warrick standing just outside the doorway. He tilted his head, and there was amusement on his face, letting her know he had overheard her sister's question.

'Rosamund?' Cecilia prompted. 'Well, is it? I would like to be forewarned.'

She smiled serenely. 'No, it's not awful at all. When you are wedded to a man you love, it's wonderful.'

Her sister studied her and her expression held doubt. 'But…doesn't it hurt?'

She caught her husband's gaze behind Cecilia and met it evenly. 'There is nowhere else I would rather be than in Warrick's arms.'

He studied her a moment before he disappeared from her view. She could only hope that he understood and would forgive her for the secret she had kept.

* * *

Warrick waited for Rosamund after she emerged from the solar. His wife's cheeks were bright, but she behaved as if he had not overheard them speaking. He followed her to the chamber they would share, but as they walked through the castle, he felt his own restlessness intensifying. It bothered him that he'd been forced to bring her here, to face her father once more. They needed a home of their own, a place where he could command his own soldiers and his own estate.

He had told Rosamund that he intended to speak with the king, to fight for Pevensham. And he would, for the sake of the people. None wished to be governed by Owen de Courcy. But he knew that Rosamund's claim to the land was feeble, at best. If there was no child, then they were powerless to help.

Even if they could not regain Pevensham, he intended to appeal to the king, offering everything he could give, in return for a parcel of land. Gaining land of his own was a means of fighting against the ghosts of his past, proving his worth.

His wife interrupted his thoughts by taking him by the hand and leading him towards their bed. 'We need to talk, Warrick.'

Truthfully, there was nothing to say. But he sat

down and she stood between his legs before she reached out for his other hand. Her palms were warm, and her eyes fixed upon him. 'I do not want you to appeal to the king. Owen can take Pevensham, and we need never see him again. We can go to Ireland, as you said. I believe Owen would keep his word and give us an estate there.'

It was clear that she wanted to take the safest path, surrendering everything. But he didn't believe for a moment that Owen would surrender land.

'Owen will give us nothing,' he said. 'He will likely sell off whatever he can to repay his debts.'

She rested her hands upon his shoulders, distracting him with her nearness. 'Or we can live with your brother Rhys in Scotland. All that matters is that we are safe.'

'And what if you *are* with child?' he ventured.

'We both know who the father is. And our son would have no true right to govern Pevensham.' Rosamund lowered her forehead to touch his. 'I would rather be wedded to you and raise our children knowing their father's name.'

Warrick had no desire to behave like a coward, knowing what Owen would do to the estate. He stood from the bed, his height towering over Rosamund. 'So you would abandon the people of Pevensham and let Owen take command? Was that what Alan wanted?'

She faltered at that. 'The people were loyal to the de Courcy name, not to me or Alan.'

'Or perhaps they were afraid of Owen?' he ventured.

Rosamund gave no answer, but slid her hands beneath his tunic to touch his bare chest. He understood that this was a distraction, a means of avoiding the truth. But the scent of her skin allured him, and he could not resist threading his hands in her dark hair.

'All of us were afraid of Owen,' she admitted at last. She moved her hands upon his heart. 'It's why I want to leave. I never want to see him again.'

'You need not be afraid of any man,' he said.

Rosamund straightened and took a breath. 'But Owen will not rest if there is the threat of a child.' She rested her cheek against his chest, and her fear was palpable. 'If you leave, he will come after me.'

Now he understood the true reason for her fear. 'Your father will guard you,' he assured her. 'He has a stronghold here and dozens of men. Owen cannot reach you, so long as you stay behind these walls.'

'I trust him not. Nor my father.' Her voice held

melancholy, and he wanted to comfort her. 'And you are still leaving me behind.'

He pulled back from the embrace, meeting her gaze. 'Owen must be brought to justice for what he did.'

But he could see upon her face that she did not believe him. 'It's more than that, isn't it?'

He could not speak reassuring lies to her, no matter what she might wish. Instead, he took a step back from her. 'I know you are tired. Rest now.'

But Rosamund reached for the laces of her gown and began to loosen them. The blue gown she wore was fitted to her arms, and she struggled to loosen it. 'Will you help me, Warrick?' Her voice was soft and inviting. Desire roared through him, though his mind warned him not to touch her.

Yet, she could not unfasten the gown without help, and she had no maidservant this night. For a moment, he rested his hands upon her gown, sliding it down to her shoulders, revealing her shift. The thin linen revealed the silhouette of her full breasts, and he wanted nothing more than to lower it to her waist, cupping her until her nipples rose beneath his hands.

But once her gown lay pooled at her feet, he

stepped away. His body urged him to claim her, to join with her until her flesh merged with his.

Yet, he gathered command of himself, pushing back the physical needs. She turned to face him, and her expression held sorrow. 'You have not forgiven me, have you?'

He shook his head slowly. 'It will take more time, Rosamund.' His voice came out harsher than he'd intended, and he tried to soften his tone. 'I am leaving on the morrow with my men,' he told her. 'Owen may follow us, but he will not find you.'

'And what if he finds you?' Her expression held uneasiness. 'You only have two men.'

'We can defend ourselves, if need be.'

She moved closer to him, drawing him into her arms. 'Do not go with anger between us.' Once again, she moved her hands beneath his tunic. Rosamund slid her fingers over his spine, over the scarred flesh. 'I wish I could turn back the years, Warrick.' For a moment, her thoughts remained veiled, though he could see the worry in her eyes.

Then her expression transformed when her hand passed over a different scar on his lower back. He tensed the moment she touched it. Then he guided her hand away, holding her palms in his.

'That scar isn't from the whipping, is it?' she murmured. 'It's a burn mark.'

'It was a long time ago. It doesn't matter.' He squeezed her hands, fully intending to leave her to sleep alone.

But Rosamund would not be deterred. 'If it didn't matter to you, you would tell me. But this bothers you, doesn't it?'

She wasn't going to relent on this, and well he knew it. And yet, he didn't want to open up the nightmares of the past.

She traced the outline of the mark, and said quietly, 'Someone burned you with a hot poker. Did your father do this to you?'

He went rigid, not wanting to speak of it. 'Let the past remain buried, Rosamund.'

But she touched his face gently and pleaded, 'Tell me what happened, Warrick.'

Warrick didn't want to relive that part of his life, especially now. But he realised that he could voice a demand of his own in return. He rested his hands upon her waist. 'If I tell you of this, then you must tell me about our daughter,' he said quietly. 'And what happened to you when you learned you were pregnant with her.'

His wife hesitated, studying him with indecision. 'And if I do, will you forgive me for my silence?'

It was difficult to make a promise like this, when he knew not if he could. All he could say was, 'I don't know, Rosamund.'

While he waited for her to speak, she took a seat upon the bed. She took a quiet breath and began, 'I told my father that I would wed Alan, and he promised to release you. After that, he took me home where the betrothal agreement was finished and signed. It felt as if I were living another woman's life for the first month. I did as I was told and was obedient to my father. But every night, I wept for you.'

She traced the outline of his shoulder. 'Then I started getting sick. It wasn't like most women who are with child and are only sick in the mornings. I was violently ill for most of the day. My father caught me one night, and he knew what was happening.' Her voice softened. 'When he accused me of being with child, I was filled with such joy, because that meant Alan could never wed me. I believed that my father would send word to you, and we would be married, as I had dreamed. Instead, he forced me to wed Alan within a sennight.'

'I came to your wedding,' he reminded her. 'And you never spoke to me. You obeyed your father's orders without even trying to leave.'

She closed her eyes as if pushing back the memory. 'He invited you to the wedding so he could use you to command me. He swore he would kill you where you stood if I refused to speak my vows.'

'He would not have done such a thing,' Warrick contradicted. Such would be considered murder in the eyes of the king and would demand justice.

Rosamund let out a breath of air. 'He had enough coins to hire any number of mercenaries to wield a blade. And I do not doubt he would have kept his word. My father wanted to control me, to bend me to his will. And so he did.'

The enigmatic look returned to her face, as if she were still haunted by it. But there was also a thread of steel, her invisible determination not to be Harold's pawn again.

She reached down to touch the scarred mark upon his backside. 'Now tell me who did this to you and why. Then I will tell you of our daughter.'

Her light touch was soft, but he had never forgotten the searing pain of the red-hot poker. 'I witnessed something I was not meant to see,' he said. He rolled to his back and stared up at the ceiling. 'My father remarried after the death of my mother, and his new wife, Analise, promised him another son. Edward never cared about a child, since he already had Rhys, Joan, and me. I was six years old, but I remember when Analise gave birth to a daughter.' A chill iced through him as he remembered the fragile infant with reddened skin and dark blue eyes that stared at him. She had reminded him of a baby wren, newly emerged from a shell.

'I was so proud to be a big brother, to have someone smaller than me. Mary cried a lot, and it seemed that she was always hungry. Analise did not have a wet nurse for her, and she told my father she would feed the babe herself. But I never saw her do so, and I thought she was starving the child.'

Which now, he believed was quite likely. Analise had never wanted a daughter and it was easiest to claim that the child was sickly.

'I heard her screaming in her cradle one night, and I slipped into Analise's bedchamber. She was not there, and I believed it was my task to protect my sister. I picked Mary up and held her, but she would not stop crying.' He spoke the words, wishing he could blot out the memory of the wailing infant.

'That night, I had brought her some warm goat's milk. I dipped my finger in it, and put it to her lips. She drank it from my fingers, and only then did she stop crying.' The coldness in his chest deepened, spreading throughout his body. 'Analise caught me feeding my sister, and she was furious. She struck me and took the babe from my arms. Then she threw Mary to the floor and killed her.' The raw memory haunted him still, and even Rosamund's words of comfort would not diminish the grief.

'I know now that she was trying to starve her daughter. Analise wanted only sons.' He let out a sigh. 'She told my father that I dropped the babe and killed my own sister.'

'Dear God...' Rosamund breathed. 'And your father believed her?'

'He did. I was punished for it when they branded me with the hot poker and sent me away. But before I left our lands, Analise warned me that if I ever dared to tell anyone about what I had seen, she would hurt Rhys. I stopped talking for a number of years, because I was afraid of her.'

Those years had been a blur of nightmares, and he had found it easy to obey her command. There was nothing at all to say—not when his own father refused to accept the truth. Warrick finished by saying, 'My father believed Analise when she told him I was simple-minded and unworthy of being his son.'

'I cannot believe he could not see her for what she truly was—a liar and a murderess.' Rosamund held him tightly, and her embrace soothed the ache.

'She died from a fall on horseback and broke her neck. Thank God, or else she might have found a way to hurt any other daughter she might have birthed.'

It was strange, but telling Rosamund what had happened had lightened the burden of the past. He drew his hand over her shift, down to her flat stomach. 'It seems cruel to lose a second infant girl, one of my blood.'

She covered his hand with her own, letting it rest upon her womb. 'I waited for a time to tell my husband about the babe, but he admitted last week that he knew I was with child when we wed. My father had told him, and Alan agreed to wed me, in spite of it. Or perhaps because of it.' She laced her fingers with his. 'I was surprised at how pleased Alan was, but I later understood it was because he believed he could not sire children. He told everyone of my pregnancy and was so very proud.'

Rosamund told him more, of the changes in her body and the time she first felt movement. 'I was lying down in bed and I felt the barest touch, as if a tiny hand reached up to me.' She smiled, but he heard the slight hitch of emotion in her voice. 'It was so very precious, a part of you that remained within me. And as the months passed, Alan brought me gifts for the baby. A wooden rattle and silk for her clothing.' She tightened her grip on his hand. 'We became friends, and I could not be angry with him.

'But a few weeks after Owen visited us, I lost the baby. I went into labour and delivered her stillborn. She was small enough to fit into my hand.' Rosamund rested her face against his chest, and he could feel the hot tears spilling on to his skin. She wept for the loss of their daughter, and his own grief welled up inside him.

'I am sorry,' he said. But the words were useless in the face of such a tragedy. It would not bring the child back.

She grew quiet, tracing the outline of his face. 'I have not ever conceived a child since I lost her. And never a day goes by that I do not think of her.' Tears spilled over her face, and she murmured, 'I named her Anne.'

His eyes burned, and he could not bring himself to mourn. A part of him ached with jealousy, that at least she had been able to look upon the face of their child. She had held their daughter before Annehad been buried and had even given her a name. Whereas he had never been given that chance.

With the greatest effort, Warrick pulled back the ragged emotions and steeled himself. He brushed away Rosamund's tears and bade her, 'Rest now, and I will bid you farewell in the morning.'

She gripped his hand in hers and drew it to her waist. 'Will you not lie with me and share the hours we have left?'

He couldn't. Not now, not with the weight of grief shadowing him. Better that he should leave his wife in peace and spend the last few hours in his own solitude. He brushed his mouth against hers in a light kiss before he left.

Just as he started to close the door to their chamber, he saw her curled up on her side, her shoulders racked with sobs. And her anguish echoed within his own heart, though he would never let her see it.

Chapter Thirteen

It had been four months since she had last seen her husband, and Rosamund could not suppress the fear that Warrick was dead. She had sent at least three missives to him, but no one had found him. He had sought an audience with King Henry in Normandy, but her messengers had all returned, admitting that Warrick had not been found among the king's men. It terrified her to wonder if something had happened to him.

There was no doubt now that she was pregnant, but what startled her most was the size of this child. It appeared that she was much further along than she had imagined, which was impossible. But perhaps it was because she had given birth to a child before.

Owen had attempted to see her on numerous occasions, but her father had turned him away, even when the man had brought half of his forces.

Not once had he allowed de Courcy to enter their gates. Rosamund was grateful for Harold's protection but knew it could not last. What worried her the most was Warrick's disappearance.

For that reason, she had begged her father to seek his own audience with the king. And now they were on their way to Canterbury, where Henry was rumoured to be travelling.

After they stopped, Rosamund rose from the litter, holding her back as she stood. The July sun was hot, and her body ached from the miles of their journey. Her father was near his horse, speaking to one of his men. She approached Harold and asked, 'Are you certain the king will be here?'

'I have it on good authority he has come to seek penance for the death of the archbishop.' Harold sounded confident, but Rosamund was not so certain. The cathedral at Canterbury had been damaged during a fire, and the men were working to restore it.

'Has there been any word from Warrick?' His absence was an ache within her, for she could not help but fear the worst.

Her father hesitated a moment. 'I learned he was taken prisoner by the king's men. They are bringing him here, along with Owen de Courcy, as a witness. He has accused Warrick of murdering his brother.'

Her blood chilled at the thought of her husband being held captive. 'When did this happen?'

'A few weeks ago. I only just learned of it last night.' Her father studied her a moment and added, 'You are looking pale, Rosamund. You should sit.'

'My husband has been a captive for weeks,' she retorted. 'Sitting is the very last thing I want to do. I need to see Warrick. You must find him for me.'

Harold shook his head. 'It is not possible. I brought you here for an audience with the king, so he would see for himself that you are with child. If he believes Alan's testimony that you were already pregnant before he died, you can return to Pevensham. Then, if you bear a son, the land will belong to him.'

She had no desire to fight for Pevensham any more. The land was lost to her, and she had no right to claim it—especially now.

'I beg of you—please find my husband and arrange for me to see him.' Though she had kept up the façade that this was Alan's heir, Warrick deserved to know of her pregnancy. She wanted to mend the breach between them, for it wounded her heart to be parted from the man she loved.

Harold reached out for her hand, and his gnarled

palm closed around hers. 'There is a rebellion happening, Rosamund. King Henry's sons and his own wife are rising up against him, and we know not who will win. These are dangerous times.'

'But my husband has been falsely accused. I cannot let him remain a captive.' Warrick mattered more to her than all else. She would not even consider abandoning him.

'And you would endanger your child by interfering with men who want to overthrow the king?' her father mused. 'There is no danger of Warrick dying, for the king has not granted him a trial yet.'

'I do not trust Owen de Courcy. He will do everything in his power to lay the blame at my husband's feet.'

Her father turned to face her. 'I know you are afraid, Rosamund. But you must think of Alan's heir first.'

Harold's demeanour towards her had altered greatly over the past few months, and he had softened at the sight of her pregnancy blooming. There was still a rift between them, of a father who demanded obedience and a daughter who held her own power. But he had made an effort to be kinder, and it had not gone unnoticed.

She rested her hands upon her swollen womb. There was a ripple of movement, the barest touch of motion. Her heart ached for this unborn child, and as much as she was afraid of losing it, she would never risk the baby's life.

'I love Warrick,' she reminded her father. 'And if he is endangered in any way, I will do whatever I must to save him. He matters more to me than all else. And I have not forgotten how you had him punished or how you forced me into a marriage with Alan.'

Her father grew sombre. 'I was angry with him for stealing your innocence. If ever you bear a daughter of your own, you might some day understand how you could easily kill someone for daring to harm your child.'

She stilled at this, for already she felt a strong bond with this unborn baby. Her father was right—she would indeed fight with her last breath for the sake of her child. 'I do understand,' she said at last. 'But Warrick and I spoke vows to one another on holy ground before I gave myself to him. He took nothing from me that I did not give willingly.'

Her father blanched at that. 'Do not speak of such things, Rosamund. Let no one hear you say that.'

She kept her expression serene. 'Because you fear I will lose Pevensham. What we had was a true marriage, was it not? Which would make my marriage to Alan invalid.'

'Do not be a fool,' her father gritted out. 'What's done is done and cannot be changed. But you may be able to save Warrick's life *and* keep Pevensham if you do as I ask.'

Rosamund was weary of lies and deception. When she said nothing, her father added, 'I do not deny that I made mistakes. I was an angry father who wanted you to have a castle of your own.'

'And you cared naught for what I wanted.'

'You were a girl.' He sighed. 'How could you know what you wanted in a husband?'

But she had known from the first moment she saw Warrick. 'You had no right to do what you did.'

He looked as if he wanted to argue with her, but instead, he kept silent. 'Whether you believe it or not, I do want you to find happiness, Rosamund—despite all that has happened. Have I not travelled across England to help you in this?'

She didn't know what to believe. He had manipulated her life, punished the man she loved, and exerted power over her.

He let go of her hand and said, 'I will speak to the king on Warrick's behalf. But I can make no promises.'

She could hardly believe what he had said. And yet, it did appear that time had softened the edges of this man. As much as she resented all that he had done, it seemed that he was trying to bridge the distance between them.

'I would be grateful,' she told him. 'But if anything happens to Warrick, I will not stand back and do nothing. I will fight for his life.'

Her father reached out and brushed his knuckles against her face. 'Just as I would fight for you and your happiness.'

'We're going to die,' Bennett muttered. Warrick eyed his friend with disinterest. They had fought alongside Henry's men near Alnwick Castle, only to find it besieged by King William of Scotland and thousands of Flemish mercenaries. The soldiers had decamped several miles south, keeping a clear distance of the enemy while they decided upon their strategy. 'There are eighty thousand men, so I've heard,' Bennett continued. 'We'll be caught in the midst of a slaughter.'

'There are *not* eighty thousand,' Warrick corrected. 'The Scottish king wants the people to believe that, but it's not true.' The power of exaggeration could provoke fear, and that was what William wanted.

Warrick wondered if his brother Rhys was involved in this battle and hoped not. An unexpected war could be a curse or a blessing. He knew his men wanted to escape their bindings and flee, but he could not join them—not until he brought justice on Owen. The man had accused him of murder. If he dared to attempt an escape from this captivity, it was as good as admitting guilt.

Bennett fell into silence, and so did Godfrey. Both of his men had refused to abandon him when he'd gone to seek Henry in Normandy. And because of their loyalty, they had joined him in captivity.

God help him, he missed his wife. Warrick had parted ways with her, unable to let go of his resentment for the past. He had finally allowed himself to grieve for his daughter, and time had made him see that Rosamund had made her choices out of fear. He knew not if he would ever see her again, and the burden of regret shadowed his mood. But if he had the chance to look upon her face once more, he would tell her how much she meant to him.

Bennett let out a heavy sigh. 'It matters not how many men there are. The problem is that we cannot fight, if we remain imprisoned.'

'I will ensure that you both are released,' Warrick swore. 'You are not to blame for any of this.'

Godfrey rested his bound hands upon his knees. 'We could offer to fight for King Henry,' he suggested. 'It would prove our loyalty to England.'

'You're daft. They'll never give us weapons,' Bennett argued back.

But Warrick wasn't so certain. He had already fought for the king in Normandy, after Rosamund had married Alan. 'There may come a time when they need every fighting man.' He shot a wry look at Bennett. 'Especially against eighty thousand who are not really eighty thousand.'

Though he tried to keep their spirits up, he felt the shadow of death resting upon his neck. Although he was a prisoner now, he had brought Father Francis with him as a witness. The priest had avoided captivity, and had promised to speak on their behalf at the trial.

Around mid-morning, one of King Henry's commanders approached him. He eyed Warrick and said, 'My men have seen you fight before. You joined our forces in Normandy two years ago, did you not?'

Warrick nodded. 'I did.' He had hired his sword

out, fighting for England wherever he was needed. The constant marching and the haze of battle had made it possible to endure each day.

'They called you the Blood Lord.' The commander studied him, as if wondering if it were true. 'You slaughtered Henry's enemies.'

He gave a nod of assent. The truth was, he hadn't cared whether he lived or died. When Rosamund had married Alan, Warrick had welcomed the thought of death. Every time he swung his sword, it was a means of fighting back against both of them.

'You want me to fight again,' he stated. And so he would—but this time, he would fight for his future with Rosamund.

'You were imprisoned because you were accused of murdering Alan de Courcy of Pevensham. But none of that will matter if we don't survive this battle.' The commander drew closer, unsheathing his blade. He sliced through the ropes at Warrick's ankles but kept his hands bound. 'Your reputation among our men has saved you. Come and fight alongside us.'

Warrick didn't move. 'Free my men, and they will join with your army. They are strong warriors as well.' It was a grave risk, but if they survived this battle, his loyalty to the king would stand true.

And it was the only means of seeing Rosamund again.

Two weeks later

'Your father bid me to say that the king has not answered your request for an audience, my lady.' The young serving lad bowed and was about to leave when Rosamund stopped him.

'Wait, please.' She was not surprised that the king had ignored her pleas, but she had another tactic in mind. Only a day ago, she had spied a familiar face among Henry's knights. 'Send word to Sir Ademar of Dolwyth that I wish to speak with him. I understand he is here, fighting with the king's men.'

'He is, my lady, but…' The boy's words trailed off with confusion.

'I have my reasons,' she said. 'Send word that Rosamund of Pevensham, wife of Warrick de Laurent, has need of him.'

The boy hurried away, and Rosamund went to sit for a moment. Ademar had been an adolescent boy when he had attempted to help them escape. She knew he had been forced to betray their location against his will. And now, he might want to make amends for it. They needed allies, and she hoped Ademar could help them.

The baby kicked within her, and she rested her palms upon her swollen middle. Her back ached, and she tried to calm the worries rising inside her. If anything happened to Warrick, she could not return to Pevensham. And she knew not if her father had the power to help them.

While she waited, she spent time embroidering a length of white linen for a baby gown. The white thread created a raised pattern, and she passed the time by stitching with her needle. As morning stretched into afternoon, her serving lad eventually returned with Sir Ademar.

He was still very young, perhaps sixteen, but he had been knighted on the battlefield by the king himself. He had grown into the height of manhood, and he wore chainmail armour. For a moment, he was silent, waiting for her to speak.

'Was it you who betrayed Warrick and me?' she asked quietly. Rosamund was careful to keep the anger from her voice, for she did not blame the lad for what had happened.

He gave a single nod. 'N-n-not by choice, m-my lady.' He tightened his lips as if trying to hold back the stammer.

'I understand this. We both know it was not your fault.' She took a breath. 'But Warrick and I have need of your help. He is the king's captive, and Henry will not grant me an audience to plead for my husband's release.' Without waiting for him to speak, she plunged forward. 'I want you to try to free my husband. He has done nothing wrong.'

Sir Ademar eyed her with regret. 'I m-must stay to fight with the K-King. But I w-will do what I can.'

It was the best he could do, and she understood this. 'Thank you.' She braved a smile at him. 'When you see Warrick, please tell him that my father and I are here.'

At that, Ademar's expression turned grim. 'You sh-should know, he fought for the k-king at Alnwick. We have not heard from them yet.'

A coldness rushed through her skin as she understood what had happened. Her husband had tried to prove his loyalty by fighting with Henry's men—but she didn't know if Warrick had survived that battle. Her heart quaked at the thought.

'And what of Owen de Courcy?' she ventured. 'Have you seen him at all?'

'N-no, my lady.' Sir Ademar regarded her with understanding, as if he understood the silent threat. But there was nothing to be done for it.

A knock sounded at the door, and Ademar answered it upon her signal. Two armed soldiers approached. 'We are under orders to escort you to King Henry,' one of them said.

Rosamund's pulse quickened, for this was what she had been hoping for. And yet, she could not dispel the rush of nerves. Everything rested upon this meeting with the king. She reached for her cloak, and Ademar followed. Although she wanted to believe that the king would protect her, she could not be certain. Beneath her breath, she pleaded, 'Do as I asked and send word to my husband, Ademar. Please find him, if you can.'

He lowered his head in acknowledgment. 'W-will you be all right?'

'Yes. But we need your help.' She pulled the large cloak across her shoulders, pinning it with a brooch.

The knight departed, leaving her with the two soldiers. They kept a swift pace, but try as she might, she struggled. The weight of the child was so low, she had to hold one hand below her girth to manage it.

'Make haste,' one of the men ordered, and she stopped walking to glare at him.

'I am with child,' she reminded him. 'Haste is not something I can do.' But she trudged onward, while one of them trailed her. They led her away from the camp towards a group of waiting horses.

'The king has brought his court a few miles outside Canterbury,' one said. 'We must travel to meet him there.'

She hesitated, for she did not know if they were telling the truth. 'Perhaps we should wait until he returns.'

'We go now,' the soldier insisted. He ordered her to step into his hand, wanting her to mount the horse. Her instincts warned against it. Something was wrong.

'I want my father to accompany me when I see the king,' she insisted. 'I will wait until he comes with us.'

In answer, the soldier unsheathed the blade at his waist. He pointed it directly at her swollen womb, keeping his hand against her ribs. 'I would suggest you mount the horse, Lady Pevensham. Else this blade might slip.'

She didn't move—couldn't move. But the other soldier came up behind her and forced her to mount. The firm pressure of the blade remained at her stomach, and a sudden rush of anger flooded through her. She would allow no one to harm her unborn child.

'You are Owen's men, are you not?'

When they did not answer, she knew it was so. But she'd had her fill of obedience. There was no doubt in her mind that if she went with these men, they would kill her and her unborn child. Instead, she dug her heels into the flanks of the horse and screamed as loudly as she could. The horse bolted at the noise, and the blade slipped against her skin. She felt the slash of pain, but she pulled away from them, riding as hard as she dared.

For their lives depended on it.

Chapter Fourteen

Warrick hardly slept at all during the journey south. Weeks ago, he had worked alongside the king's men, fighting to take back Alnwick. King William of Scotland had spread out his soldiers across thousands of acres.

There had not been not eighty thousand mercenaries, but there were indeed thousands of men. He had accompanied Ranulf de Glanvill, the Sheriff of Westmorland, along with four hundred soldiers. And thanks be to God, they had triumphed. Now, they had a valuable political prisoner.

A heavy fog obscured the grasses, and he guessed they were a full day's journey from the king's encampment. As he rode south, Warrick let his thoughts drift back to Rosamund. God, how he missed her. He wondered if she had conceived a child and if she was well and protected. At night, he ached for the warmth of her body, the softness of her skin against his.

She hadn't wanted him to seek out the king, but this was about more than justice. He wanted to prove to her that he was a worthy husband, a man respected by others.

He heard a slight noise behind him, of a horse travelling faster than the others. Warrick turned to order the soldier to fall back, but he saw Sir Ademar riding hard. He had not known the young man was here among the king's men. But he feared the reason for Ademar's haste.

'Owen's men have t-taken R-Rosamund,' he stammered. 'She c-came to seek an audience with the k-king.'

Rosamund was here? A boiling rage took hold in his veins, and Warrick gripped the reins so tightly, his knuckles whitened. 'Where is she?'

Ademar nodded in the direction of the king's encampment. 'Owen's men took her a day ago. I rode to find you as swiftly as I could.'

'And you didn't go after her yourself?' he growled.

'The king's s-soldiers were involved. I th-thought it best if I came to t-tell you.' Ademar stiffened, and Warrick forced himself to calm down. The knight could not have fought against the king's men.

'I am sorry,' he amended. 'Is my wife unharmed?'

'I c-cannot say. But I believe she and the babe are well.'

Ademar's words sank in, and Warrick could scarcely grasp what the man had told him. Rosamund had become pregnant? It had only been a few months, so how could anyone know for certain? A sudden numbness gripped him, with fear for both of them. Why had she not sent word? Had he known, he would have returned from Normandy at once.

A sudden resolution took hold within his mind. He had not been with Rosamund during her first pregnancy, but he would not leave her behind a second time. This time, he would be there for her, to guard her until their child was safely delivered.

His commander led them along the road towards the king's encampment, and Warrick had no choice but to follow at their pace. He could not abandon his duties, no matter how much he wanted to ride back to Rosamund.

The surest way to return to his wife was to protect their prisoner and win the king's favour. Only then could he gain his freedom.

* * *

Rosamund cursed herself for being so weak. Pregnancy had robbed her of any speed, and from the moment she'd tried to ride away from Owen's men, they had caught up to her.

Her body was bruised, and aching, and she prayed that no harm had come to her unborn baby. The gentle kicking within had brought her such relief, she'd nearly wept.

The men had taken her to a tent near the outskirts of the encampment. Although she was unbound, the two guards remained at the entrance. There was no trying to escape, for it would be like a cow trying to outrun a wolf. She had no hope at all.

But Ademar had ridden hard, and she believed he would return with men to help free her. Or perhaps he would get word to Warrick.

She gathered her skirts beneath her, trying to calm herself. Her fingers rested upon the swelling at her waist, and she tried to reassure her child that everything would be all right. *I will protect you.*

Time dragged onward and eventually the flap opened and Owen de Courcy entered the space. He brought with him a hunk of bread and a flask of wine. She was desperately grateful for the food and drink, despite the bearer.

'I see that you are trying to pass off Warrick de Laurent's bastard as my brother's,' he began by way of greeting.

'I see that you are still trying to take me as your prisoner.' She noted the flash of interest in his eyes, and her skin crawled with distaste. 'And I have no doubt that you were responsible for ordering Alan's murder by Fitzwarren.'

Owen shrugged. 'Fitzwarren acted of his own accord.'

'Lies. I know what happened, and so do you.'

'It was not my hand that killed him.'

'He was one of many whom you hired.' She struggled to stand and was irritated when he offered his assistance. In his eyes, she saw the greed and ruthlessness. 'Go back to Northleigh, Owen.'

'Pevensham is mine now,' he countered. 'I care not what Alan said before he died. I will not give my estate into the hands of a bastard.'

She met his gaze evenly, though he was right that Warrick's child had no rights to the land. And yet, she did not want to see her people harmed by Owen de Courcy as their leader. He had terrorised enough of them. She could not stand back and let him seize what her husband had desperately tried to protect.

He gripped her wrist firmly. 'The king will hear of my claim to Pevensham in the morning. If you tell him your child is Warrick's, from this new marriage, then I will leave you be. But if you try to seize what is mine, I will see you burned for adultery. And Warrick will die for the murder of my brother.'

He let her go, but the grip of his hand still left marks upon her skin. Deep inside, it felt as if her blood had frozen in her veins. For she knew that no matter what she said, Owen would demand her death.

He strode from the tent, letting the flap fall behind him. Rosamund sank down upon a low stool, feeling faint. God help her, what could she do? If she fled, Owen's men would only bring her back. And she had no idea where Warrick was now.

He was a prisoner, just as she was—and he was caught in the midst of the king's battle. No man could fight and survive when he was bound.

She sat for a long time, her cheeks wet with tears. Her hands rested upon the swelling at her womb, and she prayed for the life of Warrick and for their child. Finally, she rose to eat and drink, for she was starving.

Rosamund had just taken a sip of wine when she heard a noise behind her. She turned and saw Berta entering the tent.

'Don't drink or eat anything Owen gave you, my lady,' her maid warned. 'He means to do you harm.'

Fear sliced through her, and she set down the cup. For all she knew, Berta had placed herbs in the wine.

'Why are you here?' she demanded. She had doubted her decision to banish Berta from the start, but the woman's presence could not be an accident.

'I managed to take my son away from Owen de Courcy, and I brought him to stay with my mother,' Berta responded. 'Now, I intend to save your life, as you saved mine.' Nodding towards the wine, she added, 'It would not surprise me if Lord Pevensham filled that with herbs to cause miscarriage.' Berta brought out a bundle wrapped in cloth. 'Eat this instead.'

Rosamund was torn on whether to trust anyone. She was starving for food and desperately thirsty, but she feared the worst. Instead, she lied to Berta, 'I am not hungry now.'

Her maid left the food in a corner of the tent. Her face was troubled, but she admitted, 'I know you do not trust me. I never meant to poison your husband, but when a mother's child is threatened, she will do anything to save him.' Her face paled, and she added, 'I will atone for my mistakes. I promise you that.'

Then Berta retreated from the tent, leaving Rosamund to wonder what would happen now. She left the food and drink alone, curling up on the ground to rest. In her mind, she tried to think of Warrick, praying that he would be safe from all harm.

Her back ached from exertion, and the skin was stretched so tightly across her swollen womb, it hurt. She tried to change positions, to find a way to be comfortable, but her anxieties rose higher.

You will die on the morrow, the voice of fear whispered. *Owen will demand that you be burned for adultery.*

Terror filled up the hours, and she did not sleep at all. Her body was racked with aching pain, and she could find no respite from it. Though she had taken only a single sip of the wine, there was no way of knowing what Owen had put in it.

And when the morning came, she wept at the sight of blood upon her thighs.

The morning sky was tinted rose, and ahead, Warrick could see the smoke rising from fires near the king's encampment. He wanted to pull away from the others to seek out Rosamund, but there were so many at the encampment, he had no way of knowing where she was.

The Sheriff of Westmorland drew his horse alongside Warrick's. 'I will speak to the king on your behalf,' he said. 'You and your men have earned your freedom for what you did.'

He said nothing, but nodded in acknowledgment of Ranulf's words. Right now, he needed to reach his wife. He had to ensure her safety, and time was not his ally.

'I want you to stay here and guard our prisoner,' Ranulf continued. 'The Scottish king cannot escape our custody.'

Warrick hesitated and spoke. 'First, by your leave, I must seek out my wife. She is here with her father.' They were so close, he could not delay any longer.

'Protecting our hostage is far more important,' Ranulf argued. 'Your woman can wait.'

'I fear for her safety, for she is with child.' The very mention of Rosamund's unborn babe filled him with a sharp tang of fear. He doubted not that Owen would attempt to harm them. 'I have not seen her in months.'

Ranulf studied him a moment. 'You fought well

among us, and we would not have defeated our enemies without you. If it is your will to see her for a moment, I will allow this. But I will expect to see you among my men by noontide.'

'I will be there,' he swore. He glanced back at Godfrey and Bennett, in a silent command for them to follow. They pulled ahead of the others, and Warrick ordered, 'Help me find Rosamund.'

'You need only look for Owen's guards,' Godfrey predicted. 'She will be with them.'

With his men at his side, he rode into King Henry's camp. Row by row, they searched the tents until he saw one with two guards standing outside it.

'That one,' Bennett said. 'I recognise those men from Pevensham.'

Warrick dismounted, handing the reins off to Bennett before he approached the guards. Godfrey dismounted and followed. 'Is Lady Pevensham within?'

'No one may see her,' the first answered. His hand rested upon his weapon.

'Except me,' Warrick countered. He struck the man hard across the jaw, disarming him in one motion.

The guard stumbled to the ground and Godfrey

stepped forward, his sword pointed at the other. 'Don't,' he warned.

Warrick pushed aside the tent flap and found Rosamund inside. The very sight of her shocked him, for she was indeed heavy with child for one who should have only had a slight pregnancy.

'Warrick,' she cried out, opening her arms to him. 'I thought you were a prisoner.'

He crushed her into his embrace, so glad to see her. And in the moment she clung to him, he did not care about anything else. This was the woman he loved, the one he would die for. He kissed her hard, tasting the salt of her tears.

'Did they let you go?' she asked.

'I was granted an hour to see you, but no, I must return to the commander.' He was aware that his freedom was short-lived, but he intended to bring Rosamund to safety first.

She wrapped her arms around his neck, and Warrick slid his hands down her body, reassuring himself that she was all right. When he hesitated at her waist, she broke free of the kiss and guided his hands to their unborn child. 'I tried to send word to you about this, I promise. The messengers could not find you.'

Her skin was hard and rounded, and he was startled at the tightness. But when he looked upon her face, there was stark fear instead of joy. 'Are you all right?' he asked. He wondered if there was something wrong with the child.

She blanched at his question. 'I do not know. I—I began bleeding this morn.' Within her frightened voice, he recognised her terror. She had lost a child once before, and it might already be happening again.

His heart sank at the thought, and prayed that the unborn infant would be safe. This invisible battle was one he could not fight for his wife's sake. All he could do was protect her as best he could against outside threats, such as Owen de Courcy.

'Sit down,' he bade her, and she obeyed. 'Tell me what has happened.'

Rosamund confessed how Owen's men had taken her, and a thunderous rage filled Warrick up inside. 'This has to end,' he insisted. 'The man must be brought to justice.'

'I agree,' Rosamund said, 'but already both of you must face the king.'

'I intend to settle the matter in a trial by combat,' he countered. He had no fear of Owen de Courcy and doubted not that he would win. He extended his hand to Rosamund. 'Will you come with me when I speak with the king?'

She shook her head. 'If I walk, I fear it may

bring on the child. I must stay here.' Her expression grew strained, and Warrick shared her worry. But he could not leave her in this tent.

'It's not safe, Rosamund.' He understood her fears, but Owen's men had found her already. 'I will send Godfrey and Bennett to bring a litter. We must find a place of sanctuary for you.' He kissed her again and opened the tent flap, giving orders to his men.

'Wait,' Rosamund pleaded. She struggled to stand and caught both his hands. 'If there is a choice between saving Pevensham or saving your life, let go of the estate. It does not matter any more. All that matters to me is you.' Her voice filled up with emotion, and she moved into his arms. 'I love you, Warrick, and I am so sorry I never told you about our daughter.'

Her words slid through him like another embrace, and the strength of her love humbled him. He held her close, pressing a kiss against her hair. 'I was angry with you for keeping secrets. But that was in the past, and I will not let anything happen to you or to this child.' He rested his forehead against hers. 'I love you too, Rosamund. And I will see to it that Owen never bothers you again.'

She braved a smile through her fear, resting her hands upon their baby. 'Pray that it will be so.'

A noise outside interrupted their reverie, and he moved his hand to his sword. Seconds later, soldiers invaded the tent. Warrick shielded Rosamund, unsheathing his blade at the sight of them. There was no sign of Bennett or Godfrey.

'You are commanded to come with us, Warrick de Laurent,' one said. 'By order of the king.'

Three other men tried to surround Rosamund, but he shoved them away from her. 'Leave my wife alone. She is with child.'

'We are under orders to bring her as well,' another replied. 'Under charges of adultery.'

Damn Owen for this. Fury blazed through him, and Warrick fought against the men who tried to seize his wife. It was impossible to wield his sword in such a small space without risk of hurting Rosamund. He smashed his fist against one man's jaw when he heard his wife's scream, and he swung another blow at a second soldier's nose. But there were too many of them. He kept his sword aloft, trying to protect her, but the men surrounded them on all sides.

A hard blow caught his skull, and Warrick dropped to his knees.

And then there was only darkness.

Chapter Fifteen

When the men brought Rosamund into the king's presence, she could feel the cramping ache within her womb. She was terrified that she was losing this baby, just as she had before. *Please God, let him live,* she begged. The prayer was for both her unborn child and for her husband.

Warrick had regained consciousness by the time the men dragged him across the ground. His face was bleeding, and she saw another wound across his ribs. Several men had gathered, and she was not surprised to see Owen de Courcy among them. But she was grateful to see the familiar face of Father Francis. He stood at the back of the gathering, his simple brown robes blending among the other guests.

Henry Plantagenet stood with his arms crossed. The king was a stocky man with red hair and his stare held no mercy whatsoever. Another soldier spoke quietly to him, but Henry did not appear to care what the man had said.

'We have little time for this matter,' the king argued. 'But we have been asked to dispense justice over the man who killed Alan de Courcy. There is also the question as to whether Lady Pevensham was with child prior to her husband's death, which means the estate cannot be settled as of yet. Owen de Courcy claims that her child was conceived in adultery and that her child has no right to Pevensham. We will discover the truth this day.'

The king stared at Rosamund, and she felt his cold anger down to her bones. Owen's claim, that he would see her burned for adultery, terrified her. She longed to flee this place, to surrender everything to protect her unborn baby.

And yet, what would that accomplish? A dawning realisation took hold, and she understood that she had been behaving like a pawn all her life. First, her father had manoeuvred her into a marriage she had never wanted. Then her husband had commanded her to obey his order to conceive a child with Warrick. Now, Owen de Courcy wanted to threaten everyone she held dear.

The man's expression was smug, as if he fully expected both of them to die.

No. She could not stand by and let this happen. She had to stand up to him and fight for her loved ones and for the life she wanted. And even more, the people of Pevensham needed her to fight for them—for any ruler was better than Owen.

Alan had made sacrifices to protect his estate and the people. He had brought back the man his wife had loved, ensuring that she would wed Warrick upon his death. Did she not owe it to him, to do whatever was necessary to guard Pevensham and its people?

The king turned his stare to Warrick. 'You have been accused of strangling Alan de Courcy. What have you to say for this?'

'Owen de Courcy was responsible for his brother's death,' Warrick interrupted. 'He hired his brother's commander, Fitzwarren, to kill Alan. He has no right to take Pevensham with blood on his hands.'

'He speaks lies, my lord and king,' Owen interrupted.

'We did not give you leave to speak,' Henry retorted. 'This matter will be decided quickly, and with witnesses. If you cannot maintain your silence, you will be flogged.'

Rosamund knew that the king would see it done.

But she could not yet know whether justice would be met this day, especially given the violence towards Warrick when he was first brought here. She felt lightheaded, her knees trembling, but she forced herself to remain standing.

'We will hear the priest's words first,' the king said, beckoning for Father Francis to come forward.

The priest walked slowly among the people, and he did not even look at her. Rosamund felt her skin grow icy, and the room seemed to sway. She leaned against a soldier, and it felt as if the voices in the room echoed through a tunnel.

She barely heard what Father Francis was saying, but he produced a document for Henry to see.

'I am not convinced this is real,' the king argued. 'Although Lady Pevensham might have been with child, as Alan de Courcy claims, I cannot imagine he would demand that his wife marry Warrick de Laurent upon his death. Not without a dozen witnesses to sign it. And furthermore, there is no way to prove that the child was his.' He waved his hand in dismissal.

At that, an older woman stepped forward and knelt before the king. Rosamund had never seen her before, but there was a familiar cast to the woman's face. 'Your Grace, I have come to offer myself as a witness.'

The king studied her as if she were an insect. 'Who are you?'

'I am the queen's midwife,' she replied. 'I have assisted your lady wife at every birth.'

At this, King Henry's demeanour shifted. 'Go on.'

'I can examine this woman and tell you how long it will be until she gives birth. I have assisted with hundreds of women, and this may be of help.'

The king grew thoughtful at this. 'And how can you be certain?'

'If she conceived during her second marriage, it would be too soon for me to feel movement. If she was already pregnant by Alan de Courcy, this would be obvious.'

'It would not,' Owen blurted out. 'My brother—'

His words broke off when Henry backhanded him with a fist. 'The next man who dares to interrupt his king will have his tongue removed.' The king's tone held fury, and he regarded each of them. 'My own sons have risen up in rebellion, and that requires my attention.' He nodded to the midwife. 'Examine Lady Pevensham and tell me if her child is legitimate. If it is, then she will return to Pevensham to await the child's birth.'

The midwife bowed, but before she could take her to be examined, Rosamund dropped to her knees before the king. She did not dare to speak before she was given permission, but after a moment, the king touched her shoulder. He tilted her face up to look at him. 'At last, we see a woman who knows her place. What have you to say?'

Rosamund took a breath. 'My husband was very ill for a time, my lord, and we learned that he was being poisoned by a servant. The servant confessed to me that she was under the orders of Owen de Courcy. And the night my husband died, we learned that Owen hired Fitzwarren to strangle Alan.' She rested her hands upon her womb and pleaded with the king, 'No matter what becomes of my child's inheritance, I beg of you, do not let my husband's death go without justice. If Owen returns to Northleigh, he will only threaten my unborn baby once again.'

The king eyed her but there was no mercy in his gaze. 'We will think upon this while you are examined by the midwife.'

She bowed her head, and the older woman helped her back to her feet. There was no way of knowing what judgement the king would pass, but Rosamund hoped he understood her fears.

The older woman took her back to a smaller chamber and closed the door behind her. Rosamund remained standing, not knowing what the midwife would want of her.

'Lie back upon the pallet over there,' the older woman bade. Her voice was kind, and she picked up a small stool and brought it over to sit beside her. She moved her hands over Rosamund's womb and pressed upon her. Then she said quietly, 'We both know this child could not possibly be Alan de Courcy's. The man was incapable of siring children.'

'How could you know this?' Rosamund asked. The woman had never even met her first husband.

Her gaze fixed upon Rosamund, but she did not answer the question. 'I will tell the king that you will give birth to this child by All Saints Day or near to that.'

Rosamund was already shaking her head. 'I do not think—'

The midwife touched a finger to her mouth. 'You saved the life of my daughter. And so I shall save your life and the life of your child in return.'

It was then that she realised who the woman was. 'You are Berta's mother.'

The old woman inclined her head. 'I am. And she asked me to come on your behalf.' The midwife patted her hand. 'I will give you a tea to help you stop the bleeding. You need not worry—your children are safe.'

Rosamund blinked at that. 'Children?'

'Did you not wonder why you were breeding so large? It is because you were blessed with two instead of one.' The midwife smiled. 'But you must be careful, for twins are often born early. Should you wish it, I can come to Pevensham and help you.'

Rosamund felt the emotion gather up in her throat. She had doubted herself for sparing Berta's life. But now it seemed she had made the right choice. And in return, the midwife would bear witness for her sake. 'I do wish it. Thank you.'

When the midwife returned with his wife, Warrick was glad to see that the colour had returned to Rosamund's face. 'She is indeed many months pregnant with Alan de Courcy's child,' the old woman told the king. 'There is no doubt of it. She will give birth near to All Saints Day.'

Henry stared hard at Rosamund and Owen. 'And how long ago did Warrick de Laurent arrive at Pevensham?'

'A little over four months ago,' Owen admitted.

With a shrug, the king said, 'Given that Alan de Courcy acknowledged the child before his death, and the midwife has stated there is no doubt it is his heir, then you may manage your late brother's estates until the child is born. If it is a girl, you will remain the heir. If it is a son, you may act as his guardian until he comes of age.'

Warrick tensed at the king's judgement. He could not allow Owen to be anywhere near Pevensham—especially with Rosamund's pregnancy. His greatest concern was their welfare.

Owen stepped forward. When the king gave permission for him to speak, he said, 'There is still the matter of my brother's death. It cannot go unpunished.'

The king paused a moment and said, 'Both of you have said the other man is responsible for Alan de Courcy's death. We will let God decide who is the true murderer.'

Warrick relaxed, for this would be a matter of trial by combat. He could easily defeat Owen de Courcy, and justice would be served.

'It is clear who the true murderer is,' Owen countered. 'Warrick de Laurent and Lady Pevensham found my brother's body. I have no doubt of this, and my servants will give witness.'

The king turned a cold look upon him. 'We must not doubt that God is the highest witness of all. If you are innocent, as you say, then you shall prevail.' He let his gaze pass over Warrick and Owen. 'I gave penance for my grievous sins, and God granted me the victory at Alnwick. If either of you wishes to confess your guilt and offer penance, this trial will be lifted from you.'

Warrick held his silence, for he had done nothing wrong. Owen's face was bright with anger, but the man refused to confess anything.

'So be it,' the king said. He eyed each of them and said quietly, 'This trial will not be decided by combat.'

An uneasy feeling washed over Warrick. He didn't like the look in Henry's eyes, which was of a man who believed he was omnipotent. It was as if he already knew the judgement he would pass.

Warrick met Rosamund's gaze, but her face held stark fear. She tried to move closer to him, and this time, the soldiers allowed it. Her fingers were like ice as she threaded her hand in his, gripping him hard. 'I love you,' she whispered.

In answer, he squeezed her palm, letting her know without words how much he loved her. This woman was his life, his reason for being alive. And if he was asked to choose between protecting her and their child or accepting a false judgement, he would do whatever was necessary to shield them.

A sly smile crossed Henry's face. 'Since the murderer was also responsible for the poisoning of Alan de Courcy, we believe this is the truest test of finding the man who committed this crime. Thus, we will have both men drink from a poisoned cup. He who is innocent will be spared by God.'

Owen was aghast at the idea. 'Both of us will die if we drink. It is impossible.'

Perhaps that was what Henry wanted. A man as powerful as the king cared little for two lives. Warrick gripped Rosamund's hand, and she was shaking her head in horror. 'No.' But her denial was silent, her lips forming the word she could not bring herself to speak.

Tears spilled from her eyes, and she buried her face in his chest. A deep ache spread throughout his body, at the thought of leaving her behind. His hand spread into her hair, stroking it as he drew her to look at him.

'I love you, Rosamund.' He kissed her softly and then turned back to look into Henry's shrewd eyes. It was then that he understood what this was—a true test of character.

Warrick stepped forward and said, 'I am not afraid to face God's judgement. I know of my innocence.' He spoke quietly, but he could not deny the pounding of his heart. There was a strong risk that Henry did intend to poison both of them.

'And what if God judges that it is his will for you to die?' the king demanded. 'Will you freely drink from the cup?'

'I know that I am not responsible for Alan de Courcy's death,' he said. 'And if God chooses to take my life, I trust that you will ensure that my wife returns to Pevensham without the threat of Owen de Courcy or his men. Rosamund will give birth to Alan's heir and remain under the protection of her people.' He knelt before Henry. 'I have shown you my loyalty by fighting among your men. Whatever cup you give to me, I will drink from it.'

He lowered his gaze, not wanting to see Henry's

response. There was no way to know what decision the king would make. But blind obedience was the only choice, even if it meant his death. He did believe Henry would protect Rosamund, especially after the midwife had given her testimony.

A part of him had suspected his life would always come to this—death, before he would ever have land of his own. But in Rosamund's eyes, she saw someone more, a man she loved. Her words of quiet faith had struck him to the bone. And he loved her enough to give his life to protect hers.

'And what of you?' Henry turned back to Owen. 'Will you drink of the cup and trust in God?'

Owen blanched and took a step backwards. 'I— my liege, I have done nothing wrong. I swear it to you.'

'But you are afraid of God's judgement.'

'Any man would be afraid to drink poison.' Owen shook his head. 'It is not necessary, my liege. I can bring any number of witnesses who will swear to my innocence.'

The king's expression remained stoic. 'One man is willing to test God's will, while another is not.' He gestured to his soldiers. 'Seize Owen de Courcy and bind him. He may have nothing to eat or drink, save the cup of poison that we give to him.'

To Warrick, Henry said, 'As for you, you have proven your innocence before all. Any man willing to drink of a cup of poison, with no fear of meeting God's judgement, is not a murderer.'

A weight seemed to lift from Warrick's shoulders that he would not be asked to drink from such a cup. Rosamund went to kneel beside him at the king's feet. She took his hand in hers and bowed before the king. 'You are most wise, my king. Pevensham and its people will always remain faithful to you. As will my son or daughter.' She raised a shining face of joy to Henry, who rested his hand upon her forehead. There was kindness there, and a wry sense of knowing that he had passed judgement correctly.

'Go in peace,' he bade them. 'And if we have need of your alliance, we will call upon Pevensham's soldiers.'

'They are at your command,' Rosamund answered. At that, the king helped her to rise, and Warrick took her in his arms. He kissed her hard, and many of the soldiers erupted in cheers. The taste of her mouth was the sweetness of love, with the promise of hope for their future together.

She held him close, and he whispered in her ear. 'I love you, Rosamund. And we were meant to be together from the first.'

She touched his cheek. And in her smile, he caught a glimpse of Heaven.

Epilogue

He came to her late, at twilight, when the moon was just beginning to rise. Rosamund was feeding their son when she heard the door open. As soon as Warrick entered their chamber, their daughter began to cry from her cradle. Warrick picked up the infant, soothing her as she sobbed against him.

'Is Mary hungry?' he asked. 'She is trying to eat my shoulder.'

'She is teething, just like her brother,' Rosamund answered. Their son Stephen had slackened against her breast, milk dribbling from his mouth. She lifted him up to burp the infant, and after he did, she rose to lay him in his cradle.

She took Mary to her breast next, and her daughter latched on, nursing for comfort until exhaustion overcame her. Warrick sat behind her while she fed the baby, and she could feel the iron strength of his chest against her back. He kissed her neck, and her skin erupted in gooseflesh. Even after all this time, he held the power to arouse her with a single touch.

'Call your maid to stay with the children,' he murmured. 'There is something I want to show you.'

'Let me put the baby down,' she murmured, rising from their bed. Then she opened the door and called out to her maid, ordering the young woman to watch over the babies.

Warrick held out a cloak to her and offered his arm. 'Where are we going?' Rosamund asked.

'Wait and see.' He led her down the hall and towards the stairs of the *donjon*, until they were outside. She was surprised to find that he had already prepared a horse for them to share. Warrick helped her mount the animal and swung up behind her. Several of their people cast glances in their direction, and there seemed to be conspiratorial smiles.

'Will we be gone for very long?' she asked, risking a glance back at the castle.

He guided the horse to begin walking. 'A few hours, no more.' Then he led her through the gates and outside into the darkness.

The weather was warmer than she had imagined

for a clear night in May, and the moon illuminated their path. In the distance, she saw lights flickering in the forest and could not tell what it was.

When they reached the edge of the woods, she caught her breath at the beauty. There were flower petals and greenery scattered along the path. And when Warrick drew her deeper into the forest, she saw thick candles buried in the ground, the soft light gleaming.

'This reminds me of our wedding,' she said quietly.

He tightened his grip around her waist, nuzzling her neck. 'I hoped it would. And perhaps you would think of the first day we met in the forest.'

The candlelit path led towards a small stone dwelling with a wooden door. Smoke rose from a tiny chimney, and she had never before seen this place. 'What is this, Warrick?'

Her husband dismounted and tethered the horse, lifting her down. 'I had our men build it as a gift for you.'

Such a gift was far more costly than she'd ever imagined. 'You went to a great deal of trouble for me.' But she could not deny her excitement as she opened the door. Inside, a fire was lit in the stone hearth. There were candles set in sconces all around the room, and she saw her mother's embroidery hanging upon a wall. In one corner, he had given her a table filled with dozens of coloured threads, lengths of linen, and a set of sharp needles.

Rosamund exclaimed at the sight of them, hugging her husband with such joy. 'Warrick, this is wonderful!'

On the other side of the room, she saw a narrow bed and a wooden tub filled with steaming water. More flower petals were scattered upon the surface, and the thought of a hot bath was a craving she had not dared to imagine.

She realised then, that this was a place for the two of them, a retreat from the castle where they could steal away together.

'Is the bath for you or for me?' she asked softly. 'Or both?'

'I want to tend you,' he said. His voice was husky with desire, and she was already aching for this man, needing his touch.

She let her cloak fall to the floor as he closed the door behind them. In this small space, she could smell the aroma of the flower petals. Slowly, she drew the laces of her gown, and Warrick watched her undress. His eyes were hungry upon her, and she peeled away the silk, revealing her body to him.

He helped her into the tub, and the water was blissfully hot. Though it was small, she drew her knees up and revelled in the heat. The flower petals grazed her skin, and Warrick picked up a cake of soap. He dipped his hands in the water and lathered it between his palms. 'Shall I wash you?'

She leaned forward, her nipples tight with arousal as he soaped her back and drew his hand around to the curve of her breasts. A moan escaped her as he caressed her with his soapy hands.

'Remove your clothing,' she ordered him.

Warrick obeyed, and she saw his heavy erection as he removed his chausses and braies. She reached out to touch him with her wet hands, and he countered by taking her breast into his mouth. She shuddered at the delicious pleasure that coursed through her body. Her hands threaded through his dark hair, and she drew his mouth to hers, kissing him hard. His tongue slid into her mouth in a foreshadowing of what would come later.

Warrick dipped his hands beneath the water, down her stomach to her legs. Then he slid his palm between her thighs, stroking her intimately. She leaned her head back on the wooden tub, arching as he started a gentle rhythm.

He knew just how to arouse her, how to drive her mindless with need. The tremors rose up within her, the water sloshing against her skin, and she was startled when a sudden release cascaded over her without warning. She gripped the edge of the tub, riding out the storm as his fingers slid inside her.

'Warrick, I need you,' she pleaded.

He brought over several linen cloths, and she stood in the tub with shaking knees. Gently, he dried the water from her skin, and she inhaled sharply when he moved the towel between her legs.

He lifted her out of the water and brought her to the narrow bed. The warmth of the fire kept the chill from her skin and she lay upon her stomach, pulling her hair over one shoulder.

With his warm hands, Warrick slid his palms over her spine to the slope of her bottom. He replaced his hands with his mouth, tracing a path down her bare back.

'I remember when I touched you like this the

first time,' he murmured. 'I could not believe you were mine.'

She parted her legs in invitation, loving the feel of his hands upon her. 'Touch me again.'

He obeyed, following the curve of her back-slide. She arched against him, shuddering as she imagined his body joining with hers. His fingers drifted against her wetness, and she gasped at the sensation. He held such command over her, she wanted him with a force that staggered her.

But he kept it slow, teasing her as his shaft pressed against her backside. He was like heated velvet, and she craved the intimacy. She lifted her hips, keeping her face pressed to the sheets even as she offered herself. 'I want you to fill me, Warrick.'

He rewarded her by stroking her with his wicked fingers, sliding two of them inside her. 'Like this?' His thumb brushed her cleft, and she moaned. A ripple of need struck hard, and she reached behind her to grasp his erection in her palm. He hissed as she began to slide her fist around his length. Then she guided him into her wet opening, and he sheathed himself to the hilt. For a moment, he remained buried inside her, but he lifted her hips, reaching beneath her to fondle her nipples. She was sensitive there, and the jolt of feeling made her press back against him.

He began to thrust slowly, making her feel every inch of him. Warrick knew just how to suspend the moment, to draw out the heavy arousal that she craved. He experimented with the angle of her hips, until she cried out. 'There. Yes.'

His breathing mirrored hers, heavy and rhythmic as he sank and withdrew. She clenched around him, welcoming his deep, arousing thrusts. Her body was utterly wet for him, and he pressed his finger against her hooded flesh, until she felt a growing spasm inside her.

'I love you, Rosamund,' he breathed, circling his fingers as he went deep. His words were an inner caress, and it took only a few more strokes to send her over the edge. A violent shimmer released inside her, and she backed against him, welcoming his body into hers. She could feel his iron length thrusting, and she tried to meet him though he withheld his own release.

'Take what you need from me,' she urged him, but he would not. Instead, he withdrew and rolled her to her back.

She wrapped her legs around his waist, but he

kissed her lips. 'You know what I want from you, Rosamund.'

She did. There was another position that drove him into madness, and that was what he craved just now. She moved beneath him so that her legs were closed together with his erection still buried inside her. He thrust again, hissing with pleasure as she tightened her grip around him. The shallow penetration surrounded him with her essence, and he ground himself against her until his fingers dug into the mattress and he shuddered with his own release. She felt the spasm of her body and he pulled her legs around him, stroking deeply a few more times.

He kissed her softly. 'If you keep doing that, we will have many children, Rosamund.'

'I hope so.' She drew him to her, their bodies damp with perspiration and desire. Their limbs were tangled together, and he drew a blanket over them.

'Rhys wants us to come to Scotland,' he said, kissing her lightly. 'Lianna has asked us to visit.'

She knew him too well and heard the tension in his voice. 'Something troubles you.'

He caressed her skin. 'My father will be there. He has asked to make peace between us.'

'Are you not pleased by this?'

'I am not the true Lord of Pevensham,' he admitted. 'Only the guardian of the heirs. It's not the same.'

'You are the guardian of this castle and all who dwell within it,' she corrected. 'Over a hundred people rely on you to protect them and to keep Pevensham prosperous. You *are* Lord Pevensham, whether you mean to be or not.' It was true. Even the lowest serf called him by the title, and no one denied the fealty owed to him.

'None of it is mine by right.'

'*I* am yours by right,' she corrected. 'By conquest and by love.' She framed his face with her hands, kissing him again. 'And Pevensham is also yours. Never doubt that you are worthy of this land. The king himself has proclaimed it, while he burned the castles of his enemies.'

He was quiet, but he answered the kiss. 'I will guard it always, Rosamund.'

She nestled her body against his. 'I know you will. Just as you will guard our family.'

In this narrow bed, she lay with the man she adored with all her heart. He continued to touch her, as if learning her body by candlelight. It would indeed be several hours before they returned to the castle, and she held no regrets.

Their children slept within their cradles, safe in the knowledge that they were loved. Their lands were safe, and no one would threaten them again.

Just as it was meant to be.

* * * * *

*If you enjoyed this story
you won't want to miss these other
great reads from Michelle Willingham*

*THE ACCIDENTAL PRINCE
TO SIN WITH A VIKING
TO TEMPT A VIKING
WARRIOR OF ICE
WARRIOR OF FIRE*

*And, to receive an email when Book 2 in
Michelle Willingham's*
WARRIORS OF THE NIGHT *miniseries
is available, sign up for the
author's newsletter here:
www.michellewillingham.com/contact
You'll also receive a free story!*

MILLS & BOON®
Large Print – November 2017

ROMANCE

The Pregnant Kavakos Bride	Sharon Kendrick
The Billionaire's Secret Princess	Caitlin Crews
Sicilian's Baby of Shame	Carol Marinelli
The Secret Kept from the Greek	Susan Stephens
A Ring to Secure His Crown	Kim Lawrence
Wedding Night with Her Enemy	Melanie Milburne
Salazar's One-Night Heir	Jennifer Hayward
The Mysterious Italian Houseguest	Scarlet Wilson
Bound to Her Greek Billionaire	Rebecca Winters
Their Baby Surprise	Katrina Cudmore
The Marriage of Inconvenience	Nina Singh

HISTORICAL

Ruined by the Reckless Viscount	Sophia James
Cinderella and the Duke	Janice Preston
A Warriner to Rescue Her	Virginia Heath
Forbidden Night with the Warrior	Michelle Willingham
The Foundling Bride	Helen Dickson

MEDICAL

Mummy, Nurse...Duchess?	Kate Hardy
Falling for the Foster Mum	Karin Baine
The Doctor and the Princess	Scarlet Wilson
Miracle for the Neurosurgeon	Lynne Marshall
English Rose for the Sicilian Doc	Annie Claydon
Engaged to the Doctor Sheikh	Meredith Webber

1017 GEN STD LP

MILLS & BOON®
Hardback – December 2017

ROMANCE

His Queen by Desert Decree	Lynne Graham
A Christmas Bride for the King	Abby Green
Captive for the Sheikh's Pleasure	Carol Marinelli
Legacy of His Revenge	Cathy Williams
A Night of Royal Consequences	Susan Stephens
Carrying His Scandalous Heir	Julia James
Christmas at the Tycoon's Command	Jennifer Hayward
Innocent in the Billionaire's Bed	Clare Connelly
Snowed in with the Reluctant Tycoon	Nina Singh
The Magnate's Holiday Proposal	Rebecca Winters
The Billionaire's Christmas Baby	Marion Lennox
Christmas Bride for the Boss	Kate Hardy
Christmas with the Best Man	Susan Carlisle
Navy Doc on Her Christmas List	Amy Ruttan
Christmas Bride for the Sheikh	Carol Marinelli
Her Knight Under the Mistletoe	Annie O'Neil
The Nurse's Special Delivery	Louisa George
Her New Year Baby Surprise	Sue MacKay
His Secret Son	Brenda Jackson
Best Man Under the Mistletoe	Jules Bennett

1117 GEN STD HB

MILLS & BOON®
Large Print – November 2017

ROMANCE

An Heir Made in the Marriage Bed	Anne Mather
The Prince's Stolen Virgin	Maisey Yates
Protecting His Defiant Innocent	Michelle Smart
Pregnant at Acosta's Demand	Maya Blake
The Secret He Must Claim	Chantelle Shaw
Carrying the Spaniard's Child	Jennie Lucas
A Ring for the Greek's Baby	Melanie Milburne
The Runaway Bride and the Billionaire	Kate Hardy
The Boss's Fake Fiancée	Susan Meier
The Millionaire's Redemption	Therese Beharrie
Captivated by the Enigmatic Tycoon	Bella Bucannon

HISTORICAL

Marrying His Cinderella Countess	Louise Allen
A Ring for the Pregnant Debutante	Laura Martin
The Governess Heiress	Elizabeth Beacon
The Warrior's Damsel in Distress	Meriel Fuller
The Knight's Scarred Maiden	Nicole Locke

MEDICAL

Healing the Sheikh's Heart	Annie O'Neil
A Life-Saving Reunion	Alison Roberts
The Surgeon's Cinderella	Susan Carlisle
Saved by Doctor Dreamy	Dianne Drake
Pregnant with the Boss's Baby	Sue MacKay
Reunited with His Runaway Doc	Lucy Clark

1117 GEN STD LP

MILLS & BOON®

Why shop at millsandboon.co.uk?

Each year, thousands of romance readers find their perfect read at millsandboon.co.uk. That's because we're passionate about bringing you the very best romantic fiction. Here are some of the advantages of shopping at www.millsandboon.co.uk:

* **Get new books first**—you'll be able to buy your favourite books one month before they hit the shops

* **Get exclusive discounts**—you'll also be able to buy our specially created monthly collections, with up to 50% off the RRP

* **Find your favourite authors**—latest news, interviews and new releases for all your favourite authors and series on our website, plus ideas for what to try next

* **Join in**—once you've bought your favourite books, don't forget to register with us to rate, review and join in the discussions

Visit **www.millsandboon.co.uk**
for all this and more today!